THE GAMES

A Novel

Claire Carver-Dias

CLEARDAY PRESS

Copyright @ 2012 Claire Carver-Dias
All rights reserved.

No part of this publication may be reproduced, stored in a retrieval system, or transmitted in any form or by any means, electronic, mechanical, photocopying, recording or otherwise, without the prior written permission of the publisher.

Published by Clearday Press, a division of Clearday Corporation, Canada.
www.clearday.ca

ISBN-10: 1478252294
EAN-13: 9781478252290

Library of Congress Control Number: 2012912953
CreateSpace, North Charleston, SC

This novel is a work of fiction. The names, characters and incidents portrayed in it are products of the author's imagination. Any resemblance to actual persons, living or dead, is entirely coincidental.

Many thanks to Laurie, Mark, Sylvia, Jennifer, Gisela, Rory, Steve, Sue, Chelsea, Janice and Estelle, for your input and guidance. I am also grateful to my "A Team", Douglas, Ian, Deborah, Jim, Sandra, Sheilagh, FV friends, and the Carver and Dias clans, for your tremendous wisdom, encouragement, love and patience.

www.clairecarverdias.com

For Douglas, whose voice I hear above the rest.

The most important thing in the Olympic Games is not to win but to take part, just as the most important thing in life is not the triumph but the struggle. The essential thing is not to have conquered but to have fought well.

—PIERRE DE COUBERTIN

OPENING CEREMONIES: PART ONE

SAM

In the Olympic stadium, a cheer rose like a loud exhalation into the dull grey London sky. The British athletes had just entered the Opening Ceremonies—the last country in the Parade of Nations. Outside, Sam checked his watch, turned away from the crowd's breath, and wrapped his fingers tightly around the mobile phone in his pocket. His own breathing was short, shallow. A cold sweat gathered on his forehead. His body was chilled and shaking beneath his security guard uniform.

Hadn't Ellis prepared him for this moment? If he were here, Ellis would have reminded Sam to stay focused, to remember those he was saving. He would have touched Sam's face and called him "Chosen."

But Sam's mind had begun to follow the rhythm of his quickened heartbeats. It landed on the image of the female security guard twenty feet away, as she bent over and picked up an empty water bottle. Then it turned inward to consider the scent of the wet grass. Jumped to the weight of the mobile in his pocket. Then to the imagined tableau of the British athletes entering the stadium, the lightning storm of camera flashes. To Brent's little-boy eyes, upside down, peering from the top bunk. His mother's face. To the growing pain in his chest. To Ellis, cross-legged on the floor of his Toronto apartment, holding out a ring.

This must be like what happens when athletes choke. Thoughts clogging the brain.

Sam had imagined that this would be easier. That he'd be ready. He wanted to run.

Ellis, help me.

He checked his watch again; ten seconds to go.

As he counted down from ten, he ran a shaking fingertip over the four gold bands hanging on the delicate chain around his neck. His other hand clenched the phone.

He didn't think he could do it.

It was time. Sam looked at the sky and turned away from the closest security camera.

A memory came to mind. He was seven, standing on the three-metre diving board, ready to jump off for the first time. With every second of hesitation, he felt the board rise higher, the water retreat. His knees knocked together almost audibly as he leaned forward and looked down. His six-year-old brother Brent waited in the water below, laughing.

Sam swallowed, and his fingers found the right key on the dial pad.

The sensation of falling through air.

WINTER–SPRING 2011

JAYNA

For the second time in a week, Jayna arrived drunk to her university basketball team practice. It was 5:50 a.m., and the previous night's make-up was still evident on her face. There were mascara smudges under her eyes and dried-up pink lipstick residue around the edge of her mouth and on the tips of her teeth. She had somehow managed to change out of her clubbing clothes and into an oversized green sweatshirt, black tear-away pants, and court shoes. Her practice gear was underneath. She couldn't remember where she had gotten changed. In the sticky bathroom at the club? In the parking lot?

Clothing, practice kits, and stretching teammates sat in quiet lumps around the gymnasium. Jayna located a space along the edge of the gym where she hoped she could stretch in silence for the remaining ten minutes before practice. She dropped her large bag in a heap on the floor, a red high-heeled shoe poking out where the zipper should close, and faced the cinder-block wall. She placed her large palms flat against its cold grey surface and leaned forward to stretch out her hamstrings. The painful discipline of staying awake. Worse than thirty chin-ups. She studied her anklebones. *They stick out like Will's ears.* A memory like a phantom touched her now: Will's hands hard on her back and her body pressed against his in the middle of the dance floor. Bobbing heads all around them and music so loud that the sensation of heaviness filled her ears. Will's fingers, widening and slipping downward as a ripple of anticipation ran up her spine.

The gym floor began to slide beneath her feet. She stood up slowly and prepared herself for what might come next. At any moment, someone would attempt to talk to her. Someone would ask her to do a partner stretch or start warm-up laps around the gym, and she would have to shake off the shadow of the night's partying and launch into the motions of what she needed to do to become an Olympic basketball player. Among her university teammates, she was the only one with a shot at the Games, so the others watched her every move. Some vacillated between admiring her and hating her. They cheered for her, hung out with her, complimented her, and then criticized her behind her back. She knew that every shooting error, every missed rebound, was stored away in their minds. Yet, they'd rush to be in her group for drills or her partner during warm-up.

She'd rather sway with her ghosts. Though not the uninvited ones.

She looked up at Coach Nate, his tall body leaning against the orange office door. His brow was creased in thought as he studied something on an old chipped clipboard. Despite his habit of wearing vintage-looking Nike tracksuits and faded baseball caps, he was a stunning man. Especially in silence.

JAYNA

In the moments before practice, caught in deep solitary concentration, he appeared mysterious and sensual. But when he raised the whistle to his lips and took control, he assumed the trappings of coachiness. His basketball knowledge and strategy were delivered, alongside clichés and motivational quotes, as though he believed that this was the standard language of sport—a belief reinforced by four championship titles and being named Olympic Assistant Coach. Up until a few months ago, Jayna had admired his broad shoulders and lovingly watched the strong line of his jaw, even as he spewed his pep talks. But the desire to reach out and touch him had fled. He was *too* powerful now. His whistle commanded. The pencil dangling on a string could record and erase the names of players as he pleased. With the Olympic Games looming on the horizon, this power was terrifying.

The players called him Coach Nate. Or just Coach. The title bestowed upon a trusted instructor. *Or a bus*. He had begun to tweet coaching advice and had been invited to write a coaching column for the university paper. He had a following. To Jayna he was more like a Greyhound bus, bearing down upon her as she lay on a strip of asphalt. A scream snagged in her throat.

Some of the other girls told Nate jokes in the locker-room or dressed up like him for Halloween parties. A few of the players, mostly those who were known as the regular benchwarmers, cried, shouted, and complained in the showers about the injustice of his decisions. The girls laughed hysterically as they discussed what it might be like to sleep with someone like Nate. It would start with a lot of pep-talking. He would set out the rules and details of the foreplay. He would wear his baseball cap, call his lover by her last name, and shout out dirty things in his deep, raspy voice. When it was over, he would offer constructive feedback and suggest some drills for his lover to practice at home.

Jayna knew that out of all the things the girls said, only the last name part was accurate. *Bentley*, he had called her. Over and over again.

He was not a joke to her.

The score clock sounded to indicate it was 6:00 a.m. The piles of clothes around the gym grew as the girls stripped off their sweats, revealing long, awkward limbs, oversized basketball shorts and old t-shirts. She wasn't sure if she'd make it through the warm up without vomiting, but she forced herself to start jogging around the perimeter court and settled in beside Vee. They circled, now in lock step. She was dizzy, and her calves were killing her from dancing in heels all night. She forced herself to stay in the rhythm of the jog and keep up with Vee. It would be over soon. Left. Right. Left. Right. The gym echoed with the squeaking of rubber soles. After about ten minutes of jogging, there was the shrill sound of Nate's whistle, and the women hurried to huddle around him at centre court. This is what they did five times a week. Show up. Stretch. Run around. Hear a whistle. Gather. Like a herd of obedient animals.

"Morning, ladies," said Nate.

He removed his cap, smoothed his dark hair, and covered it up again.

The sounds of hard breathing. Jayna tried to slow her heart.

"Where's Castiglione?" he asked the group, without looking up from his paper.

Jen, the girl who believed all questions should be answered—and answered by her, even if she didn't know the answer—spoke up. "Haven't seen her, Coach."

There were few muffled giggles from some girls.

"Actually, Helen's sick today," said Vee, glancing at Jayna.

The team knew that Helen had gone to the club with Jayna. They had told everyone they were going out, updating their teammates via Twitter with pictures of the two of them clinking shot glasses. Probably a stupid move. She should be more careful about what she shared with her team. Helen had disappeared before midnight with her boyfriend. She could have been anywhere this morning. She was relieved that Vee hadn't said anything but felt anxious that she now owed Vee. That's the way she saw these things working: a cycle of give and take.

"Okay, thanks," said Nate. He jotted something down on his board, then let go of the pencil. Jayna stared at it, dangling there on its string, as Nate returned the whistle to his lips.

Tweet.

"I want to start practice by reading you something Vince Lombardi once said." He flipped over the top page on his clipboard and started to read. "'Winning means you're willing to go longer, work harder, and give more than anyone else.' Remember that, ladies. I want you to give more. You need to do what it takes and give me everything you've got. Clear?"

He glanced up. Jayna was certain he was looking at her, reinforcing the message that she had to give, give, give, more than she already had, to win. He returned his focus to the clipboard, and she was suddenly aware of a deep exhaustion, like thickened blood in her veins.

"Okay, today we are going to focus on fundamental ball-handling skills. Split into groups of four."

He picked up the whistle again and held it an inch away from his mouth, reinforcing that he had the absolute power to make the drills commence at any moment. To make the women burst into a frenzy of activity at his command. He gestured violently with his right arm throughout his instructions, delivering forceful karate-type chops into the air, then pointing sharply with a rigid arm at the various areas around the court.

Jayna's vodka buzz was clearing, and in its place a grey-green haze settled around her head. She couldn't focus on what Nate was saying. She peeked at the giant digital clock on the wall and saw, through bleary eyes, that one hour, forty-three minutes and thirty-eight seconds remained until the showers. She wiped the side of her hand underneath her right eye, leaving a long black smear and small flecks of dried mascara on her thumb.

"Okay, ladies, let's make it happen," said Nate, followed by the shrill blow of his whistle.

She watched as he emptied a large rack of basketballs onto the gym floor, and each girl grabbed one. The thumping of the balls across the floor was a sound that had once energized her. She used to race her teammates to be the first to pick one up. Now she waited for the balls to stop rolling. She bent down slowly to grab one. Nate was right there, taking up so much space around her, stealing control of her senses: the memory of his touch, his taste, his smell, his breath. He must have seen her wobble as she stood and turned. He didn't reach out a hand to steady her, and she didn't look up to see him. She stared at the pebbling on the ball instead, maintaining control over that one sense. She held the basketball so tightly that her knuckles went white.

With her group she began the slaps, pounding the ball from palm to palm. The repeated impact reverberated through her cloudy head and aching body. She imagined that it was Nate's head, slamming back and forth between her open hands: *forty-four, forty-five, forty-six.*

She had a sudden memory of the time he took her head firmly in his hands, pulled it towards his face, and kissed her hard, directly on the lips. It had been four months earlier. Practice had just ended; the other girls were in the locker room, and she and Nate were seated face-to-face on wooden chairs in his office.

"We just need to review an offensive play," he had said to get her there.

Strategic plays were what he was known for. In the past, whenever he reviewed these plans with the team, he had gathered the women close, removed his baseball cap, and spoke in a hushed, serious tone, as if in a war room. In those moments, Jayna sank into his brilliance, admired the perfect line of his nose, was absorbed by the deep hum of his voice, felt the throb of attraction.

Alone together in his office that day, he had pulled her out of the chair towards him. She was standing above him and responding to his kiss, aware of the droop of her tank top, the display of cleavage, and the spirals of butterflies in her stomach. Simultaneously frightened and curious about what was going to happen, she did not back away or protest. He moved his hands tenderly from her head, over her shoulders, down her back to her waist, then forcefully pulled her forward so that she straddled his lap. Perspiration, still fresh from her training session, ran down her face, and he moved to lick it. His tongue had followed the line of sweat down her neck to her chest. With each passing moment, her curiosity dissipated. She hoped he would stop, but she continued through the motions. She needed it to stop. She wished it had ended with the kiss. But he was fully into the game, and she was suddenly outside herself, watching the play—seeing her own long arms link around the neck of this married man, her coach, as he picked her up, walked to the dimly lit back corner of the office, and awkwardly deposited her on a pile of exercise mats.

She lay there, petrified and silent, with her head pinned between the rough cinder-block wall and some old weight plates. He had lifted her tank top until it covered her head and flipped up her sports bra, so that the elastic band held the dry-wick fabric against her face. He pulled her shorts down and half off, so that they lay limp around her right ankle. It was difficult to breathe, and she couldn't see anything but a vague silhouette through the grainy film of her shirt. She smelled its sweaty fabric.

And she had felt everything: her heart pounding, the painful swell of panic in her throat, his hands and mouth and sweat and body moving against her and inside her. And she wished it would all stop. She had heard sounds that would never leave her: his breathing, and the endless repetition of her last name.

Jayna's head pounded as she finished her slaps. Beside her, Jen counted the reps aloud. Nate circled the group as they progressed to more complex and demanding drills. He shouted corrections or sounds intended to make the players move faster or pass harder, like *Hup, hup, hup! Heeya! Heeya!* Like they were all horses.

SAMUEL

In a University of Toronto lecture hall, Samuel checked his watch. Professor Klein's lecture was half over. Normally Samuel would type notes directly onto his laptop, but over the past week, the letters *R*, *U*, *S* and *N* had stopped working, turning his notes into a confusing mass of typos. So he had left the laptop at his apartment, substituting it with a black ballpoint pen, and he was already suffering from an aching wrist and hand.

There were just three months left of class before his final paper was due, and his second degree would be complete. Then he and Callie Hawkins, who was finishing up her M.A. at McGill, would head out on a two-month backpacking trip through Europe. They had been planning their trip for more than a year, emailing each other lists of the museums they wanted to visit, the festivals they would attend, and the romantic locations where they might kiss. Usually, Samuel went out of his way to shun clichés and refused to watch romantic comedies, but early on in their relationship, something about Callie led him to write poetry. Nothing overly gushy, rhyming or pastoral, but something in the spirit of e. e. cummings (*i, we, find love (if this is that) in each other and in us*).

It was these early poetic efforts that won her over, she had told him. And the pressure of knowing this had paralysed his creativity and cut his poetry writing short. Since then, he had lived with the fear that he was somehow disappointing her—he was sure he could hear the boredom in her gentle exhales when they kissed, and he imagined he could feel her frustration in the way she pulled her hand out of his to open a door or pick up a leaf.

She was a beautiful lapsed Baptist, whose parents disapproved of the relationship because they feared Samuel's faithlessness would prevent Callie from coming back to church. Despite these objections, Callie and Samuel carried on, making their globe-trotting plans; and whenever she was visiting Samuel in Toronto, they stopped to peer into the Birks display case on Bloor Street, eyeing the smallest of the solitaires (all he could afford).

He had always loved rings—as a child he used to take his mother's hand and twist her wedding ring around and around her finger. He adored the smoothness of the gold beneath his touch. He loved that she never took the ring off. Even later on, when she came unspooled, she still wore the ring. It stood for a kind of permanence and normalcy. He dreamed about seeing his ring on Callie's finger. Old-fashioned as it was, he looked forward to the ceremonial exchange of bands that would mark Callie becoming Mrs Samuel Gottschalk.

He cherished the sound of that name.

Six years earlier, somewhere in the air between Toronto and Vancouver, on his way to begin his undergrad degree at UBC, Sammy Gottschalk had decided to become Samuel Gottschalk.

"Just call me Sammy," he had said on the first day of school, every year since kindergarten, when his new teachers read out his name on the attendance sheet. But then on his way to Vancouver, at thirty thousand feet, when the man sitting beside him introduced himself and initiated a conversation, Sammy spoke without hesitation: "Hello, I'm Samuel."

Instantly he liked how grown-up it sounded. He liked that he had the power to choose a name and take on the persona that went along with it. "Sammy" had seemed small and inconsequential. "Sam" would be too much of a punctuation mark. A dark blot of ink, severe and final. "Samuel" was who he chose to be now. His younger brother Brent never needed to play around with nicknames. Athletic, opinionated, and blunt, Brent lived up to the meaning of his name: to burn. And he did a lot of burning, always ready with an insult hidden in a compliment.

"At least you're smart," Brent had said frequently when they were kids. After a fraternal tussle in the backyard that left Samuel with a sprained wrist and bruised forehead. After a game of street hockey, where Brent's team scored ten goals and Samuel's team managed only two. After a race home from the bus stop. "My school bag was too heavy with books," Samuel had used as an excuse, too many times to be believable. No one likes excuses from losers, anyway.

At least you're smart. In the world of a young Canadian boy, being smart would never be better than having an explosive slap shot.

At least Samuel was a strong name.

"Hello, I'm Samuel," was also how he introduced himself to Callie Hawkins when they met during freshman week activities, two strangers sharing a washcloth to wipe down after a dip in a kiddie pool full of green Jell-O. She turned to him, a glob of green on her perfectly plucked eyebrow, and had said in a mock serious voice, "Well, hello, Samuel, I'm Callista," and then she giggled. It hadn't been the reaction he hoped for, but the way she had looked him in the eye and winked afterward sparked a longing in him. Immediately he wanted a chance to convince her that he could be taken seriously. So in preparation for the time they spent together, he created lists of topics they might discuss. Sometimes he researched these subjects on the internet to make sure he was well-informed and ready to contribute. He never let Callie see the lists, and their conversations never unfurled in the way he imagined. She loved to interrupt, challenge, and change subjects unexpectedly. She was apt to stand up and launch into a little jig, just for fun, when they had been seated too long. It threw him off. She preferred to talk about people, their clothes and idiosyncrasies, rather than discuss the Wye River Memorandum or the Keystone Pipeline.

Once, in a playful mood after sex, while buttoning up her shirt, Callie had done one of her little happy dances. He lay on the bed, watching her, pleased at her apparent satisfaction. In the midst of the dance, she looked sideways at him, cocked her head and duck-walked across the floor, half-naked and giggling. He saw a perfect imitation of his own posture and gait—remembered sitting slumped over a textbook at his childhood kitchen table, while Brent had walked round and round, whispering *"quack, quack"* each time he passed by.

Feeling deflated, Samuel covered his naked body with the bed sheet. Callie lay back down on the bed, placed her hand on his cheek, and spoke softly in her sweetest voice. "Why aren't you happy? I thought you'd like my little dance."

SAMUEL

Despite the lump building in his throat, he had shrugged, doing his best to make it appear like everything was okay. She had kissed his nose, sat up and continued dressing. He couldn't wait to immerse himself in his schoolbooks and forget the humiliating slap-slap of her bare feet duck-walking across the floor.

At least you're smart.

Professor Klein finished up his lecture, and while most of the students crammed textbooks and laptops into their bags, a few in the front rows raised their hands to ask questions. Samuel sat silently near the back of the auditorium. He had learned over the past few years not to ask questions. The answers were always disappointing. Instead, he thought about how a few classes and ten thousand words hammered out on his laptop (once fixed) separated him from hanging another degree on his wall—and from his future with Callie. A graduate degree was something people would admire. Two more letters added to his name.

VINCENT

Vincent Beaulieu grunted through a set of fifty sit-ups and then lay his head down on the deck. There was no towel beneath him, just poolside tiles. He turned onto his side, abs burning, closed his eyes, and thought about Yasmine. Her hard, slim body in the water, just twenty metres away. He wished he could run his hands over her stomach and thighs.

"Ten seconds," shouted his teammate Adam over the loud sounds of the aquatic centre.

Vincent turned onto his back and waited for Adam's signal to begin crunching their bodies again. His pulse pounded in his ears, along with the synchro swimmers' loud music. It was the same piece, played perpetually in twenty-second bursts. Sometimes the synchro coach clanged a steel karabiner against the metal pool ladder to keep the girls on a steady beat during their routine. Vincent couldn't escape the metallic tapping and music. It was always there, during land training and rests between swim sets. His ex-girlfriend Hayley (dubbed *The Synchro Chick* by Adam) used to play her routine CDs in the car.

"It helps me internalize the rhythm, Vince," she had said.

While they were still a couple, her routine music had been a soundtrack that played in his head over and over again. Vincent began to swim slower whenever she rehearsed in the morning. He imagined her long, thin legs moving through the air, first rising from below the surface, glistening with beads of water, opening into a split position, then snapping shut like long, white crocodile jaws and spinning back down into the depths.

Fortunately for his swim times and future athletic career, Hayley had retired seven months earlier, after she was cut from the World Championship Team. She had left Montreal to return to her hometown of Regina. They never broke up officially, but they said goodbye in the driveway of the house where she was billeting, and they had not spoken since. This was the way relationships in the sport world worked—if one person left that world, there was nothing to keep the couple connected.

"Go," said Adam, Vincent's Canadian teammate and fiercest competitor. They began another set of abs.

The two swimmers competed at everything. Even fifty abdominal curls were a kind of competition. Vincent watched Adam out of the corner of his eye. Pushed to lift his body higher and hold the last curl for longer. He silently celebrated these small victories.

Soon, he and Adam would hit the cold water and begin a five-thousand-metre workout, the details of which were written in red on the whiteboard behind the blocks. They would swim in side-by-side lanes, matching each other stroke for stroke, trying to gain advantage over the other with a strong push off the turns or powerful flutter. These challenges were not overt. The men celebrated the end of difficult sets with high fives, but Vincent craved the delicious rush of being the first to touch the wall. The winner would always say "Good job" to the other. To the loser, that was the worst phrase in the world.

Vincent sat up and looked at the pool. Several swimmers were already doing some drill sets, and there in lane eight was Yasmine. She was a long-distance runner who did four pool-running sessions weekly as a part of her Achilles surgery rehab. She made her way slowly down the lane, water at her chin, looking uncomfortable and desperate to breathe air that was not accompanied by water drops. Her short black hair was plastered to her head, because she didn't wear a bathing cap like the swimmers did. A red aqua-jogging belt wrapped tightly around her narrow body. He wished he were that belt. Sometimes Vincent would go underwater between swim sets and watch Yasmine's lean, muscular legs scissor back and forth; the sharp definition of her calves contrasted with the smooth lines of the swimmers' legs. He watched her bony, calloused, bare feet move through the water—feet that had been used to propel her hundred-pound body forward on hard, cold Montreal roads and university tracks for hours each day.

She was Canada's top female marathoner, fighting to overcome injury and surgery, and hoping to earn a berth for the upcoming Olympic Games. Sometimes he watched her when she stood poolside after her workouts, hair dripping, as she chatted with his teammates Melanie and Renée. Her wiry arms, tiny hands, and narrow shoulders contrasted with the female competitive swimmers' broad backs and large paws. On land, the swimmers were in Yasmine's element, and they looked apelike, with their forward-rolled shoulders and unusually long arms. She was thirty-one and married to the coach of the Canadian women's basketball team (whom Vincent guessed was at least ten years her senior) but that didn't stop him from watching her in the water, from loving that for a few hours every week. This nimble land athlete became a part of his aquatic world.

"Boys! In the water now! Let's go, let's go, let's go!" their coach, Robert, screamed from the other side of the pool. "You having a tea party over there or what? Get in the pool, or you'll be doing an extra thousand metres today."

Vincent reacted immediately, standing and moving towards his backpack. It was only in sport, or the military, that an adult could get away with shouting like this at other adults. The hierarchical coach-athlete relationship allowed space for these small threats. And, generally, it worked.

He grabbed a protein bar out from his bag and clamped it between his teeth, so he could wrap a towel around his waist, shed his shorts, and pull up two overused, chlorine-faded Speedo suits. He headed towards the starting blocks, taking large bites out of the bar. When he arrived at the edge of his lane, he swung his arms in windmills and kept an eye on Yasmine. She was climbing out of the pool two lanes over, water running down her sculpted legs.

Suddenly, he felt the pressure of hands on his back. He fell towards the water. The image of the runner disappeared as a splash, then bubbles, rose around him. Underwater, he looked up at the surface. There was Adam, leaning over the side, laughing, with both arms still outstretched. A small triumph for his rival. The water was cold around Vincent, but his face burned with embarrassment. He streamlined to the surface and began to swim his eight-hundred-metre free warm-up. Trying to get a head start on Adam. Letting his face cool down and his body warm up.

Samuel

It was 11:40 p.m. on a Tuesday when Samuel's television stopped working. A narrow, horizontal black line had appeared across the centre of the screen and, over the course of the ensuing hour, spread vertically until a pixelated blackness covered the whole scene. The sitcom characters had continued to deliver their lines, even as they drowned in the growing rectangular pool of black. Samuel slammed both fists against the top of the set. The canned laughter continued, making him want to kick the TV. He grunted and shut it off, stood for a few moments trying to think of something to do, then turned towards the desk to grab his laptop. It wasn't there. Still at the shop.

He picked up his cell. Callie was in class, so he couldn't call her. He dropped the phone onto the desk, sighed, and cast an accusing glare at the television.

The old set had belonged to his parents, and he had acquired it when he left home for university. It took up too much room in this tiny basement apartment. He had to squeeze between it and the wall to get from the living room to the kitchen, but he was reluctant to let it go. It was his past, heavy and calling for attention.

It hadn't seemed so imposing back in his childhood home in Elora. Samuel, Brent, and their dad had spent hours each Sunday on the sofa in their living room, watching sports on it. Samuel's mom, an elementary school principal, was usually tucked away in her home office, reviewing papers and getting ready for the upcoming week or school board meetings, while the three males watched pregame shows, drank litres of pop, and downed bags of chips. Samuel followed Brent's lead, shouting at the referees when they made bad calls, standing up in the crucial moments leading up to a touchdown, high-fiving his dad when the "good guys" scored. His dad seemed to love these occasions, liberally distributing nuggies and making toasts to the Gottschalk men.

Those were the days before his mom took a stress leave from her job. The days before she began to unravel. Or maybe the unravelling started first, he wasn't sure, and he would never know for certain.

She had come home late from work one Thursday, mascara running, her tight bun unpinned. Brent and his dad were out at a hockey game in Toronto, but Samuel had stayed home to study for a test. He was in the kitchen, waiting for his mom to return, his calculus textbook open on the kitchen table. She was the one who sat with him each evening since he was in first grade, as he worked his way through his homework; who brought him home newspaper articles about global affairs and national politics; who encouraged him to join the school debate team; who hugged him on the mornings of important tests.

SAMUEL

That Thursday, she had stumbled into the kitchen, left the door to the garden wide open, and dropped her briefcase on the floor. The laptop inside rattled. She touched her cheek. Thinking she might be ill, he stood and rushed to take her by the arm. She turned her head towards him. Her vacant stare frightened him.

He crouched slightly to look directly into her eyes. No recognition. "Mom? You okay?"

She turned away and mumbled something. She was unsteady, and Samuel felt helpless.

"Should I call Dad?"

She shook her arm free of Samuel's grip and walked towards her bedroom. A shaky sigh escaped her mouth, and she spoke, "Just tired."

She stepped into the darkness of her room and shut the door. The quiet click of the lock sent chills up his spine.

That night he had stared blankly at the pages of his calculus book. He was distracted by every sound in house: the blast of the furnace, the clinking of the ice machine, the scratch of branches against the window. And with each creak and click, he looked up, hoping it was his mom.

Brent and his dad had come through the door, long after midnight, and stood laughing about something in the dim light of the kitchen before they noticed him seated at the table. It was in Samuel's state of heightened awareness that he saw something he had never noticed before. The way his dad looked at Brent. Pride. Friendship. The same way his mom looked at Samuel while they debated Bush's policies or the benefits of a minority government. It was the delightful favour of a parent. Something that's just there and can't be earned. After a few seconds, the two men glanced up and noticed Samuel. The third wheel. An intruder in their private moment. Samuel didn't know why, but he chose not to tell them about what happened with his mom earlier that night. Perhaps in the hope that the next day she would wake and put on her suit and pin up her hair and wink at Samuel over a piece of toast. But the gnawing ache in the pit of his belly warned him that something had changed forever.

He had stayed at the table and listened to his father knock on the bedroom door and whisper, "Hannah?"

He heard Brent suggest to his dad that he give up. "She's probably just in a deep sleep," he had suggested. Then there was the groan of the couch springs as his father lay down for the night.

Samuel's mom had not gotten up for work the next day. She stayed in her room, only rising to shuffle in slippered feet along the carpet to the family bathroom.

And in the ensuing months, Sunday afternoons in front of the television had changed as well. For Samuel, there was the constant awareness of the closed bedroom door. Or the agony of ignoring his mom as she passed behind the couch, slumped and slow, on her way to the toilet. She spent her days in her room with the lights off. Brent and his dad seemed to huddle closer to each other on the sofa. The space between the pair and Samuel grew wide, cold, and empty.

Doctors and counsellors came and went, too, talking to Samuel's dad in hushed tones. Too many shrugs and handshakes. Sympathetic glances at the two teenaged boys, hovering near the kitchen doorway.

Sometimes when Samuel lay in his bed at night, he overheard his parents talking inside their dark room. "Hannah, please get up tomorrow. The boys need you."

And her sobs.

SAMUEL

One night, when the crying went on longer than usual, he had turned away from the wall that separated him from his parents' room. Brent shifted on the top bunk.

"Brent?"

"Yeah?" His younger brother's voice was clear and alert. Obviously, he had not been sleeping either.

Samuel realized he had nothing to say. "Goodnight," he mumbled.

Their mom's breakdown was not something the brothers discussed. They didn't have words to categorize it. It was just something that had happened, was happening, in their lives. Something they watched together from doorways or heard mumbled through walls, but never openly acknowledged.

Even the day Brent fought with two boys from school, Samuel stayed silent. He had heard the pimple-faced bullies in the cafeteria, teasing Brent about his crazy mom.

"I heard your mother went postal on the vice-principal at her school," one said.

"I heard she bit a student," said the other.

"She should be in some kind of asylum. Do you have her chained up in the basement or something?" The boys laughed loudly, and Brent, red-faced, stared into space. Samuel, one grade older and two tables over, knew that his brother wouldn't let it go.

So when Brent walked into their bedroom later that day with blood on his face and cuts on his knuckles, Samuel fetched a wet cloth and Band-Aids, but they didn't talk about what had happened.

That summer Samuel had received a scholarship to attend UBC, the school his mom had urged him to apply to. He stood outside her room for an hour before building the courage to go in. The air was thick with the smell of sweaty sheets and muscle ointment. A housecoat lay in a heap on the wooden chair in the corner. A tray of food sat untouched on the dresser. Narrow streams of light filtered through the thick brown curtains, casting a sepia tone on the room. His mother was curled up on her side beneath the duvet, her mop of matted brown hair peeking out.

"I'm moving out West. I'm going to UBC."

There was shifting under the covers.

"I'm leaving in a couple of weeks."

He waited for a response. There was only soft, breathy weeping coming from the bed. It went on for what felt like hours. Samuel stood and waited, painfully. She did not rise from beneath the duvet. He left the room.

The last time he saw her was the day of his departure for university. She had emerged from her cave in a pink nightgown tucked into old blue sweat pants. She stood on the driveway leaning against Samuel's father, with her arms crossed over her body and her hair pulled back into a messy ponytail. Rather than have to look at his mother's exhausted face, Samuel had focused on rearranging the bags in the trunk of the car he was about to drive across the country. He stopped only when Brent came out of the house, carrying the large television. His arms were flexed and powerful under its weight. Samuel could never have carried the monstrous thing alone. His dad said loudly, with undisguised admiration, "My god, look at that boy's strength!"

Samuel couldn't wait to get away from all of this.

They all stood and watched in awe as Brent approached the front passenger side of the vehicle and levered the television onto the reclined seat. Then his dad rushed over to help Brent adjust the angle of the machine, finally giving him a hearty slap on the back. Irritated by the scene, Samuel turned to his mother. She appeared frail and lost, swaying alone on the crumbling asphalt. She was nothing like the headstrong mom with proud, perfect posture that he used to adore. That mom would have loaded his car with books and sent him off with a crushing hug. This woman felt thin and limp in his arms when he finally wished her goodbye. She dropped her head against his chest and cried, shaking violently. Brent and his dad had looked in the other direction, busying themselves with talk of the tire pressure. Samuel drove away that day without looking into the rear-view mirror. He thought of his mother, returning to her sepia-toned room and retreating under the covers.

That Christmas he had stayed in British Columbia and ate a huge turkey dinner, followed by six beers, at his friend Harold's house in Kitsilano. He was full and drunk and contemplating taking a walk with Harold down to Jericho Beach when his phone rang. His dad's number popped up on the screen. It was already midnight back at home in Elora.

"Hi, Dad," Samuel said. "I was going to call you guys, but I was so busy eating that I didn't—but anyway, Merry Christmas. Did it snow at home today? Were there any sports on TV? No one here wanted to do anything but eat…it's a good thing I only watch sports and don't play them…."

Samuel kept talking so he could ignore the hairs that stood up on his neck and the loud sniffles of his dad on the other end of the line. He had a sense that something was very wrong. That it was about his mother. The beer was heavy in his stomach, his head light, and he talked on about the mashed potatoes and his roommate's "buffet pants" and Harold's yappy dog and everything he could think of so that he wouldn't have to hear whatever it was that his dad was going to tell him.

When Samuel finally stopped to take a breath, his dad spoke. "Your mother is dead."

YASMINE

She hated rehab training. The cold slap of the water at 6:00 a.m. was a thousand times worse than the sharp intake of frigid air during a winter run. But there she was, in Montreal, well into her fifth month of water running, because her doctors and physiotherapists had said her Achilles wasn't yet strong enough for road running.

The hours of back-and-forth in a pool lane gave her time to reflect on how much her life had gone wrong in the nine years since she had met her husband, Nate.

Yasmine had been on her last year of a sport scholarship at the University of Oregon, running ten thousand metres for their track team, when she met Nate at an NCAA meet. Her teammate Jeanette introduced her to him at a campus bar after their events were over.

"This is Mr Morgan, my old high school basketball coach from Montreal," she had said. "He was at the coaching conference connected with our meet."

Yasmine stared at this beautiful man: six-foot-five with large hands and thick brown hair. He leaned towards the two girls and spoke.

"I've moved up in the world since way back then." His voice was deep and full of confidence. "I coach university basketball now. Call me Nate."

He turned and smiled directly at Yasmine. His lips were pink and full. There was a swell of fluttering in her stomach.

The bar was packed with loud college students, and whenever Nate spoke to her throughout the rest of the evening, she could barely hear him. She loved having that excuse to lean towards him and ask him to repeat himself. He spoke closely and directly into her ear, his lips touching her lobe, sending bolts of electricity through her body. He talked about coaching and basketball, and showed deep interest in her running career and aspirations. Compared to the fraternity boys she usually hung out with, he seemed powerful and stoic. As an athlete who, in most circumstances, was in full control of her body, she was thrilled by the way it responded to him. Her heart raced, her back arched, and she found herself reaching out involuntarily to touch his arm. She yearned for him to lean against her. At the end of the evening, when Jeanette left the table to grab a last drink from the bar, Nate slipped his business card into her palm.

"Come visit me soon," he said softly. "You should consider training in Montreal once you finish up school this summer."

Then he leaned over and ran his lips along her right collarbone. He planted a kiss in the space between her clavicles with such tenderness that she almost let out a quiet moan. She didn't want the evening to end. She imagined this mysterious man taking her by the arm and leading her out of the bar to somewhere they could be alone. But he stood up slowly, touched his fingertips to her flushed face, and walked away. As he made his way through the crowd, she sat there, breathless and aching for more.

He had complete control over her right from the beginning. She had called him the next night, and he hadn't picked up, leaving her feeling desperate and helpless.

The night after that, he had answered. "Hello?"

"Oh, hi, Nate. It's Yasmine…the runner." She hated the way her voice shook with nerves.

"I'm glad you called," he said, and she felt a surge of relief.

In the months that followed he said very little on their phone calls. She had filled the conversations with stories of her track training and injuries, and he offered words of advice and gave her a number of practical reasons why she should train in Montreal. He offered for her to stay with him. But he rarely spoke about himself. She revealed more and more personal details in an effort to draw him out, but he never capitulated.

By the day of their graduation, Yasmine and Jeanette had made plans to drive to Montreal together.

"I know you only want to go because of Nate," said Jeanette, while she and Yasmine packed up their apartment in Oregon.

"Not entirely. I've always wanted to go to Montreal…and everyone thinks I'll be a good long-distance runner. If I'm going to make the switch to marathon, I need to do it now, right?"

The lie had been obvious to both of them. She was going for Nate. Training was the secondary attraction.

"Whatever," said Jeanette.

Jeanette had listened to her on the phone with Nate almost nightly for the past four months, often making lewd sexual gestures or pretending to make out with her pillow while they spoke.

When it came time to make the journey, Yasmine jammed her life in Oregon—trophies, medals, and school texts—into one cardboard box and two suitcases full of clothes and shoes. She and Jeanette stuffed their belongings into a beat-up red Toyota Tercel and set out on their long drive across the continent.

Even though Yasmine was eager to get to Montreal and start her adult life, they had planned to drive North through Washington State, cross the border into B.C., and head directly to Yasmine's parents' home in Surrey to drop off her stuff. Then they would embark on a five-day drive across the country. Excited by the idea of speeding across Canada towards a new man, a new athletic discipline, and a new city, Yasmine spent hours meticulously planning out their route in highlighter on a large map. As the line of fluorescent yellow lengthened, doubts crept in: *What if I don't like it? What if he doesn't like me?*

It was 1:00 a.m. when they arrived in Surrey, but her parents and nineteen-year-old brother were in the living room, waiting for the girls with a champagne bottle and a large cake with *"Welcome Home Champ"* written in red on the white icing. Yasmine ran to embrace her mom and inhaled the comforting scent of Nivea cream and fabric softener. It was the same scent that greeted her at the finish line of the one-kilometre and five-kilometre races she ran when she was a child.

Her dad high-fived Jeanette, then pulled Yasmine into a bear hug, lifting her off the ground. "It's so good to have our little Yazzie home."

His stubble scratched her cheek. Same as always. These familiar sensations were the security of home. Each held a memory that anchored her to a past and a real identity.

Her brother interrupted, "Okay, everyone, enough with the hug fest. Let's have cake!"

She separated herself from her dad and flopped down on the old yellow-and-blue flecked couch. She sank into the overstuffed pillows and watched as her best friend and family dug in to the dessert. She tried hard to imagine Nate standing in her parent's house, eating her mom's cake, but she couldn't manage to juxtapose her image of the strong, imposing basketball coach with the easy comfort of her childhood home.

Her focus drifted to the idea of Montreal. The new and the mysterious. And there would be the reunion with Nate. She felt her body tingle slightly. Her heart raced. Yasmine wasn't sure what would happen or whether she was ready for it all. She thought about future training runs past the cafes and restaurants of downtown Montreal. A life propelling forward into new climates and terrain. She wondered if this mix of nostalgia, apprehension, and excitement was a trait of adult life.

Her dad walked over with a piece of cake. "Tired, Yaz?"

She accepted the plate, sat back, and took large bites. "Thanks, Dad."

The grape jelly filling was the happy taste of childhood birthdays in her house. She never used to notice these things, but they were hitting her now, along with a sadness she couldn't shake.

When Yasmine woke up the next morning, she was lying on the couch, still in the clothes from the night before, covered with one of her mom's afghan blankets. She checked her watch: 5:45 a.m. She put on a pair of running shorts, sport socks, a tank, and running shoes from her suitcase, and walked out into the wet Surrey air, inhaling the familiar smell of pine needles. She passed the old house where the hoarder lived, with old newspapers stacked up against the inside of the windows; the garage door closed to about a foot from the ground, stuffed animals, small appliances, and stacks of books creeping out underneath.

She passed her old elementary school and the tree where Mikey Szabados pinned her and tried to steal a kiss during a game of tag at recess. She passed the homes of her childhood friends Alison (who used to be a bone rack but recently posted a series of photos on Facebook, showing off her 290-pound body and four kids) and Eunice (whose parents always tried to get Yasmine to eat some kind of squid). She picked up speed and passed into the next neighbourhood, before she turned around and ran home, using different streets and rushing past old memories. She did not think of Nate.

Back at her parents' home, the scalding hot shower poured over her, and she enjoyed the strong throb of blood moving through her legs. This is what it felt like to be fully alive, fully in control of her body, and able to push further than her conscious mind thought possible, able to go fast and then go faster—and able to do it all knowing that tomorrow she would be back up again and ready for more.

Once she was dressed, Yasmine found her mother in the kitchen. Her back was to the doorway, and she was busy moving clean dishes from the dishwasher to the cupboard. A bowl of fruit salad and fresh coffee cake sat on the counter.

"Didn't see you there," her mother said with a wink. "Glad you're up. Come sit with me and tell me about the Montreal boy."

Yasmine swallowed hard. She had not expected the topic of Nate to come up so soon, but her mother's questions came fast.

"What was his name again? Nathan? Are you going there because of him? You said you might be staying with him when you get there?"

Yasmine had only mentioned Nate once in a brief phone conversation, but she must have said his name or talked about him in that certain way that can make a mother take notice.

"I'm going to Montreal to train, and yes, there's a guy, but he's not exactly a boy." She wanted to get the age gap part of the conversation out of the way. She spoke fast. "He's older, like mid-thirties. He's a university basketball coach, actually."

Yasmine's mom looked down at her hands for a while. She said nothing, maybe out of restraint, maybe out of shock. The age thing.

"Don't worry, he's a great guy and my priority will be training….He said he can get me immediate access to gyms, a physio, and coaches…and maybe even an agent." Yasmine sensed she was moving into the territory of saying too much. A rising tide of insecurity about the move drove her to keep selling the plans. And all the while her mom said nothing. Just like she had remained silent two years earlier, when Yasmine chose to attend a track meet instead of returning home to accompany her family to her grandmother's funeral. There had been dead air on the phone line that day. She wondered whether these tight-lipped moments held some particular significance: a rite of passage; a parent letting a child make a mistake so that the child can learn from it; an acknowledgment that she had relinquished her parental control years ago when Yasmine left for university. Whatever the reason, her mom's silence drew her awareness to the apprehension growing in the pit of Yasmine's stomach. She just wanted to know if her mom approved or not, but she would never ask. She was afraid of the answer being stated aloud.

Her mom simply poured some tea into her emptied cup and told Yasmine that she was welcome to come home whenever she wanted. And that was it. All that was left were Nivea-scented hugs, and then she would be off with Jeanette, leaving the past behind, on the road east.

Within the hour the two women, armed with a large Ziploc bag of sandwiches and homemade snacks, were back in the Tercel, speeding along the TransCanada, singing "Life is a Highway" at the tops of their lungs.

"To the future," Yasmine said, raising a bottle of water into the air.

When they crossed over the Ontario-Quebec border several days later, Yasmine stared out the window, looking for evidence of being in a Francophone province. She was disappointed to see that beyond the French-only road signs, a slight hike in gas prices, and bumpy road conditions, it appeared the same. Same big-box stores. Same green grass. Same dented guardrails. Same roadside fast food stops and types of cars. She was told by friends and acquaintances that she would be moving to a place that was a little taste of France in Canada, but she was dismayed to see that, so far, everything looked pretty ordinary. She had been hoping for something new and exciting.

They entered the city from the highway north of downtown, passing through kilometres of nondescript streets lined with bleak grey duplexes. Then they weaved their way through older streets flanked by long rows of three-story buildings with the spiralling wrought-iron walk-ups and multicoloured doors. As they approached the Plateau neighbourhood, Yasmine had the urge to go for a run. Running had a way of making her happy. But first there was the matter of reuniting with the man she had met in person only once. *Will I sleep on the couch, or will he expect me to share his bed? This is insane.* She wondered if there was a lingerie shop near Nate's house. She needed one of those miraculous push-up bras, the kind that made her look more feminine. She didn't relish the moment when she'd undress and he'd recoil at the straight lines of her body.

They pulled up to Nate's home at around 5:00 p.m. From the outside it seemed to be a tiny, slightly tilted, and rather disappointing cottage-style home (sympathetically, Jeanette suggested that it was cute), with small windows and a dark doorway that contrasted with the majestic stone steps of the three-story walk-up next door. A small, square front yard sat between the house and the sidewalk. Nothing grew there. It was a flat plot of hard earth, covered with the various droppings of the neighbours' large trees. Originally, the riskiness of the move appealed to Yasmine. It was something someone in their early twenties should do once, but the sight of hard-packed earth and dark doorway changed the whole thing from a fun, crazy idea to something real, with threatening shadows and hard surfaces.

"You should stay with me for dinner," said Yasmine, trying not to sound terrified. She did not want to face his front door alone.

But Jeanette seemed desperate to head home to see her family. "I'll wait in the car until he comes to the door, okay? We can get together tomorrow, I promise."

Yasmine stood outside the little house with her suitcases next to her and beads of sweat gathering on her forehead. She felt absurd, even embarrassed. She had no idea what this man really wanted from her. What would Nate say or think when he realized that she came with more than just a pair of running shoes and a desire to train for the marathon event? That she came with ideas and fears and memories? She knocked and waited, her stomach knotting up.

Nate appeared at the door, with a huge smile and an uncomfortably firm embrace, and invited her in. "I'll manage your suitcases."

It was that simple. Jeanette shouted goodbye out of her car window and drove away, and Yasmine walked through Nate's door.

He moved the cases into his office, where he had made up the single bed for her. He seemed so casual about the whole thing, as though he regularly invited young women to move across the continent and live with him.

That night they dined at one of his local haunts, and he ordered for her.

"The young lady will have the chicken with a side salad." Then he turned to Yasmine. "Limit the fat in your diet right now. Fat and fast don't jive." And he winked.

Maybe he likes my childlike shape? Then she doubted that was true.

She longed for the sexual energy of the night they met, but this was much more like a meeting of a coach and athlete.

In the middle of the meal, he opened up the laptop bag at his feet and handed Yasmine a binder full of paper.

"What's this?" she said, disappointed.

"First section's your training plan. In the second section, there's info on your new coach, Frederic. I went ahead and spoke with him and gave some stats on you." He left no time for her to respond. This was so different from their phone conversations. "There's a calendar of the next two months at the back…and there's a meeting scheduled with a potential shoe sponsor."

Despite her disappointment over their first dinner together, that night she had let him guide her back to the house, let him kiss her and run his hands over her body until she was breathless. It made her think it might be fine in the end. She was relieved at his urgency. He carried her to her room, where he laid her on the bed and announced that he was going to be a good boy and let her get some rest. She was gutted. She said nothing. She felt she didn't have the right to say anything. She longed for her mom's embrace.

"Anyway, you have to get up and train in the morning," he said. "I arranged it already. McGill gym at six. Good night. Sleep well."

He left, shutting the door behind him. She sat up, hugged her knees, and stared into the darkness. She wondered how this new life of hers would turn out after all.

During her first months in the city, she had convinced herself to feel grateful for the way he organized her life. He walked with his hand on the small of her back, made suggestions about who she should hang out with, left her lists of things she should do during the day, and seemed to make acclimatizing to a new home much easier.

At the end of the second month, when she returned from a long run, exhausted and wanting to spend some time stretching in the family room, Nate met her, smiling, at the door. He had insisted she go up and get changed right away. She obeyed, not knowing how else to respond to him. At the top of the narrow staircase, she pushed open the door to her room and found it changed: no pyjamas on the floor, no suitcases in the corner, just a bare bed and a desk. She panicked. *Is he sending me away?* She didn't know what to do. Her heart pounded hard and quick. Her legs, still burning from the run, began to shake.

Nate's hands were on her shoulders. He was standing behind her. This was the part when he would send her home. *You don't have the right stuff to make it*, he would say, and she would feel the confidence built up by all her athletic wins crumble away. She would feel skinny, flat, and unfeminine. She would be forced to rent a car and return back across the country, the same route in reverse.

Instead, he had said, "I moved your stuff into the master bedroom!"

And she began to cry. She felt the tears bubbling up from some deep cavity in her chest, like they had been waiting there all along for a good time to come out. They slid silently down her cheeks. Nate didn't seem to notice her tears. He was too busy reaching his arms around her, moving his hands over her chest and belly. She leaned back into him to feel the pressure of his body behind her. He turned her around and bent to kiss her in that space between her collarbones.

"Mine," he had said.

She was fully his.

Within two months they were married at City Hall. When he asked her, she said yes, hoping it would help her feel more secure. Nate had reassured her that getting married would make things easier. As far as she could tell, all it did was upset her parents and inspire Nate to sometimes call her "Little Morgan," even though she had not taken his last name.

It was early on in their marriage when Yasmine had begun to feel an urge to roll her eyes when he spoke. She would pretend she couldn't hear him when he shouted something to her from another room in the house. He began to exhaust her more than her long hours of training or a marathon race.

Her failed attempts at meeting the Canadian qualifying time for the 2004 and 2008 Olympic Games was a topic he brought up from time to time to motivate her to push harder. She had become aware of a nagging twinge of irritation when he spoke. She wondered if it had always been there, like a tumour, growing silently in her brain.

YASMINE

She was now injured and stuck in a pool, struggling to strengthen her broken body so she could run again. The water was a slow medium, with no real propulsion or speed. The slowness of working her way up and down the lane seemed futile, even stupid. She knew that the male swimmers watched her between sets, maybe even joked about her. They probably thought she was old and awkward. And she was powerless in their element. Sometimes she would watch the backstroker named Vincent swim by, his long, powerful arms slicing the water. As he surged along the surface in the next lane, she would reach under the rope to try to touch him. But he was elusive as a fish—offering nothing but a cold current of water against her hand.

It occurred to her one day that no one would ever do backstroke or butterfly to save her life. At least as a female marathoner, she could run faster than most men, train anywhere, and save herself by running away if she ever needed to. If she weren't injured.

Yasmine's last real shot at the Olympic Games was just over a year away, and it frustrated her that she could do nothing but attempt to slosh through water to strengthen her body. She was trapped.

That night over dinner, Yasmine admitted her fears to Nate. "I'm not recovering fast enough," she said. "I'm afraid I might not be able to do what's necessary to qualify for the Olympics. I'm starting to ask myself why I'm doing all this anyway."

She immediately regretted sharing these concerns with him. Nate had just come in from supervising his team's strength and conditioning session. His face was flushed, his dark hair slick with sweat. Yasmine figured he had worked hard spotting his athletes in the weight-room. She never asked him about the team or the basketball practices, because long ago she had learned that his answers would be lengthy, and she would have to struggle to appear interested. He was still handsome, but Yasmine no longer felt any attraction.

"You have to just stick to the physio's plan," he said. "You were born to do this sport."

Nate returned his full attention to his food, and she sat there, staring at the man she married.

"Mmm," he said, mid-chew. She wasn't sure if he was speaking to her or the food.

Yasmine had nothing left to say. She stood up and pushed in her chair. Nate was still focused on his plate.

"I'm going to do my physio exercises," she mumbled, as she walked out of the room.

"That's the spirit. Stick to the program!" Even his words of encouragement inspired a build-up of irritation in her chest.

In the family room, she flicked on the news and started her exercises, focusing on the proper alignment of her leg and the activation of the right muscle groups. She tried to block out the sound of Nate clattering plates in the kitchen.

All of a sudden, he was there in the room with her, watching her and adjusting her leg angle. His touch was perfunctory, like a factory worker pulling a lever on the assembly line. She cringed. Perhaps he moved his players' bodies in the same way, with the same sense of ownership? Did they allow him to freely manipulate their limbs, touch their abs, adjust their posture? In a sense, she knew this was all in the rights of the coach, but Nate had a way of taking more than he was given permission to.

One time, shortly after they got married, Yasmine's parents had come for a visit. On the day they arrived, she spent hours preparing a nice meal for them. It was laid out on the kitchen table, candles lit, when they sat down to enjoy the food. She interrupted her mother's compliments to run upstairs for the cloth napkins she had forgotten. Nate abandoned her parents at the table and followed her up the stairs. He waited behind her as she rummaged around in the linen closet. After she collected the napkins Nate took her by the hand and pulled her into the spare room where her parents would sleep. He closed the door, pressed her up against the wall and began to kiss her on her ear. She giggled at first but then tried to move. He used the weight of his body to pin her.

"Not now," she had said, uncomfortable. "My parents...."

He moved his mouth over hers so she could not finish.

He began tugging at her jeans. She pictured her parents seated in the kitchen and staring at her roast chicken as Nate unbuttoned his pants.

She spoke firmly this time, "I want to go back down."

He placed his index finger over her mouth and said, "Shhh."

She heard her mother's voice calling from below. "Don't worry about it, Yaz. We can use paper towels."

Nate pressed harder against her, panting. There was the sound of feet moving slowly up the stairs.

Yasmine had shoved him, whispering, "Stop."

He dropped his hands heavily and stepped back, breathless. "We'll pick this up later," he said. She had hoped he'd forget.

Nate leaned back on the couch and watched Yasmine continue her exercises, occasionally throwing her a correction, or leaning over her and manhandling her body to adjust her alignment.

On the TV, there was a news story about a 2012 medal hopeful who was caught taking a banned substance and wouldn't be eligible to compete.

"A Canadian hero caught cheating. Today, one of Canada's sporting icons let down a lot of fans…" said the reporter.

"It's stupid to cheat, but even more stupid to get caught," said Nate.

Yasmine did not respond. Nate swung his feet up onto the coffee table and didn't seem to be moving any time soon, so Yasmine collected her mat and stretch cord and headed to their bedroom. As she entered the room and began to remove her clothes, adrenaline coursed through her body. It was a race to put on her pyjamas, clean her teeth, and be in bed, asleep or pretending to be asleep, before Nate made his way up the stairs. While she hurriedly brushed her teeth, she looked into the mirror and stared into her own eyes, something she used to do as a pre-race ritual—study them to see if she could identify any doubt or weakness inside. Tonight all she could focus on were the heavy bags, the dark emptiness of her pupils, and her chlorine-scented hair. She moved to the bed, pulled the covers up high, closed her eyes, and hoped for sleep to come quickly. She'd be back in the cold water, running on the spot, the next morning at 5:30 a.m.

SAMUEL

Samuel was in the back row of a small auditorium, looking down at the fifteen rows of students in front of him. People had their laptops open and were switching back and forth from note taking to dating websites, game sites, Facebook, and Twitter. *Totally bored in Poli Sci* was probably the current Facebook status of half the people in the class. It bugged Samuel that the proliferation of this kind of non-news sharing was further encouraged by the hordes of people online who read these mundane status reports and clicked "Like." At the same time, he got it. He imagined that since the beginning of formalized learning, students had felt compelled to report "being bored." It seemed to be a normal, maybe even necessary, part of learning. Perhaps there was even some value in celebrating the trivialities of everyday life. It kept people fulfilled, he guessed. But Samuel was convinced that, for him, fulfilment would only come the day Callie put on his ring and assumed his name.

He looked away from the array of open Internet windows and focused on the back of the head of the girl two rows in front of him. Her loose brown ponytail, slightly stringy at the ends, like it needed a good brushing, reminded him of his mother. *I should have brushed her hair for her. I should have sat on her bed after school and told her about the mundane details of my day....I should have said, "I was totally bored in math class, Mom." Maybe she would have liked that. Maybe she would have smiled.*

A quiet ding from his newly repaired computer drew his attention away from the girl's hair and memories of his mother. An email from Callie had come in. Without hesitation Samuel clicked to open it, guessing it would be a list of links to travel websites.

Samuel,
I've been giving this a lot of thought, and I've decided that we shouldn't stay together any longer.

A horrible, sick feeling struck Samuel. He kept reading.

I know that we've gone through so much together, but I've come to realize that it just doesn't feel right. We were getting carried away with the idea of getting married and living an adult life.

He was unable to breathe. Sinking.

We don't need to talk this over. It's what's best for both of us in the long run.
Love,
Callista

SAMUEL

He thought he might vomit. He instinctively pressed reply, then decided against it. He considered for a split second that it was a joke. Then he wondered if he had misread it. His throat burned, and his temples pounded. He reread the email slowly. Then again. The words didn't make sense. He stared at the letters on the screen, blurred by tears now. He studied the punctuation. He chose not to believe her message. *It's not true. No, no.* He was speaking aloud. The students around him turned and glared.

His memory went back to that fateful day, to his dad's breathing on the line. "Your mother is dead." Samuel had frozen. Not able to speak or hang up. There was the sound of crying on the line. His dad's voice again, raspy. "She committed suicide. Brent's here with me, so I'm okay."

The lecture hall shrunk around him. His body launched into an erratic dance of quick movements: he closed and opened his laptop, scratched his cheek, pulled at the collar of his shirt, picked at a hangnail, crossed and uncrossed his legs, ran a hand through his hair, breathed faster and faster.

The professor continued to lecture from the front and the students continued to tweet relentlessly about nothing. Samuel sweated. Panted. He struggled to stand and stumbled out of the auditorium.

All he needed to do was talk to her. He dialled her number. It clicked to voicemail.

"Hi, Callie…please call me back." Tears came faster now.

He disconnected and tried a second time. Her voicemail again.

"Please. I just want to talk. Call me."

He rushed towards the bus station. He had to see her. Had to get to Montreal. Go to her. He dialled her number over and over as he walked, leaving increasingly desperate messages.

Pacing the bus station, he tried again. Her recorded voice. Click.

"I bought a bus ticket. I'll be with you soon."

Two hours to departure. He dialled again.

Her beautiful, deep voice: "Hello."

His heart raced. "I'm coming to see you."

Silence on the line for too long. He heard her sigh. Fear rose. "Samuel…"

It was in the way she said his name. Exasperation. The tone of a parent speaking to a misbehaving child. Then her silence.

"Callie, I'm coming…." It came out more as a plea than a statement.

"Please don't. There's no point." Her voice far away. Given up. Cold.

His fingers loosened, and the bus ticket slipped to the concrete floor. The punishing drone of the dial tone.

At unexpected times in the weeks that followed, rage welled up in Samuel, and he would turn to whatever solid surface was around him and hit it. He made two holes in his apartment wall and had fresh cuts and dark bruises on his right fist.

While studying at the library one day, he stood up suddenly and swept his arm across the table covered in textbooks. They crashed to the ground, causing everyone nearby to look over. Some students whispered, "Shhh!" while others returned to their studies. No one asked if he was okay. No one offered to help him clean up. Samuel surveyed the rows of tables and realized that he hated all of the people there. He hated the tops of their heads as they bent over their books. He hated the way some of them tapped their highlighters against the table. He hated the way one girl sniffed her nose repeatedly. He hated the undergrads flirting in the corner. He hated the people on iPhones and the ones draped over textbooks, asleep. *Self-centred idiots.* He packed up his bag and left the library.

Once out in the cold winter air, he began to walk. Off campus, out to the street, fast. Not heading anywhere in particular, just needing to move. Trying not to think about Callie. Or his mother. Or his father and Brent. *Just keep moving.* An uncontrollable anger boiled inside, turning to stabbing pain. He grabbed his chest. His heart beat too fast. His hands trembled. *I'm going to die.* He reached out to balance himself on the wall of a bus shelter. The pain increased. Sweat dripped down his face. He had to rest. He staggered over to the icy steps of a church and sat. He placed his head in his hands and squeezed his eyes shut, hoping the agony would stop.

It took several minutes before his breathing slowed and the tight fist around his heart began to unclench. He was vaguely aware of someone sitting on the stone step next to him. When Samuel finally opened his eyes, a slim, grey-haired man in a black coat was looking at him with concern.

"Keep breathing. You're going to be fine."

The stranger's voice was calm and without condescension. Samuel felt an unexpected rush of gratitude towards him. The pair sat there for several more minutes, until Samuel's hands stopped trembling.

The man spoke again. "I didn't introduce myself...I'm Ellis. I'm just meeting a group of friends in the church here."

Samuel had not known they were on the steps of a church, and the mention of it made him uneasy. Suddenly he was aware of the numbness in his feet and bottom from sitting so long on icy stone.

"Listen, you should come on in and warm up inside while the group meets. We plan to discuss food security and poverty. Join us."

Samuel responded quietly. "No thanks."

He hated going into churches. As a child Samuel had gone to Christmas Eve and Easter Sunday services with his mom, dad, and Brent. Back then he had enjoyed the comfort of sitting in the pew between his parents, sucking on a candy his mom had pressed into his palm, and dreaming about the gifts and chocolates that awaited him at home.

After his mom's death, Callie had thought that a trip to church would help him deal with his sorrow. She had sworn off regular churchgoing long before and only went when she had some big request to make of God, or when there was a death or wedding in her family. But she had dragged him to a charismatic service in downtown Vancouver. It was an altogether different church experience than what he remembered from his childhood.

The small sanctuary had been crammed full of worshippers, pressed up against one another and sweating while they sang. The congregants were so loud and boisterous that as the band at the front played, Samuel could not hear his own voice. They reached their arms up towards the ceiling, wrists crisscrossing all around the room; some shouted out, some spoke in languages Samuel had never heard, some screamed variations of *Hallelujah*. Noticing Callie, who was no longer a regular churchgoer, fall into the sway of the crowd, he had closed his eyes and tried to join in. The words that came out were not what he had expected: *Where are you, God? How could you let this happen to me? Help me. Help me now.* They were angry sounds thrown up into the cloud of noise. When he looked around, the room was exactly as it had been before, absorbed in chaotic communal praise of a god he did not know. And no answers came. Even Callie was shouting things into the air. Although she had been beside him, and there were bodies pressing in from all directions, there was a space, wide and empty, all around.

Ellis gently placed a hand on Samuel's shoulder. There was warmth and reassurance in his touch. Samuel realized he wanted to stay with this man. What would he do if he went home, anyway? He needed a break from checking Callie's Facebook page, where, on the day of her breakup email, she had changed her relationship status to "single" and had more recently changed it to "in a relationship." From what he could tell from the new photos in her album, she was dating a swimmer from Montreal named Adam. There were shots of the two of them poolside, her wearing yoga pants and a large Canada sweater (his, obviously) and Adam in a bathing cap and Speedo, pecs buff, hairless and shimmering. Yesterday Adam had posted on her wall: "Let's celebrate! I got a PB in 200m back. I need a congratulatory smooch!" Thinking about the message, broadcast into cyberspace for all to see, sparked Samuel's anger again.

"I didn't catch your name?" Ellis was standing and reaching down to help Samuel up.
"Samuel."
"God heard."
"Excuse me?" He was hit by sudden fear. Was this man, who had been so kind and comforting, going to turn out to be some kind of Christian fundamentalist freak?
"The Hebrew meaning of Samuel. I've always liked the name." With that, they shook hands, and Ellis turned and walked up the steps.

Samuel hesitated for a moment and then followed Ellis to the red door of the church, calling out, "Okay, I'll join you."

They stepped inside the building and removed their coats and scarves. It was warm, and there was a strong smell of wet carpet and paint. Samuel surveyed the rows of empty wooden pews, worn and concave from so many years spent supporting the weight of congregants. To his surprise the place was empty and still. There were no holiday service crowds; there was no one shouting at the rafters. From the church window, an image of Jesus draped in a white sheet looked down at him; outstretched arms; eyes wide and sad; brows raised in small arcs of apology; lips slightly open as though he was about to speak; a colourful but silent multitude all around him.

Samuel imagined that if he waited long enough, he might hear the glass Jesus speak. He knew it was a silly, superstitious notion, but something anchored him there. Waiting. Only a brief moment passed before he heard the clearing of a throat.

Out of the corner of his eye, he noticed Ellis watching him.

"Let's get going," said Ellis.

Samuel followed.

The two men joined eleven other people in a dimly lit hall in the church basement. There was the sound of their shoes on the parquet flooring as they made their way to a circle of folding chairs. There was a hippie couple, dressed in matching colourful ponchos; five university students, with backpacks under their chairs; an old, bearded homeless man, wearing filthy blue pants and a wool sweater; a bald man in jeans and a navy rugby shirt; and two women, both dressed as though they had just come from a board meeting.

The group turned their attention to a video that had begun to play on a screen at the front of the room. It was a montage of photos: a baby with a distended stomach, covered in flies, lying on a mat on the ground; an emaciated man holding onto the post of a barbed wire fence; a group of skinny men staring blankly at the camera, cheekbones and clavicles protruding; a pile of skulls; a skeletal child in a field; an undernourished baby wailing in her mother's arms; more living skeletons; more dying babies.

Samuel sat and stared at the onslaught of horrific images. As the video played on and on, he was mesmerized by the looks of pain and suffering in the faces of the people on the screen. They were looking directly at him. Blaming him. His chest ached. A woman two chairs away from him began weeping loudly. For fifteen minutes they watched as pictures of people, somewhere between dying and dead, flashed on the screen. There was a short pause in the video before the image of an obese child appeared. Then an overweight woman; a fat family of four posing in front of their large home; a woman carrying an armful of boutique shopping bags; a sprawling subdivision of mansions; an all-you-can-eat buffet restaurant; a famous, overpaid basketball player covered with tattoos and bling; a politician brandishing a giant novelty cheque. The montage ended with a photo of a mother squatting on a field of dry, cracked earth, holding a dead child.

Samuel realized it was propaganda, but it made the anger start up again. His head and stomach ached.

The bald man rose, went and turned up the lights, and gave some papers to the hippie guy to hand out. The weeping of the woman two seats over had turned to muffled sobs and nose blowing. Samuel heard her apologizing to no one in particular.

Without identifying himself by name, the homeless man rose and began to speak. "Screw the politicians and their self-interested, snail-paced commitments to change." He had everyone's attention. He pulled up the waist of his dirty pants. "We are here because we know that we need to take things into our own hands. Our fat, rich society sees that there are children, real human beings, dying of hunger, but they don't do anything about it."

The bald man cut in to invite others to contribute to the discussion. One of the students spoke out with the practiced force and slightly angry tone of a charismatic preacher. "James one-twenty-seven says that the *religion that God our Father accepts as pure and faultless is this: to look after orphans and widows in their distress and to keep oneself from being polluted by the world.* We are compelled to help. We. Are. Compelled. To. Act."

One of his friends winked at him and said, "Amen, brother!"

Someone coughed. Samuel glanced at Ellis, who rubbed his chin and appeared to be listening intently.

A paper was passed around. It listed statistics about famine and hunger-related deaths around the world. It also showed figures on how much Americans spent on fast food the previous year; how much Canada spent on hosting the 2010 Olympic Games; how much the NHL, NBA, CFL, and NFL teams spent on athletes' salaries; how much Canadians spent on spa and salon treatments; how much Americans spent on plastic surgery. And the list went on, column by column, front and back.

The homeless man spoke again. "We need to act. These numbers grow, and we sit in this hall every month and get all up in arms about it but do nothing. We should despise ourselves for this complacency…we're no better than the greediest of people."

Some people chimed in with ideas on how the group could make an impact locally. A bake sale for the hungry.

Volunteering at a soup kitchen. Bring more people to these meetings. One of the students suggested an online awareness campaign. Another student recommended a campus-wide hunger strike, but when asked by one of the businesswomen what would need to happen for them to end the strike, the student couldn't answer, and the idea was dropped.

The hippie woman stood up. Her hair was a mass of dirty blond dreadlocks. "I know what we should do. We should put on an art show that totally hits the world in the face." She cleared the phlegm from her throat and continued. "We've got to use art to show the community about the reality of the universe."

"Right on!" exclaimed the other hippie.

Samuel became irritated by their ideas and longed for the stillness he had felt upstairs minutes earlier. Their reach would be short and generally a waste of energy and time. He wanted to stand up and yell at them. Shout and swear and tell them they were a bunch of powerless idiots, wasting their time brainstorming in an old church hall. As he considered this, it was Ellis who stood up and addressed the group instead.

"I've been listening to the wonderful ideas shared here today, and it's obvious that we all feel strongly about doing something meaningful for this cause. We are serious about helping the hungry and impoverished people around the world."

He talked slowly and clearly, in a soft voice. A few side conversations that had started now stopped, and everyone looked to Ellis. He paused, then walked slowly around the outside of the circle, occasionally placing his hand on a shoulder. Everyone watched and listened. Samuel felt goose bumps rise on his arms.

"While the rich world is engrossed in possessions and busyness, we are immune to the reality of hunger elsewhere.

We turn on our televisions, go to work or school, and we are able to tune out the cries of those dying children. We play sports and get involved in clubs and meaningless activities. Pursuits without meaning are simply pastimes, and humans should not have the luxury to simply pass the time."

He stopped speaking for a few moments. Long enough for Sam to take note of his own attraction to Ellis and his words. Something stirred inside him.

"Time is short. So, my friends, we need to strip away the stuff with which we distract ourselves. We need to see the futility of the western way of life. We need to remove the noise and distractions to hear the cries of the impoverished. And we need to rage against the greed of the world."

His energy and volume picked up as he spoke. The group listened with rapt attention. When he finished speaking, they applauded. There was a moment of silent reflection, and the discussion began to flow again. Pamphlets and speeches and letters to the editors were suggested. Nothing was agreed on. Samuel kept his eyes on Ellis the whole time. After another half hour of debate and discussion, the bald man dismissed the meeting.

Ellis turned to Samuel and, in the same clear voice he used earlier to address the group, asked him over to his apartment for a chat. Samuel was desperate to get to know this man and agreed. Ellis led him out of the building through a side door.

They sat side by side in silence as the subway roared westward. When they emerged from the underground, they turned onto the main street and walked past a huddle of underdressed, tattooed, skinny men exchanging goods. They went inside through an old blue door next to a Portuguese bakery. At the top of a narrow wooden staircase was a grey door, covered with dents and scratches. Ellis unlocked and opened it, entered, and switched on a light. Samuel followed him inside.

SAMUEL

It was like a scene out of a movie: a single bulb, dangling from the ceiling, flickering and buzzing. The room was small and mostly empty, with a stack of books, a single mattress, two plastic chairs, and a folding table. In the corner was a small kitchen, with empty spaces where the appliances should have been. Next to the kitchen was a door, presumably to a bathroom. The apartment walls were bare, except for a curtainless window looking out onto the street. The open closet featured only two dark suits, dangling limp on drooping wire hangers, a couple of chunky woollen sweaters, and a pair of jeans folded neatly on the floor. Samuel found the scene creepy, but Ellis moved with an ease and confidence that made Samuel feel safe. Ellis removed his suit jacket and laid it across the counter top in the small kitchen. He filled cups with tap water, handed one to Samuel, and invited him to sit down on the white plastic chair in the centre of the room. Ellis sat on the floor next to it and stretched out his long legs.

"You know that homeless guy at the meeting, his comments were pretty insightful. He seemed passionate about the issue," said Samuel, feeling compelled to say something.

"Frank isn't homeless, actually, just retired and eccentric," said Ellis. "He used to be a professor at York. Of English, I think. He certainly has a fire in his belly, but he depends on others to act. From him, there will be a lot of rage and angry words but very little action. And action is what is needed."

Samuel sat back in his chair and thought for a second about what else he should say. There seemed to be nothing worthy to utter in the presence of this man. He was struck by the absurdity of his own closet full of clothes, grad school education, and expensive textbooks crammed with useless theories. He thought about the emaciated faces of the children in the video and the body of the rich basketball player, taut with muscles he'd no doubt worked on for thousands of hours. He thought about that swimmer, Adam, spending his days moving back and forth in a pool lane. All for what? So he could wear a Speedo and not be laughed at? To win the attention of women? To steal other men's fiancées? Samuel's heart began to race. Aggravation rose, and the tremble returned to his hands as he imagined Adam and Callie together.

He pushed the anger back down into his belly.

For several minutes he focused on grey paint peeling from the floorboards. Wind screeched against the apartment window. He looked up and saw Ellis, sitting with his eyes closed and a finger over his mouth to indicate that silence was in order.

Ellis finally said, in a voice deep and serious, "It's too easy to be angry about the wrong things."

The goose bumps returned to Samuel's arms. He put his hand flat against his chest to try to slow his heart. He tried not to think. Suddenly he was aware of the sounds of traffic on the street, a distant police siren, and shouts from one of the neighbouring buildings. It was like he was inside a warm bubble, so peaceful that he could hear everything in the space beyond it and yet be undisturbed by it. Keeping his eyes closed, he focused on Ellis's words, typing them out over and over again in his mind, but replacing the words *wrong things* with the faces of people and objects. Callie. Adam's pecs. His mom's oak casket. His father's voice on the phone, *Your mother is dead.* Samuel sank into the warmth of the bubble, listening to the slow, drawn-out sound of his own breathing.

When he opened his eyes, he was lying on the floor. He must have fallen asleep. The light was off, and the room glowed red from the neon signs outside. He was hungry and confused. The sound of traffic had faded, and Ellis leaned against the wall a few feet away, absorbed in a book.

"What time is it?" Samuel whispered.

"Around two."

"I must have been tired. Sorry, I didn't mean to fall asleep on you."

"You did what you needed to do."

Samuel wanted to thank Ellis for the strange peace he felt. "Deepest sleep I've had in a long while."

"I could see that you needed rest. You are weary."

"It's been a pretty rough couple of months." He rubbed his eyes and yawned.

"Go back to sleep. You can go home in the morning, but I'd like to meet with you again soon. Sleep on my mattress tonight if you want…I'll be fine over here." Ellis returned his attention to his book.

Samuel had so many questions he wanted to ask, but the desire to go back to sleep was too strong. It was almost painful to be awake. He walked to the mattress, lay down, and fell asleep.

In a dream he met up with his mom. She stood at the foot of his bed in her old orange housecoat and touched his feet. "Sammy. My Sammy." She wept.

"I'm here," he said.

"This little piggy went to the market…" she began. He reached out to grab her hand, but it was gone.

"Sammy?"

"I'm still here."

Her hands were on his feet again, but her face had disappeared. He was losing parts of her slowly. They faded in and out like bad radio reception, until she was entirely gone and there was simply crackling static in the dark air at the foot of the bed.

He woke up alone in the small apartment. The sunlight filtered through the window. Ellis had already left. Samuel struggled to make sense of the memories of the night before, but he was rested and happy. He whistled while he scanned the apartment for a note from Ellis, finding only an old business card (*Ellis Shepherd, Charitable Donations Consultant*), left on the floor near the door.

JAYNA

She slumped down on the court. Nate blew the whistle to stop the scrimmage. She had been hit hard in the stomach by a pass she hadn't seen coming. She knew it was just a matter of time before her diaphragm spasm would stop, but the inability to breathe scared her. Jen, the teammate who had delivered the unexpected blow, crouched beside her and was rambling on in a quiet, panicked voice: "Oh my god, I'm so sorry...so sorry. I thought you saw me there....You were open....I'm so sorry."

Jayna just wished she would shut up.

It was never good to hurt a teammate, but it was especially bad to take down your star player. Good thing she wasn't really hurt, just temporarily grounded. She should have seen the pass coming from her left. Normally she had a kind of sixth sense about the ball, but she had been too busy glancing up at the clock, counting down the minutes until the practice's end. Something she never used to do.

Now Nate was beside her, wrapping an arm around her and helping her stand.

He whispered, "You gotta keep your eye on the ball and head in the game, Bentley."

She could not wriggle out of his strong grasp. Her breathing wasn't back to normal yet.

"Keep playing," Nate shouted at the players scattered around the court.

They were almost at the bench when she felt her stomach relax and lungs fill with air. The physical relief was overshadowed by the discomfort of his hands on her body, of the smell of his sweat in her nostrils.

She tried to pull away. "I'm okay." Her words were shaky, unconvincing.

Nate did not release her; he eased her down on the bench, pressing his fingertips too deeply and painfully into her armpit.

"I'm good, Coach." Words pushed through clenched teeth.

His hand was heavy on her shoulder, his words quietly cutting. "No, you're not. Just rest here. The scrimmage is almost over." Then, louder, towards the court: "Helen, cover your man. Cover your man!"

He moved away from her suddenly, adjusting his hat as he rushed down the sideline shouting instructions at players. The pressure of his hand lingered.

Jayna turned her attention to the game: the quick movement of feet along the hardwood; players' fingers spread wide, waiting and hungry; beads of sweat on cheeks and foreheads; the beautiful arc of the ball into the net. An audible swish. A call to dance. She blocked out Nate's barks from the sideline. This game was her beloved dance form, and he was an off-key soundtrack. Usually on the court she weaved gracefully among the players. Her body instinctively knew where to be, the way to move, and how to respond to the ever-changing environment and unknowns of team sport. There was euphoric beauty in each step. But here on the side, she was useless. Her hands hung limply in her lap as she watched less accomplished artists move mechanically along the floor.

After what seemed an eternity, the buzzer went off, and the women exchanged taps and slaps. Jayna joined her teammates filing into the ladies' locker-room. Nate moved to the door quickly, half-blocking the entrance to the showers, and high-fived the players as they passed through. Smack. His palm hard against hers. Hot and accusing. She was of no use to him on the bench. A disappointment to him, to the team, to herself. She was a lame dancer. And she was no good to anyone on the court if she wasn't at her best. There was no valid in-between state at her level of sport. You were either high-performing or worthless. Injured athletes, even temporarily injured ones, were silently reviled.

In the shower, she let the water run over her face. Jen entered the room a few minutes later, walked over to her and spoke apologetically, "Coach wants to see you when you're ready."

Despite the hot shower, Jayna felt a chill. She wouldn't let Jen see the fear. "Okay."

"Look, sorry about the pass."

"Okay."

"Really, I...."

"It's okay."

She kept her eyes closed and head tilted back towards the flow of the water. Jen eventually moved away.

She dressed slowly. The rest of the team was long gone by the time she closed her locker, threw her school bag over her shoulder, and turned back towards the gym. *I should just leave.* But a spot on the Olympic team might be at stake. *I'm an adult. I can deal with this.*

She wasn't sure how long she had been standing, immobilized, in the midst of the lockers, when Nate's voiced echoed through the room. He called from the door. She could not see him; he could not see her. It was like after swim lessons, when Jayna was nine years old, and her dad, impatient with waiting, opened the change room door an inch to call loudly into the room, "Jayna! Are you coming?" Inevitably she would have been seated under the wall-hung hair dryer, pulling on her socks and chatting with a friend.

"Bentley? You there? You coming?" Nate called.
I can do this. I'm an adult.
She spoke as calmly as she could manage. "Coming."
He was behind his desk when she slid quietly into his office. He gestured to the chair facing him. "Sit."
At least this time, there was a barrier between them.
She balanced her school bag on her lap. Her heart beat hard, painfully hard, against her chest. Her hands shook. The room spun. Nate spoke to her while rustling around in his desk, looking for something.
"Look, you need to step it up a bit. There's a chance you might get called for Olympic selection."
She knew all this. She wished the room wasn't spinning so much. Then she could respond intelligently, reassure him that she was ready for the hard work and challenge. But she said nothing.
"There will be lots of great NCAA and professional players out there. It's going to be a tough race. You're going to have to show us what you've got."

She hated what was behind his words. She looked at her nails but couldn't find her focus. Bile rose in her throat. She imagined Nate crouched behind her, his breath warm on her skin, his calloused hands along her neck.

"Bentley?" He was still behind the desk, waiting.

She *had* to reassure him. That's what athletes did with disappointed coaches. They jumped up and vowed allegiance to the coach and the training plan. They thumped their chests and promised to sweat and bleed and do whatever it takes.

"I will. I will." There was fear in her voice. He stared. She had to leave quickly.

She stood, unsteady on her feet; her school bag thumped against the floor, and her physiology textbook spilled out. In the back of the office, she could see the ghost of herself, motionless on the mats. With his hands all over her, pulling at her clothes.

She collected her things, left his office, and rushed to join with the other students moving anonymously along the building corridors.

A thought crossed her mind as she walked out into the bright sunlight. That day, months ago, in his office, when she could no longer stand the sound of his breathing and the horrible weight of his body, her mind had drifted into a vision of the 2012 Olympic Opening Ceremonies. In her head, she had circled the stadium with cameras flashing out of the dark crowd. She had shielded herself with the cacophony of cheering in every language and then stepped into the fire burning in the Olympic cauldron.

SAMUEL

On his way home from Ellis's apartment, Samuel got off the subway a few stops early, so he could pass by the church. He approached slowly, stood on the same step where he had met Ellis the day before, and stared at the red door.

In his mind there was a confusing confluence of the events and feelings of the past day: the pain and panic, the open-armed Jesus, the magnetism of Ellis. Samuel's heart raced, and he felt an inexplicable desire to go in. As a modern academic, he was supposed to shun the world of faith—the belief in things unseen. He was trained to look at everything that happens beyond that red door as manufactured, coercive, and irrational.

Over the years he had joined several of his professors and fellow students in fervent and angry dialogues that slammed organized religion, insisting that it was a source of hatred in the world.

"We must engage in the pursuit of unfettered scientific inquiry, without thinking we need a god to answer our questions," Samuel had insisted once, caught up in the excitement of a rant session.

Two of his classmates had nodded eagerly in agreement, and the high-pitched conversation railed on. It was the same kind of feverish noise he had noted both at that church service with Callie and in the church basement discussion the day before. He saw now that raised hands and amens might have flowed just as naturally in that meeting of academics, if they had allowed it.

He stood and studied the curve of the doorway, fighting the urge to enter. Going in alone would be tantamount to surrender. He wasn't ready for that. He remembered Ellis reaching down for his hand and the comfort of his touch. He recalled the peace he had felt last night. That was something he could pursue. Something much less scary.

Andrea

Practice was over. It was time to telephone JJ. Their daily post-training call was something she used to look forward to but had now begun to dread.

Andrea was in North Carolina training with the Canadian National Canoe and Kayak Team. Even though she was an American athlete, the Canadian coaches agreed that her presence at their training camp would encourage friendly competitive spirit and raise the level of performance, so they had let her come. She was meant to keep everyone on their toes. There were some athletes who were really aggravated by her being there, but she didn't care much about any of that. She had just needed to get away from San Diego, from her home, and kayaking was her only ticket.

"Let me train where I can stop thinking about what happened," she had said to her coach Randy, at practice just days after the incident. "I'm paralysed here."

Finally, Randy made some calls to the Canadian coaches and set it up. "Go and work this out," he had said, as though the pain she felt was just superficial. Something she could slough off through vigorous movement.

This wasn't how she had imagined her pursuit of Olympic gold. After a silver medal finish in Beijing, she had sat down with Randy and the team psychologist and laid out a comprehensive four-year training plan that they labelled *"My Games. My Gold."* Silver wasn't enough for them at the time. Winning was the endgame. According to the plan, she should have been training in California with her American teammates, but she couldn't face one more sympathetic tilt of a head or the threat of a reassuring arm around her shoulder. The good intentions and pity were suffocating. She preferred the cold glares of the Canadian athletes and the sparse feedback she received from their coaches. Out on the water, thousands of miles away from the place where she had found Danielle lying dead on the locker-room floor, she listened to nothing but the swish of water racing past her kayak and enjoyed the lactic acid burn.

She often thought about when she and JJ first met. It was the previous summer, after the World Championships in Poland. She and Danielle had taken the train to Lucerne, Switzerland, to cheer on the American rowing team at their World Cup. It was not something she would normally do (*Rowers are weird*, she and her teammates often joked. *They do it backwards*), but Danielle had a crush on one of the male rowers and had convinced Andrea to join her on the trip to Lucerne. After watching the men's lightweight fours final, the girls sat down on the grass with a couple bottles of beer. Close by, JJ was slumped in a white plastic chair in a cordoned-off area, next to the washrooms that were being used for doping control. There were three empty Gatorades under the chair, and he was staring down at the half-consumed bottle of water in his hands. His red unisuit was pulled down to his waist, exposing rippling waves of ribs and abs. Next to him stood a very short man dressed in a navy blue FISA t-shirt, holding a clipboard.

"I'm ready to go now," JJ had said to the man.

She knew this scene well. Doping control. He meant he was ready to pee in a cup.

"We must wait until the Italian athlete inside is finished," said the man in heavily accented English.

"Seriously, sir, I *have* to go now."

"You must wait."

"Listen, I've had a lot of liquids, and if we wait much longer, I'll explode and we'll need a boat to row ourselves outta here!"

That was when Andrea burst out laughing, and JJ looked over. His hair was the colour of sand and his smile was the broad, close-lipped smirk of a mischievous boy. He laughed too and waved. The doping control man crossed his arms over the clipboard and furrowed his heavy brows as Andrea stood up and approached. Danielle giggled in the background.

"I see you're waiting your turn," she said to JJ, admiring the dark blue of his eyes and the light brown freckles on his tanned face.

"I'm trying not to think about it. The rest of my team is already celebrating somewhere, and I'm stuck here overhydrating myself." He took a swig from the plastic bottle, then reached out his hand to shake Andrea's. "I'm JJ. A rower... obviously. Canadian."

He pointed at the maple leaf tattooed on his chest. Then he pointed at her face. "I see you're rooting for the enemy."

She touched the temporary American flag tattoo on her left cheek.

"Don't worry. We all have our faults," he said.

She liked this good-natured teasing.

"I'm Andrea. I'm a kayaker. K-1 and K-2. Here with a lovestruck teammate." She motioned behind her at Danielle, who waved. "I peed in a cup a couple of days ago too…at Worlds in Poland."

Only athletes and moms with children in diapers talked about urination so openly. It was a badge of honour, something that differentiated them from the rest. The presence of a doping control officer indicated that an athlete had crossed the threshold into true high-performance sport. The first time Andrea was drug tested was at her second Junior National Championships. She moved her kayak to the dock after a race, and a woman with a clipboard and pink paper form was there waiting for her. Even though she had been well-prepared for the occasion and cautious about what medication she took, she was struck by doubts: *Maybe my multivitamin or the Red Bull I drank before the race will show up on the test?* But later, when the test was over, she felt a sense of pride—that she was good enough for them to check and make sure she wasn't cheating.

JJ's doping control officer cleared his throat. Obviously she was too close to the cordoned-off area for his liking. She wasn't sure if there was a rule against her being there. There were always so many rules. She ignored the man.

"Great race today. You happy with the bronze?"

"Better than fourth, I guess. We could have stepped it up in the last five hundred. I had no juice left…legs like lead."

She knew what that was like: the pain of those last seconds of a race as you fought your body to keep going, and the torture you felt if that battle started too soon.

ANDREA

"How did Worlds go for you?" he said.

"Two golds."

She paused to see how he would react. She found that her frequent wins made some men squirm.

He appeared distracted. "Excuse me for a sec." JJ turned to the doping control man. "Can I pee now?"

The man shrugged his shoulders.

JJ looked back at Andrea. "Why don't you hang out with me later? We're going to Pickwick's at nine. We can show off our medals and get free beer."

That night she had happily joined the Canadian rowers at the crowded bar. A couple of the men were already drunk and heavy-lidded. JJ took her by the arm and introduced her to his teammates. "Brent, this is the illustrious kayaker, Andrea; Andrea, this is my loudmouthed, jock-headed teammate."

Brent looked up from his collection of empty glasses. His eyes were unfocused. He stood up on his long, wobbly legs and shook her hand. He wore his bronze medal.

He had turned to JJ and spoke as though she was not standing right there. "She's hot. Check out those pipes, man, they're bigger than yours."

JJ put his hand firmly on Brent's shoulder. "Take a seat, Bud." Brent sat down unsteadily and turned back to his beer.

JJ made a few more introductions, then led her outside, past the crowds of rowers and coaches. She loved being led by someone, not leading for once. And from his smile, she could tell he was happy to be the one in control. They walked towards the city centre. The wind was strong.

"Sorry about Brent. You just have to get to know him. He's primarily focused on rowing and winning medals. It's his entire life."

She was amused at the way he made excuses for his teammate. She had let him continue.

"If you ever need someone to *cliché* you into working hard, he's the guy. Ten minutes on the phone with him is about as good as reading an entire motivational book. I dare you to try it," said JJ.

"You don't seem like the cliché-loving type to me," she said.

"Every athlete repeats a little cliché or two to keep going. We're expected to, and sometimes it works."

They both laughed, and she let him pull her closer as they walked.

"What do you do besides row?" she asked him.

"Not much these days."

"All I do now is eat, sleep, and train, but I used to do a lot of photography," she said.

JJ stopped suddenly. He pulled a small digital camera out of his tracksuit pocket and handed it to her. "Take a picture of us, then."

He pulled her even closer. She liked the pressure of his strong body against hers. There on the sidewalk, they pushed their cheeks together, and Andrea held the camera at arm's length to take a photo. As she pressed down on the button, JJ shifted position and kissed her on the lips. His mouth was warm and soft.

The photo turned out to be a blurred image of the back of JJ's head. His sandy hair. He had sent it to her by email, and she saved it as her phone wallpaper. She used to look at it and imagine the delicious warmth of his lips. With anticipation and excitement, she'd dial his number, armed with the latest tale from training. But when Danielle died, her life had taken an unexpected turn.

In North Carolina, Andrea was billeting with a local family. She slept in a windowless room in the basement of their old home. She had no TV of her own, just a futon, a brown duvet, and a desk. It was dark and lonely in the room, just like she wanted. The perfect place to cry freely.

She rarely called home. She couldn't deal with her mom bombarding her with questions about what had happened to Danielle and how she was coping. It was easier not to think too much about what had taken place.

But no matter how hard she tried to avoid these memories, they assaulted her unexpectedly. Random sounds and smells would remind her: the bang of weight plates in the gym, the wide hands of a Canadian kayaker, a door closing. When she was least expecting it, these occurrences, though completely unrelated to Danielle, would trigger the memory. The image of Danielle lying facedown on the floor of the locker-room. And she was sent back there in her mind, staring at Danielle's lifeless body. No one else in the room. No help. Danielle's National Team backpack, still zipped up, was on the bench. There had been something in the tightness of its zipper, the mocking teeth of metal, that had unlocked Andrea's mouth to scream. She wished she hadn't been the one to find Danielle. The first person on the scene is expected to be the hero. That person is called the first responder. Her own response was a high-pitched shriek.

In the hospital waiting room, two hours after finding Danielle, she couldn't stop shivering. Still in her tight blue training gear, holding onto her coach Randy's hand, she waited for news from the doctor. Danielle's parents arrived and sat huddled in the corner, magazines open and ignored on their laps. They sat staring at their nails or each other or the walls. She had hoped whatever news came through the doors would be good, delivered authoritatively by a medical professional. Something like, *No need to be concerned. She was just dehydrated*, or, *She was just tired. She was sleeping soundly.*

A doctor pushed through the doors and walked towards Danielle's parents. Danielle's mom inhaled sharply and placed her left hand over her mouth as he approached. A reflex.

He had a Looney Tunes scarf wrapped around his head like a cap. On it were Bugs Bunny and the Tasmanian Devil. The doctor sat on the arm of a waiting room chair and spoke in hushed tones. From across the room she heard the words *rupture of a dilated aorta* and *hidden cardiovascular condition* and *nothing we could do*, but nothing else. She watched as Danielle's father's shoulders began to shake and Danielle's mother stood up and walked around the corner, still holding a hand to her mouth.

Andrea tried not to break down. She focused on the whirlwind around the Tasmanian Devil. Death was the same. It alternated as the villain and hero, but would always bite through just about anything, the strongest of muscles, Olympic dreams and friendships, to get at what it wanted. She stood up to go to the washroom, to get away, to be anywhere but around other people. She needed to keep moving. She could only be heroic on the water, it seemed, and no amount of fast paddling could have saved Danielle.

Randy grabbed her arm to keep her still. "Be strong."

They were well-intentioned but empty words.

She snatched her arm back. "No." She had spoken too loudly, not able to control her volume, and a nurse rushed over to guide her gently out of the waiting room.

"Try to stay calm," the nurse whispered.

"No. No." She tried to extricate herself from the nurse's grasp. She couldn't stop. She heard herself and hated that it was all like a scene out of a movie. But it just came out, everything she was feeling, as a pathetic refrain of *no*.

Her mom came to pick her up at the hospital later that day; she pulled up in her black Mustang convertible, with a Starbuck's cup in hand and one waiting in the holder for Andrea. It reminded her of the time before she could drive; her mom would cart her to and from practice, often waiting in the car with a smile and the latest protein bar or supplement for her to try.

"Got you a latte," her mom had said, as Andrea slid into the passenger seat.

There was a lump in Andrea's throat. She was drained and wanted to sleep.

"Tell me about what happened," her mom said.

"Not now." *Probably never.*

For weeks following that day, she imagined the Tasmanian Devil crouched down inside her pulmonary artery or behind the left ventricle, waiting for the right moment to attack.

"I'm so sorry for your loss," she had struggled to say to Danielle's parents at the funeral viewing. "If we had only known."

She hadn't finished the statement. *If I had known, then what?* She would have convinced her to stop training for the Olympics? Nothing could have convinced Danielle to stop training, not even the threat of death. Andrea knew this, because she had been the same way up to that point. Before Danielle died, Andrea had been a devout athlete. Now she was a backslider.

She waited for JJ to pick up the phone and half hoped he wouldn't. The only remaining benefit of their short daily exchanges was that they helped keep her from sinking too deeply into her mourning. These days, she and JJ commiserated about their various aches: the tendonitis in his wrist that flared up when it rained; the sore back that kept her from completing a dead lift set at training; the bruised forearm that had faded to a strange shade of brown.

She hoped it would be one of those calls when JJ interrupted their conversation to pass the phone to Brent: "He wants to say hi. Here he is." Then Brent's voice would come on, loud and enthusiastic, and Andrea would settle in to listen carefully. He did not share her doubts about whether the forty-hour training week was worth the investment.

"I think of rowing as my calling," he had said once in complete seriousness.

And like a priest who wept publicly in awe of God, Brent's unrestrained fervour could either inspire or repel those who listened to him. His raucous incantations about putting it all on the line when he trained made her more aware of her growing apathy towards her sport career. His passion for sport helped make it clear to her that she was no longer in the mindset to pursue and win a medal. Strangely, it felt like she was released.

JJ did not answer the phone. Perhaps she would try again later.

SUMMER 2011

YASMINE

In the lanes to her right, the swimmers had removed their bathing caps and goggles and were finishing up their workout with a kick set. They held onto multicoloured flutter boards, dipped their mouths into the water, and spat to the side every few seconds. Round and round they went, up one side of the line, down the other, their large feet propelling them.

Yasmine made her way slowly up her own lane, her legs moving in large, running strides, and saw Vincent watching her as he sped by. The red circles around his eyes from wearing tight goggles gave him an angry look. Like he saw her as an intruder. A frail old woman wrapped in a floatie and dropped into his pool.

Her face burned with embarrassment. More than ever she longed to get out of here and onto the road. She missed tying up her shoes at the front door and setting out on long, early morning runs that took her further and further away from her and Nate's house. Now, her life was centred on getting healthy and being released from the tedium of rehab. She spent long days focused on strengthening one small tendon. A fibrous tissue: her shackle.

"Soon," her physio had told her two days earlier, in a formal meeting with Yasmine and her coach Frederic. "Be patient."

A gentle splash in the face reminded her where she was. It was the swimmer named Adam.

"Earth to the little gazelle," he said as he fluttered by. He glanced back over his shoulder to flash a wide, warm grin. A smile spread across Yasmine's face.

Gazelle. *Soon.*

SAMUEL

Samuel let himself in through the unlocked grey door of Ellis's apartment, removed his shoes, and went directly to the faucet to pour a cup of water. It was warm and tasted of rust, and he drank it in small sips. Ellis was not home.

In the months since that first evening at the apartment, he had met with Ellis every day or two. At first he showed up at Ellis's place hoping to get back to the place of warmth and peace he found on that first night. Within the first few conversations, Ellis had unravelled the anger coiled in tight bands inside him.

But it wasn't long before Ellis began to rant about the idiocy of the first world.

"Your anger was misplaced," Ellis had said one night. "Rage against greed. Rage against a society that runs around wildly and consumes everything in its path. It wants more, eats more, dreams more, kills more, hates more." He slammed his fist against the wall before continuing. "They love their things, and they feed their appetites, but they hate everyone else and feed no one else."

Samuel had sat down and remained silent.

A flickering memory of the incident in the library: the books crashing to the floor, the students' eyes staring at him, and the burning hatred he had felt. Maybe Ellis was right.

"Don't be like them," Ellis said through clenched teeth. He turned slowly, stepped towards Samuel, crouched down, and whispered into his ear. "The *they* that I speak of are the marketers. Capitalists. Ad people. This society. Pop culture. Our neighbours. All of them. We're programmed to want all the things the people around us have and to hate the people around us for having them."

Street noise filled the room. It was a rainy Tuesday, and Ellis was at a meeting—his workdays consisted of lunch dates, where he advised corporate bigwigs on their charitable involvement and not-for-profit initiatives. He was an encyclopaedia of information on Canadian-based charities and their activities. Ellis described his loathing for how these corporate execs threw money around; his hatred of the way they obsessed about their oversized luxury vehicles, overaccessorized children, and large homes.

Often these executives took Ellis out to fancy lunch spots around the city, from where he brought home leftovers. The food was enough to feed Ellis for three days, but the meetings left him exhausted and angry and often got him talking about taking action.

"The best thing these corporate guys can do is help us," Ellis had said, cryptically, to Samuel after one of those meetings. "When we are ready to take action, they'll help to fund our work, and then I'll quietly cut them out. They understand the way business works. We will not let the left hand know what the right hand is doing."

Samuel carried his cup of water and plastic chair over to the window and looked out. There was a line-up of people at the bakery across the street, a steady stream of cars on the road, and pedestrians walking the sidewalks—mothers with fancy hydraulic strollers and designer diaper bags; emaciated men with stooped shoulders, dirty clothes, and cigarettes in hand; small groups of giggling teens. Some people wove in and out of shops, carrying out plastic bags with various goods. Five people waited in line at the ATM for their turn to grab money and go. They did all of this without appearing to stop or reflect, smile, or show any hint of gratitude for each new item in the bag or extra bill in their wallet. He watched a tall redheaded woman park her SUV along the curb, climb out of it, and look irritated as she inserted her credit card into the parking meter. Samuel thought she must be bothered that the parking wasn't free, and that she'd probably think it should be free. Like the air she breathed and polluted with her oversized car. Like her luck at having been born in a rich country and having access to the things she needed and wanted.

Ellis had challenged Samuel to watch Canadian urban life unfold around him and hate what he saw. He had told Samuel to despise his own past. Reject things.

Now, when Samuel looked at old photographs of himself at undergrad parties, wearing a Hollister sweater, a beer in hand, Prada glasses on his nose, his arm around Callie, he detested his own image. He began to recognize that all that mattered to him before he met Ellis was his own pursuit of knowledge, his longing for a stylish wardrobe, and his ravenous hunger for Callie—food, sex, recognition, money, and success. Now he felt revulsion towards who he had been. In the past month, he had closed his Facebook account, let his hair grow, sold his textbooks to the university bookstore, given his designer glasses to charity and picked up a simple pair from the local pharmacy, and stopped drinking alcohol. The braces-perfected set of teeth he saw in the mirror each morning was one thing he could not undo, and he had developed a sense of guilt about his perfect grin. When he caught the white flash of his smile in the subway or bus window he looked away quickly or covered his mouth with his hand.

The redhead on the street below Ellis's apartment walked over to the ATM line. Samuel imagined her hair on fire.

Ellis would be back soon.

In the past two weeks, Ellis had started to speak about the leading role Samuel could play in his plan to send a message to the rich world. He had placed an arm around him and called him *Son*. He made Samuel feel like they were the only people in the world. He made it clear that they had an enlightened view of society. Samuel had handed his passport, credit cards, and bankcards over to Ellis with the giddy euphoria of someone who discovered he had absolute faith in someone else. He listened carefully to every bit of Ellis's advice.

"Keep your mind and life free of clutter, so that you can see things as clearly as I do. Do not rush to find a job. Roam this city and watch people. Observe the reckless confusion of their lives. See the waste and the hectic pace. Overhear the silly conversations. If you need something, ask me, but do your best to want nothing. Eat only when you must," Ellis had said.

The previous week, Ellis had sent him to roam the sprawling pathways under the city to watch people pass through during rush hour. The crowds of men and women in black suits crashed through the doors and poured into the halls. Everything was swallowed up in the black rush of unsmiling people. After each of these activities, Samuel and Ellis had spent hours discussing the fruitlessness of Western culture with growing intensity and disgust.

"You know what Jesus did to the tree without fruit?" Ellis had asked Samuel. "He cursed it."

The previous day, Ellis had sent Samuel to sit for five hours at a table in the food court at Yorkdale Mall. And he went eagerly, watching groups of trendy moms coming and going with shopping bags that overflowed with stuff they didn't need. They sipped fancy espresso drinks with long hyphenated titles and talked about their lives and diets and kids and fitness regimens. Samuel sat, listened, drank nothing, ate nothing. He let the ache of hunger swell, along with his dislike for these women. Then he used his last subway token to return to Ellis's almost empty apartment to sit quietly, wait for Ellis, and reflect on a world without shopping malls and manicured moms.

After their debrief discussion, Ellis had moved closer to Samuel, pulled a tiny black box out of his pocket, and opened it up slowly. Inside was a simple chain necklace with a single gold band pendant on it. Samuel's heart began to beat faster. He sensed that something significant was about to occur.

"I selected you, Samuel. This chain symbolizes our connection and your belonging."

Ellis had pulled the chain and band slowly out of the box and reached behind Samuel to fasten it around his neck. Samuel exhaled to calm his heart. He ran his fingers against the smooth gold ring. This was an important ceremony. He relished the impression that, at that very moment, the universe was looking inward at Ellis and him.

Ellis clasped both of his hands around Samuel's. "I am proud of you," he said. "You've earned this ring. It is the first of five. This ring symbolizes our connection. The next four rings will be even harder to earn."

There was a Hollywoodness about the whole interchange. Samuel knew that what he was thinking and feeling would seem like fiction to others, but it was real to him. In his former life, he would have rejected such melodrama, but he loved the adrenaline moving through his veins, the goose bumps, and the intensity of Ellis's stare.

While looking out the window, Samuel fingered his new chain and replayed the previous day's ceremony in his head, each time experiencing a fresh ripple of excitement in his belly.

Ellis entered the apartment quietly, slipped off his shoes, and placed his bag next to the door. He was wearing a new grey suit, pink shirt, and blue tie, all part of a recent gift package from a corporate client who had begun to complain that Ellis's suits were looking worn and inappropriate for a man with his level of influence. In other words, the client was embarrassed to be seen with him. This had amused Ellis. After recounting the story, Ellis had said to Samuel, "If someone has to feel a little bit of discomfort to give me what I need, that's fine with me."

Today in the apartment, Ellis leaned against the windowpane next to Samuel. "I could see you up here from down on the street."

The stern tone surprised Samuel. He tried to explain. "Oh...I was watching the people. They're aimless."

Samuel had imagined Ellis would be impressed by this show of initiative, but his mentor's eyes darkened. "You must be more careful from now on. Do everything I say without asking why."

Samuel's stomach tightened. *Have I done something wrong? Is Ellis mad?*

After a pause, Ellis changed to a friendlier tone. "We've moved beyond theory now. It's time for you to show real commitment."

Ellis moved away from the window and lowered his voice. Samuel focused on his face. He was desperate to communicate that he was listening.

"No fancy job, degree, or town hall meeting is going to accomplish the kind of change we're looking for in the world. Everyone is given a special gift and purpose. I have the vision, and I know without a doubt, that you were born to change the world."

A surprised gasp escaped Samuel's lips. The words reminded him of his mother. Each night when he was a little boy, she had tucked him into bed, stretched out beside him on the covers, and let him ask her whatever he wanted.

"Mommy, why are all our ceilings painted white?"

"They're meant to remind us of the clouds up in the sky. Why do *you* think they're painted white?"

"Probably because the clouds are up, and the ceiling is up, too."

She had laughed.

"Mommy?"

"Yes?"

"Clouds are where God has his house, so now the ceiling makes me think of God and his big beard."

"You're sweet, Sammy. I love your imagination. It's your gift. Everyone is born with a special gift, and I think that's yours."

She had kissed him gently on the cheek.

"Pay attention," said Ellis sharply.

Samuel turned his face towards Ellis, who was pacing the room. *I need him to see that I will do anything.*

"This is what you will do. I've booked you a flight to London. You will go there, and I will tell you what you need to do. You leave in two weeks."

JAYNA

She could never quite get away from Nate's touch. Her sister brushing past while she stood buttering toast at her parents' East Coast cottage counter pulled Jayna into the memory of Nate's hands over her back and throat. When she sat on the back patio, the wind was his breath in her ear. And her mother must have seen the full-body shudder that ensued, because she went inside and returned with a heavy red blanket, placed it around her daughter's wide shoulders, touched her hand to Jayna's forehead, and said, "You must be coming down with something."

Jayna had shaken off her mom's gentleness, slapped away the old, familiar hand, and insisted, "No, I'm fine." To succumb to that tenderness would lead to tears, to confessions, to complaints, and likely…eventually…to the death of her Olympic dream. It was easier to numb herself to these things. She drank beer first thing in the morning to get started on that process, downed cocktails on the beach in the afternoon, and stalked the cottage at night with a glass of wine in hand, trying to exorcise Nate from her body.

But the summer break was much too short to accomplish that feat. In early August, Jayna returned to Montreal to attend the summer basketball training camp. Will met her at the airport. When she walked into the greeting area, he was facing away from her and speaking into his phone. Seeing him scared her now. Somehow the month of long-distance calls and daily texts made him seem slippery and no longer firmly hers. When she had called, he seemed distracted, like he might be simultaneously playing a video game on mute or holding up a finger to silence someone else in the room. And she wasn't there in the flesh to win back his attention—to pull his head towards her and plant a kiss of invitation on his lips.

Now that she had returned, she would work hard to solidify his commitment to her.

She walked up to Will slowly enough to catch him saying, "I put you on the VIP list for tonight. No worries, Sweets. I'll see you there."

There was a sudden uneasy stirring of heat in her gut. A firing line of questions inside her head: Who was he speaking to? Was it just a friend, or one of his little blond muses? What did he get up to while she was away? Did he want her anymore?

Her cheeks burned. She couldn't let him see this lack of confidence. She stood tall instead, reached out, and touched his back. "Will."

He turned slowly, a smile spreading across his lips. No hint of being caught red-handed on that call. Maybe it was just a friend or acquaintance? He wrapped his arms around her and kissed her cheek. With her flats on they were about the same height. She wished she was a normal sized, so she could look up at him helplessly and bat her eyelashes or press her ear against his chest. She was too big to be cute. Too big to be cherished and protected. And there was always the threat of leaning in and looking eye to eye. She suspected it was a matter of time before he would cringe at the touch of her big hands and move on.

As they drove to her apartment that evening, Will said something about needing to get to the club early enough to put up posters and meet the new bartender. Jayna knew she couldn't let him leave her without capturing his interest. She would need to put on her game face, entice him, and then push him away before there was any chance of boredom creeping in. She would leave him wanting. And she hoped the pressure of his body against hers would scrape away Nate's lingering presence.

He pulled into the visitor parking space, and before he was able to undo his seatbelt, she climbed over him, her head bent to the side, and pressed against the roof of the car, and began her performance. Jayna experienced the moments that followed almost entirely as an outside spectator: the reclined chair, a leg bent at a strange angle, the arch of her back, the glow from the streetlamp shooting through the space between their stomachs. It was a film that ended abruptly when she blew a kiss and shut the car door behind her.

She walked slowly to the entrance of her building, conscious of Will's gaze from the car window. She did her best to make her hips sway from side to side and shake away the sense that Nate was hovering inside her, somehow complicit in the making of this movie.

SAMUEL

Brent was breathless when he answered Samuel's call.

"Yo." There was the sound of crunching gravel and loud voices in the background.

Samuel hadn't spoken with him in more than six months. Last time they had talked only briefly. It was on Christmas Day, when Brent was away at a winter training camp. There was the usual exchange of flat holiday greetings and questions about the weather before Samuel passed the phone over to his dad.

Ellis had instructed Samuel to make this call. He told him to cut ties. "He's a grown man who spends forty hours a week turning his body into a machine. For what greater purpose?"

Samuel had had no response. He had leaned back against the cold apartment wall, arms limp at his sides. Ellis stood above him and spoke through gritted teeth. "His goal is to move a boat backwards between markers, get faster each day, and prove he's a better man than his competitors. He worships his own body. He's his own idol. It's all a religion for him—an empty, wasteful, heretical religion."

Samuel recalled the palpable tension in the apartment that day—the way he had instinctively pulled his knees tight to his chest; the tremor in Ellis's voice as he ranted and paced and shook his hands like an athlete psyching himself up for an important game; the sound of the door hitting the wall when Ellis pulled it open and departed suddenly.

Afraid to leave, Samuel had waited there until Ellis returned the next morning.

"Brent?"

The crunch of the gravel was louder than Brent's voice. "Sammy!"

It was the childhood diminutive, coming from his baby brother.

"I'm calling to let you know that I'm moving away."

Brent did not say anything at first; he seemed to be speaking under his breath to someone else. After a moment, he responded, "Sorry, Sammy? What did you say? I missed it."

It was exactly like when they were kids: Samuel making a comment about the school curriculum or about an NHL management change, and Brent only half-listening—busy tossing a tennis ball against the bedroom wall or retaping his hockey stick. The old anger and frustration pulsed in Samuel's fists, his throat, and his mouth: "Listen to me! I'm moving."

Brent cleared his throat, "Oh, cool. Where to?"

Brent's disinterest was evident. He always had the habit of throwing out a question and not really listening to the response.

"London. I don't plan on keeping in touch."

The sound of gravel had picked up again, accompanied by loud grunts.

"Sorry about the noise on my end...I'm helping transfer some of the equipment from the boathouse to...." The end of Brent's sentence was indecipherable.

Suddenly Samuel realized this conversation was pointless. The only remaining connections with Brent were his grainy memories. They had already said dozens of meaningless goodbyes throughout the years. It seemed there was nothing left of their relationship to cut off.

"Sammy...You should follow me on Twitter...."

Not even a tenuous thread left.

Samuel hung up.

ANDREA

"What's your mantra?" the television reporter asked Andrea.

In the three days since she had returned to San Diego, she had been interviewed by various news and sports networks. They asked all the usual "one year countdown to the Olympics" questions, but what they really wanted to know was how she felt about Danielle's death, two months after the fact. They wanted to capture the tragic image of athlete/medallist/Danielle's friend, crumbling and sobbing into a microphone. This particular reporter had not gotten to that question yet. Andrea would sense it coming, and she would not let herself break down. Leading into it, the reporter would take on a solemn, sympathetic tone, with halting preamble, as though responding to his line of questioning was optional. It wasn't. The media wanted to publicize her pain and struggle. It was the perfect story. If she didn't answer, they would probably film her standing there on the brink of tears, or focus the camera on her back as she walked away.

THE GAMES

To this point, she had given each reporter the same response, exactly what the team's PR manager recommended she say: "Danielle's death was a sad turn of events for our sport, for her family, and for our team."

What she really wanted to spit out was, "Death puts everything into perspective. Go mourn your own dead."

The reporter cleared his throat to remind Andrea he was waiting for her to address his mantra question.

"It's *go hard or go home*, because there really is no point in training or competing if you can't give it your all," she said reflexively. It wasn't really her mantra. It was what people expected her to say.

The reporter's voice softened to introduce his next question, the Danielle topic. Andrea steeled herself against the images that entered her head as he reminded the viewers of her terrible locker-room discovery. She stared at her reflection in the lens of the camera until the reporter was silent. Her eyes were tired. Then she gave the PR manager's answer.

After the interview finished, the reporter shook her hand and left. Another interviewer was waiting in the training centre. The media attention would only build as the year progressed. This was the strange by-product of excelling at a sport in America: full-time athlete, part-time public motivator. Andrea knew that sooner or later the public would see through her empty words and notice her blank stare into the camera. The nation looked to athletes like her for inspiration. They expected them to achieve perfection. They wanted them to rise above the stuff that pulled normal people down. They forgot that things blew up in athletes' lives, too.

Seated on an exercise ball in the corner of the weight room, she watched the last of today's reporters leave. "Bring back the gold," said the cameraman. Andrea feigned a smile.

She opened a container of quinoa and tuna, bland and unsatisfying. Twelve more months of all this seemed intolerable. Four years ago, she had loved the media build-up, the brutality of training, and the discipline of her nutritional regimen. She thought of Brent and his bull-headed determination; there could be real beauty in the wholehearted chase of an Olympic dream. A lukewarm relationship with that dream would lead to failure and pain. It was like falling out of love.

The beep of a call coming in from JJ shook her. The photo of the back of his head popped up on her caller ID.

She spoke before he had a chance to say anything. "I'm taking a year off. I'm not mentally in the game for Twenty-twelve." She felt a wash of cool relief.

They had never before discussed a future that excluded the London Olympics. He cleared his throat to start to speak but stopped.

"I just decided," she said. She gave JJ a moment to respond.

"But you're favoured to win a medal?"

"I already have an Olympic medal....It's not about that. You know, you just get to the point where you realize you're mortal, and that changes the game."

"What?"

"We're all going to die one day. Do you want to spend the best years of your life doing this?"

She knew he wouldn't get it. He wouldn't understand the decision to step away, deliberately, from a legitimate shot at Olympic gold. Few people would. But for Andrea, the idea of taking a year off, or more, had been born. She had spoken it aloud, so it became anchored to reality. Maybe no one could talk her into caring about winning again.

SAMUEL

When Samuel stepped off the bus in Guelph, his father ran up the sidewalk to meet him. His dad's bald head was covered in beads of sweat, his yellow t-shirt wet in the pits—he had never managed well in the heat of summer.

Damp arms enveloped Samuel. He stiffened his body and stared at a bird flying off in the distance. *A vulture perhaps?* Its wings widespread, the bird dipped and soared on the wind. His dad whispered something in his ear. Samuel tuned in the roar of a passing bus.

Ellis had warned him that physical contact might disarm Samuel's resolve. "Keep the wall up. Focus on something else or on the things that bother you about your father."

"That's going to be hard. I haven't seen him in over a year."

"What you need to remember is that your family ties you to everything you hate. They taught you to want things and to love things. They initiated you into the lie that houses should be comfortable and filled with stuff, and that success is found in athletic triumphs, a high-paying job, or beauty."

When Ellis had finished speaking, Samuel thought about his parents' bungalow on their quiet cul-de-sac. Each winter, his dad laid down plastic, dug post holes, and put up plywood for the backyard skating rink. On weekdays the neighbourhood kids had run home from school, dropped off their school bags, picked up their skates, and headed to the Gottschalk yard for a game of shinny. His dad laboured over the rink, re-stapling the plastic to the boards, filling outside gaps between the wood panels and the liner with rags, scraping the ice with a shovel on snowy days, and resurfacing the ice with the hose each night. The kids had nicknamed him Daddy Gretzky. He used to lean over the sides and watch the kids skate with a pleased look on his face. He had instructed the kids to practice their passes and stickhandling and told them to avoid slap shots above the boards. Nevertheless, he had laughed every time Brent, much too tall and strong for his age, whacked a puck out of the rink, and his dad was forced to run through the deep snow into the woods behind their house to retrieve it.

Samuel had spoken more loudly and boldly than he usually did in Ellis's presence, hoping that increased volume would convince both of them. "I think my dad's a decent guy."

Ellis responded in the soft, apologetic tone of someone conveying condolences. "That's nostalgia speaking. He was your father, and you want to think of him as a good person, but memories lie. Everything he ever did for you and your brother stemmed from a selfish motive."

Samuel thought about early mornings at the community indoor hockey rink, his dad in the stands with the other parents while he and Brent practiced. Samuel had loved seeing the parents gathered together, hands hugging Tim Horton's cups. Were they only there to make sure their kids had every chance of making the NHL? So they could brag and feel like great parents?

Samuel had never consciously thought about his dad this way, but Ellis was helping him think clearly. Ellis had led him through an inventory of memories and showed Samuel how flawed family could be. The exercise had precipitated an onslaught of images.

Another memory came to mind. Samuel had pushed open the bathroom door. Thirteen-year-old Brent was seated on the counter, his face covered by a thick layer of shaving cream. Their dad knelt below Brent, rummaging under the counter for a new razor. "Dad's teaching me to shave," Brent had said excitedly, his mouth a small black hole opening and closing amid the fluffy white. Samuel lifted his hand to touch the dark brown, never-shaven peach fuzz above his own upper lip. He was fourteen. Embarrassed that he was about to cry, he backed out of the bathroom and shut the door.

Outside the bus station in Guelph, Samuel inhaled and focused on the stench of his father's body odour, mingled with the exhaust of the bus. They headed across the street to where the car was parked. A woman with platinum hair was fully reclined in the passenger seat, with her sneakered feet up on the dash. *Who the hell is this?*

"I want you to meet someone special," his dad said tentatively, as he opened the passenger car door.

The woman's eyes popped open. She removed her feet from the dash and pressed the button to adjust the seat back.

"Hi, Sammy!" She used his childhood name. "I'm Rebecca, but call me Bex."

Samuel noticed the small wrinkles that lined her pink lips, evidence of a smoking habit. *A sixty-something-year-old named Bex? Really?*

"I'm sure I told you about Bex in one of my emails, right, Sammy?"

"No, you didn't," Samuel said coldly.

"I know I told Brent...and I'm sure I told you too."

"Come on, Davie, you didn't tell him about me?" Bex whined.

Davie? There was a lot of reinventing going on.

"I'm sure I did, Bex, he's probably just kidding around... .I'm just so glad that two of the most important people in my life can finally meet. I wish Brent could be here too." Davie wiped sweat away from his upper lip. "Let's head home."

Samuel glared at the couple, repulsed by the way Davie rubbed his hand up and down her forearm—just like he used to do to Samuel's mom.

On the drive to the bungalow, he listened to Bex drone on and on about her old house and how she was slowly moving in with Davie. *Moving in?* These people were already irritating him.

Bex pointed out the building where her now-grown twin daughters had taken ballet, the strip mall where she used to run a small consignment shop, the park where her innocent mini-schnauzer suffered a premeditated attack by a poodle. Samuel's dad smiled, laughed, and continued rubbing her forearm as she spoke. Samuel reflected on how easy it would be to leave these people later on.

At the bungalow, Bex prepared a salad in the kitchen, and Samuel walked around the home, noticing the way his mother's imprint had been rubbed out and replaced by this new woman's things. The wooden "Home Sweet Home" sign that used to hang next to the kitchen door had been replaced by an oval mirror. A framed wedding photo of his parents that used to sit on their bedroom dresser had been replaced by a silver framed photo of Davie and Bex.

There was still the wooden chair in the corner, its surface partially obscured by tank tops of various colours. And there were photos of Brent at the Olympics all over the place.

The three of them ate at the picnic table in the backyard. The wide expanse of grass where the hockey rink stood in the wintertime was now covered over with a greenhouse.

"We just erected it about a month ago," said Davie. "It's a beauty, eh. Bex is growing some veggies, and she put in a few bees, too."

"My very own tomatoes are in the salad," said Bex, her mouth full of food.

The glass building was cheap-looking, with chintzy white embellishments across the peak.

"Bex grows the juiciest tomatoes," said Davie.

Sam wondered whether these were the kinds of things they discussed each day. A life full of meaningless small talk. Samuel pushed the tomatoes off to the side of his plate.

There was a long silence before Davie spoke again. "Brent's doing really well this year, eh?"

"Says he's in peak shape," said Bex.

"We spoke with him yesterday," said Davie.

"Such a wonderful young man," said Bex.

Samuel had nothing to say to them. More silence ensued. He swatted away the mosquito buzzing in his ear. There were the sounds of chewing.

After a moment Davie spoke with a full mouth: "Any job prospects in Toronto?"

It was time to let them know.

"Change in plans…I'm moving to London."

Davie clapped his hands like an excited child. "London, Ontario?"

"No. London, England. I'm leaving this week."

He watched the reaction: the shaking of his father's head, the open mouth, and the way Bex reached out to take Davie's hand. Samuel wasn't feeling a thing.

"This is so sudden. I thought you, me, and Bex would be able to spend more time together." Davie's voice trailed off.

Or Samuel stopped listening. His attention was on the greenhouse now. He could see the series of stakes lined up, tomato vines tied to them with nylon stockings. He imagined lost bees buzzing around inside the glass house, looking desperately for a place to pollinate.

They ate the rest of their meal without speaking. Davie sniffled from time to time.

When they headed back to catch the bus, Bex stayed behind at the bungalow.

"You can just let me off here. No need to park," Samuel said as they approached the station. He was ready to leave and never come back.

"Are you sure about this London thing, Sammy?" His father's voice was shaky.

"Yes." *He cannot change my mind.*

"Okay, well, then…can I drive you to the airport?"

"No, those plans have been made already." *Ellis will take care of me.*

Davie spoke more forcefully, "I would like to. Do you need…."

Samuel didn't let him finish. He didn't care to hear one more word. "No, I don't need you."

SAMUEL

He got out of the car quickly. He felt nothing. He could almost laugh. The coach was idling at the curb, ready to take its passengers back to the city. Samuel kept an eye on the bus as he leaned down and spoke through the open window.

"Bye."

VINCENT

He flip-turned, pushed off the wall, streamlined, and fluttered. On the pull, he turned his head slightly to keep an eye on Adam in the lane next to him. They were neck and neck. It was supposed to be a steady, slow-paced training set, but they were both pushing it. He was breathing hard by the time he touched the wall, just slightly before his rival. *Yes!* To hide his smirk, he turned his back to Adam, watched the red hand make its way towards the top of the clock, and readied himself for the next rep. Adam breathed heavily behind him.

Vincent placed his feet against the wall and bent his legs for the push, just as his coach, Robert, reached down from where he was standing on the deck above him and grabbed his wrist. "What the hell are you doing? This is a slow set!"

Red on top: Adam launched off the wall. Likely with a smile on his face. *Dammit, he's going to get ahead.* He watched

Adam surface a few metres down the lane, then he turned to Robert, who was red-faced and fuming.

"Do you think this is some kind of joke, Vince? That I design these sets on a whim or something? When I say slow and steady, I mean slow and steady!" He released Vincent's arm and pointed at the clock. "Black on top."

Adam was already nearing the other end. These were the little defeats of training.

SAMUEL

Samuel stared at the red door of the church. He came here often, drawn to the memory of the stained-glass Jesus and the stillness of the place, but he never went inside. He sat on the stone steps and tried to evoke the curious sense of anticipation he had felt the day he followed Ellis over that threshold. That first afternoon was the only time he had entered. Since then he wondered what would have happened if he'd waited a little longer to hear what the open-mouthed and open-armed glass saviour had to say. He could not bear the thought of its potential silence. Instead, he chose to focus on the comfort of Ellis's company and wisdom. Somehow, going inside the church again seemed like betrayal.

The air was heavy with humidity. Sweat soaked the back of his t-shirt, and he longed for a drink of cold water. He fanned himself with his hand in an attempt to cool down, as three well-dressed men turned from the sidewalk to climb the stairs. They moved purposefully in their white dress shirts, dark suit jackets folded over their arms. They did not speak. The red door opened and then squeezed shut behind them, pushing out a gust of delicious cool air from inside. The thought of relief from the heat added a new layer to Samuel's temptation. He ached to enter. The pull was strong. Excuses formed in his mind. *I needed to get out of the sun. I needed water.*

A tall brunette in a white sundress climbed the stairs. Samuel's chance. He stood and rushed to hold the door open for her. She gave a sideways glance and a closed-mouthed half smile and entered. He slipped in while the door shut slowly and hovered there, listening to the rhythmic clicking of the woman's heeled shoes as she made her way down the hallway towards the basement staircase.

Once she was gone and the place was silent, he emerged from the shadowy foyer and slid quietly into one of the worn pews. For a minute he sat still enough to let the air cool his overheated body. He closed his eyes and bowed his head. His heart beat fast. He wasn't sure what to do. He let out long, slow breaths and did not look up. From somewhere on his right he heard murmuring, a voice speaking into cupped hands. His heart rate peaked again as he sank deep into his seat, trying to make himself as small as possible. What if it was Ellis? What would he say?

The muffled noises continued. Now he wished he had stayed outside and wondered how he could escape the church without being seen. He opened his eyes and lifted his head to peek over the edge of the pew. Two rows up to his right, there was a woman with a wild mop of wavy black hair, kneeling in the aisle, hands covering her face. Her nails were painted blood red. He was mesmerized by her, as she moaned and shook and spoke in small emotional bursts. She did not seem to notice him scrutinizing her from just metres away. Suddenly, she released an audible, helpless, "Oh God," inspiring ripples of energy to course through Samuel's body. He gasped loudly at this sudden surge of feeling and covered his mouth. The pew creaked as he sat up straight. The woman did not seem to hear. She remained engrossed in her prayers. He admired the beautiful angles of a body bent in prayer, the stunning vulnerability. This was what he wanted. Her words were distorted by the sobs and emotional reflexes of her body, but Samuel heard these noises as tender music. He loved the sensation of the warm swell of tears in his eyes.

A familiar whisper from nearby tore him from the quiet moment.

"Samuel."

There was a sudden tightening around his heart. He turned, slowly, hoping he was wrong, that he was hearing things. But there was Ellis, his face thin and wise, in the row behind. He glared at Samuel. No softness in the look. His mouth was tense. "You shouldn't come here."

Samuel remembered all the excuses: the summer heat, the need for water. A child awaiting grounding, he wished he were anywhere else. He said nothing.

"Go only where I tell you to."

The build-up of tears from earlier had begun to trickle down his cheeks. They seemed at odds with this moment, and he wiped them away hastily.

Ellis's voice turned hard and cold. A warning. "You must leave now. Go to my apartment and wait."

Samuel nodded and stood up. He wanted desperately to apologize but hoped obedience would say more. Ellis remained still in the pew, eyes focused on the woman kneeling in the aisle, as he rushed by. When Samuel reached the door, he heard the brunette in the white dress retreating quickly down the hallway, betrayed by the click of her shoes.

ANDREA

Andrea lay awake, thinking about how she was going to tell her coach Randy that *"My Games. My Gold."* was due for the shredder. *Establish a single-minded focus on doing what it takes to win* was one of the primary objectives listed in the plan, and she knew that was no longer possible. The idea of waking up without an alarm and staying in bed until she felt like getting out of it made her giddy, as did the thought of spending her days somewhere other than on the water heading in a straight line. *I'll tell Randy tomorrow that I'm done.* She imagined his stunned silence in response and smiled at the thought. She hoped that it wasn't just midnight bravado that had stirred up her resolve.

She turned over onto her stomach to try to fall asleep.

A memory passed through her mind. Danielle was sitting on the back of Andrea's knees as Andrea struggled her way through a long set of back arches. *Twenty-four, twenty-three, twenty-two.* She grunted with each repetition. At about number eleven, Danielle spontaneously burst into a fit of laughter, setting Andrea off as well. Randy yelled at them for not taking the exercise seriously. They tried to stop laughing, but for the rest of the workout they occasionally snorted and giggled.

After practice, Randy had pulled them both aside. "Girls, if you want to succeed at the Olympic level, you need to understand that every rep counts. If you can't focus and do it seriously, you're going to have big problems."

"We hear you," Danielle had said, and Andrea nodded in agreement.

It had made total sense at the time. It was crucial to have a rock-solid belief in the all-American sport glory story—that the relentless pursuit of an athletic goal was noble and serious business. The moment athletes saw cracks in that story, rational thoughts crept in and drowned their determination.

Those cracks had now widened for her. In her bed, Andrea dreamed about all the things she'd be able to do in the coming year. She'd be able to go downhill skiing again, something she hadn't done in the decade since she signed a national team agreement that disallowed high-risk activities. She'd be able to take decongestants if she got sick and not have to worry about doping tests. It was the little things that excited her the most.

Andrea switched off her alarm clock and fell asleep thinking about sleeping in.

SAMUEL

Samuel woke up on the bare floor of Ellis's apartment with a folded sweatshirt under his head.

After returning from the church the day before, he had paced the boiling hot apartment, panting and sick with fear. Ellis returned hours later and did not acknowledge or speak to Samuel. He undressed and lay down on his mattress to sleep. Samuel pressed up against the wall and waited until Ellis's breathing deepened and slowed. Then he curled up on the hard floor with his makeshift pillow and slept fitfully.

He was leaving for London in two days. A week earlier, he had handed in his final apartment rent cheque, packed his only remaining belongings in two ragged suitcases, and moved them to Ellis's place.

He wiped his eyes and yawned. His stomach growled. He hoped that forgiveness had come in the night. Near him, Ellis sat cross-legged, sorting through the open suitcases, occasionally throwing an item into a pile close to the door.

Tentatively, Samuel walked over to see what had been tossed on the heap. There were two pairs of perfectly good shoes, a couple of sweaters and t-shirts, and a small photo album that had spilled some of its contents.

The photo on the top was one of his favourites. He was six years old, with his mom, standing waist-deep in Lake Huron and beaming. He had been afraid to swim in the open water, so his mom had taken him by the hand and walked him along the shore to search for lake monsters, gradually edging him further in. He was up to his hips and comfortable before he realized her trick. She had made him feel safe.

That was before she unravelled.

Samuel leaned down to pick up the photo. Ellis watched.

"I thought I told you to let go of those people," said Ellis.

"I have."

"I don't think you have, so I'll help you. From now on, you will not contact anyone here. No family. No friends."

Ellis continued to sort through the suitcases as he spoke. A pair of sunglasses landed in the pile.

"You'll be taking only what I include in just one suitcase." He paused and then spoke again. "Now rip that photo."

Samuel studied the image, noting the way his face was turned up towards his mom. He ran a finger gently over the picture and wished he could feel the warmth of her skin. *Why did you leave me? Wasn't I enough for you?* He didn't want to know the answers. He held it by the edges. *I can't do this.*

"Don't hesitate. Just do it." Ellis flashed the same cold look from the day before in the church.

A deep ache swelled in Samuel's chest. He longed for his mom. He wanted to call out to her like he used to when he was a child. But Ellis was there, listening and watching.

Ellis moved from his position on the floor and embraced Samuel. He spoke in a different tone now, soft and nurturing. "You are stronger without her, and you are better without her." He paused and added, "I'm your mother, brother, father."

Samuel exhaled and relaxed into Ellis's arms, the photograph in his hand now pressed against his chest. They stayed like that for several minutes. Ellis spoke into his ear.

"This is your chance to prove to me that you're ready."

Ellis separated himself from Samuel, maintaining eye contact, and opened up his fist to display the small gold band in his palm.

"This ring symbolizes sacrifice. Prove to me that you can make sacrifices."

Samuel looked at the ring before Ellis returned it to his pocket.

I must do this. He held his breath and ripped the photograph, tearing his mom and himself apart. Parting Lake Huron. Something inside of him slammed shut.

"Good," said Ellis, while returning his gaze to the baggage.

Samuel slumped down on the floor and wondered anxiously if Ellis would present him with the second ring after all. He worried he had hesitated for too long. Perhaps the withdrawal of the ring was a punishment from yesterday.

He waited in silence while Ellis finished sorting. He imagined Ellis rejecting him, taking back the chain and ring and sending him away. He shuddered with fear.

After a long while, Ellis closed the suitcases, stood up, and approached Samuel.

"Kneel," he said, sharply.

Quickly, Samuel raised himself to his knees. He was ready to do whatever Ellis asked of him and win back his approval. Ellis stood over him and held out the ring.

"If you want to earn the rest of the rings, you can't falter. What we are going to do is important and will require courage. Now take this and remember how close you came to failure."

Samuel held the ring tight in his palm.

"One last thing. From now on, I am going to call you Sam. It's stronger."

JJ

Seated on the floor of the boathouse, legs spread in a wide V and bent forward in a stretch, Brent picked at a loose thread in the seam of his training suit and grumbled something about the quality of the new gear. JJ leaned against the wall, leg bent in a quad stretch, and thought about the warmth of the bed he left at 4:00 a.m. There was never much need to make the bed, because he'd get back into it after practice. He was early to training because Brent had insisted on getting there in time to do a thorough warm-up on dry land before starting in the boat. Today Brent was his ride. Joe and Mark, the other two lightweight crewmen, their coach Pete, and the heavyweight athletes were not yet there.

JJ switched directions to stretch his other quad. Despite the early starts, this was where he wanted to be and what he loved to do. The boathouse odour of damp wood was something that energized him. The delicious pull of muscles tightened by the previous day's weight workout engendered an almost sexual satisfaction.

He did not fully understand how Andrea could be ready to give up these moments. At their level of sport, they were part of one of the most exclusive clubs in the world. Headed to the Olympic Games. They understood the beauty of pain. He knew that as soon as athletes left the world of training and competition, they quickly forgot how wonderful it felt to be this strong, this determined, this consumed. Once they were gone, they could no longer relate. He wondered what their relationship would become, now that Andrea was leaving the club.

Since the afternoon they met in Lucerne, they had spoken every day. They shared the highs and struggles of training. One time they managed to sneak in some time together while on an overlapping layover in Frankfurt. They separated from their teams and cloistered themselves, for two hours, behind an unused gate desk. They held hands, kissed, and said very little. Though JJ had dreaded their boarding announcements that would require them to part ways, he knew that separating again would keep their relationship fresh.

When he had a day off during spring training camp in Sacramento, he had borrowed one of the team trucks and drove to see Andrea. They had only three hours to be together. They parked on the side of the road halfway between Sacramento and Andrea's home in San Diego and sat in the bed of the truck eating turkey sandwiches, while cars whizzed by. When she pulled a thick photo album out of her bag, he had felt a sudden wave of disappointment. He did not want to spend their rare time together running through an inventory of her childhood memories, past relationships and daily life. He said nothing.

JJ

"I never show my photos to others, so you're a very special exception," she had said, lifting a hand to gently sweep his hair away from his eyes. He felt a pang of guilt.

When she opened up the album, he had been relieved to see that the photos were not vacation pictures and high school party poses, but artistic candids of strangers and objects. There was an appealing transience about the shots, like the photographer was capturing casual moments as she passed by. He had barely flipped through the first few pages before he gave his verdict.

"I like them."

"Oh, shut up. Don't make fun of me."

"I'm serious."

She had snuggled close as he flipped through the rest of the book. When he put it down, she looked up at him and he could tell she wanted him to say something more. She wanted praise or feedback, but he couldn't think of what else to say.

After a moment of silence, he managed to spit out, "Thanks for showing me. I'm not an expert or anything, but I think they're good."

She had grinned.

It was safer to not venture too far into discussing her work. There was an awkward vibe when they talked about something other than sports. He was eager to share stories about his crew, the insanity of their latest plyometric circuit, the pressure of the upcoming Olympic season. Or simply enjoy her body. Her touch. He had turned to her, cupped her face in his hands, and kissed her.

The boathouse was quiet, dark, and damp, the smell of the lake in their clothes and nostrils. Once the full crew arrived, they began to set up on the water. Waves lapped up against the old wooden dock, which was slippery with goose droppings.

None of the enthusiastic local retirees had yet come to brush it clean. The athletes placed the quad sweep on the water next to the dock, put their oars in the oarlocks, and closed the gates to secure them in place. They eased down onto their seats, positioned their knees up, and secured their track spikes. After checking the seat movement on the runners, they pushed away from the dock, extending the oars to the side and laying the blades flat on the water. These were the kinds of things they did without stopping to think.

JJ held onto his oar handle and breathed in the cool mist that rose from the surface of the lake. They rowed out to Point One, where Pete met them.

Pete spoke clearly, with a tinge of reprimand in his voice. "Today I want to see better synchronization on the release, especially as you tire. More consistent back splash and less sloppy than yesterday. We'll focus on getting some volume in."

JJ didn't relish the idea of high-volume training the day before a race simulation, but there wasn't much he could say to change Pete's mind. It was just the way it worked with their crew. Pete had a master plan, and the athletes trusted that it was the best plan. More than once Pete had preached to them about the importance of training the body to deal with lactic acid. The longer the body pools and buffers lactate on race day, the better. It didn't really matter what Pete's rationale was, anyway. They would have done almost anything he asked of them.

About thirty minutes into the row, the sun began to burn away the mist, and JJ removed his long-sleeved shirt and pulled his sunglasses down. He struggled to keep focused on each stroke to ensure exact placement, relaxing on the recovery, only to feel the pain of his calloused hands as he put pressure down on the handle. He removed the blade from the

JJ

water and onto the feather, then rolled it back into his fingers and onto the square. He focused on exact placement in unison with a solid press from the legs and back. His lungs burned as the boat propelled smoothly through the water and the crew breathed in synchrony—one powerful creature. Words from a book he once read went through his mind: "Like Einstein," the author wrote, "we wish to know God's thoughts. We shall attempt to pry them loose with an oar." He could see how the author could find a glimpse of something divine space in the midst of physical strain and the streamline surge of the boat.

On the way home from the lake that day, he reclined the passenger seat and listened to Brent talk.

"Take a nap this afternoon, JJ. Rest your body so we can kick ass tomorrow. No hot and heavy phone calls with *Andrea*."

Brent drew out Andrea's name as if reciting a childhood taunt. JJ didn't take the bait. He had no desire to discuss his relationship with Andrea, as Brent would inevitably guide the conversation towards an analysis of her physical appearance. Despite his claim of being an impartial outside observer and advisor to JJ, Brent's infatuation with Andrea had become obvious. It was like she was a trophy girlfriend he wanted to win.

JJ focused the conversation on the time trial instead. "We're competing against the clock tomorrow. No one else will be there, so how exactly will we be kicking ass?"

"It's a race simulation. We need to get ourselves into the right mindset and feel the kind of stress and focus we'll feel at the World Championships or Olympics. We're kicking the clock's ass." Brent smiled as he came up with the last line and repeated, "We are kicking the clock's ass!" He punctuated the sentence by holding down on the car horn.

"Right." JJ closed his eyes. Arguing with Brent was never worthwhile. It was simply best to agree.

"By the way, I'll borrow my mom's car and drive tomorrow. Pick you up at five," said JJ.

Later that day, JJ dropped a sliced bagel into the toaster and thought about how, for the rest of the day, he would have to limit his portion sizes and prepare for the weigh-in the next day. He never had much trouble weighing in below seventy kilograms, but since the average of the rowers in the boat couldn't exceed that amount, he knew he had to do his best to keep his weight as low as possible, in case someone else came in above. No one had suspected they would (weight was something they discussed frequently), but it was best to be safe—even if it was just a simulation.

The next morning, JJ woke up and went straight to the scale in the washroom. It read 69.3 kilograms. *Perfect.* He threw a handful of energy bars, two bananas, his large water bottle, and two packets of electrolyte powder into his bag. His throat was scratchy, like a cold was on the way, and he told himself that it was all in his head. *The mind tells you strange things on race days. Ignore it.* Later, in the car, Brent insisted on playing a CD of pump-up music to get them ready for the simulation.

At the boathouse, Pete was waiting with the scale and a note pad. After last-minute runs to the washroom to flush out any excess fluid, they each stepped up. JJ exhaled with relief as Pete read off their weights. "Mark, sixty-nine point one; Brent, sixty-nine point eight; JJ, sixty-nine point three; and Joe, seventy. So far, so good. Now you need to refuel. I'll meet you at the dock in an hour."

JJ sat silently and downed one electrolyte drink, loving the cold rush of liquid pouring through his parched body. He then devoured two bananas. Brent drank a Red Bull while holding an energy bar aloft in his other hand. No one spoke. At a

JJ

competition, the boathouse would be filled with the distracting noise of other competitors, but today it was eerily quiet.

Pete gave his usual pre-race talk at the dock. "Alright, I wanna see direct catches. Hold the finishes, boys. Keep it simple and effective. Just let the boat do the work for you."

The rowers slid into the boat and moved out into the warm-up area. There were ten minutes of light paddling, ten minutes of short and powerful race pace bursts that lasted from thirty seconds to a minute in duration, and a final ten minutes of light paddling. There was the lingering taste of banana in JJ's mouth.

Pete yelled a five-minute warning through the megaphone.

They manoeuvred the boat into the lane set up for them by one of the assistant coaches. There were three minutes to go. JJ felt the nerves rising.

"This game of make-believe is pretty realistic," said Joe, balancing his oar.

Mark spat into the water. JJ yawned, as he always did when he was nervous.

"Focus, boys, focus. Just breathe," said Brent.

JJ looked up at the sky in an attempt to ignore the knots in his stomach. The thick grey clouds seemed close. The air was humid. The white lane markers on either side of their boat bobbed up and down with the rippling of the lake surface. They reminded him of the pool lanes he used to circle before quitting swimming to take up rowing. He loved the tidiness of lanes—everyone knew where they needed to be. There were very few unknowns in rowing, except for the weather; and he found it reassuring to know that wherever he raced, there would be the same boats, the same straight two-kilometre course set up, with the same kind of markers. *Just breathe. You've done this a thousand times before.*

Eventually, Pete blew the horn, and they were off.

The crew struck a rate of forty-eight strokes per minute off the start and kept that up for the first forty-five seconds before settling into their race pace of thirty-nine strokes per minute. At the thousand-metre mark, the boat surged forward. JJ's focus was on twenty solid strokes to set up the last half of the race. His breath was hot, and his throat burned. He dug in and grunted with each move.

At 1500 metres, the crew drove the stroke rate back up to forty-two for the final sprint home. The white markers switched to red for the last 250 metres, and the crew launched into their all-out sprint of forty-five strokes per minute. The crew grunted on each drive, inhaling loudly on the recovery. Though the team moved in unison, so close together, JJ was hauled inward into the isolation of his physical pain. His vision narrowed. His lungs were on fire. All he wanted to hear was that horn. Primal sounds escaped his mouth. Ten strokes to go. Nine, eight, seven. Burning. Burning. Three, two.... The horn blew.

The crew collapsed forward. Breathing was too hard. JJ groaned. There would be another minute of agony as he started to recover. The strange dichotomies of sport were contained in one race: pain and euphoria; fear and relief; team synchrony and complete isolation. He waited and breathed.

"Five fifty-nine, boys. Awesome," Pete shouted over the megaphone.

The exhilaration began to push its way through slowly. JJ high-fived his teammates. Brent slapped his back. Mark let out a loud holler. They all laughed. It became something dreamlike and emotionally beautiful in a matter of moments. It was similar to the rush of post-race adrenaline he experienced at real regattas. The feeling was hard to describe. The

JJ

drug of athletes. The high that kept him coming back for more.

The rain began to fall in little circles on the water as the men finished putting away the equipment.

"I'm going to run home to cool down," said Brent. The drops were coming down hard now.

JJ rolled his eyes. "Okay, but stay on the sidewalk, and have a good day off."

He ducked into the car. When he turned the key, "The Final Countdown" blared over the speakers. He ejected Brent's motivational CD, tossed it onto the backseat, and drove out to the street and into the rain.

SAM

Passport and e-ticket in hand, Sam waited in line to check in his small suitcase. The couple in front of him argued about who would get to sit in the window seat for take-off.

"You always sit in the window seat," said the lady.

"That's not true, dear. Remember the trip to Russia? You got the good seat on the way there *and* on the way back," said the man.

"I don't think so. You're making that up. I never get the good seat, because you're always blathering on about needing more leg room."

Irritated by their pettiness and the growing whininess of their voices, Sam stood taller and thought about how naïve and self-focused these people were. He heard his old self in their pointless discussion and relished the feeling of being superior. *I am changed.*

At the desk, Samuel placed his suitcase on the conveyor belt. The attendant opened his passport (returned to him by Ellis that morning), glanced up, and nodded. She printed and affixed the baggage tags, and that was it. No suspicious looks or questions. Although he knew that he wasn't carrying anything illicit, he wondered if the disgust and hatred he felt for the people around him was somehow detectable. His palms were sweaty, his breathing rapid. He continued on to security and moved smoothly through. He was not taken aside to be searched. He was not taken to a windowless room to be questioned. You cannot fly with liquids, aerosols, or sharp objects, but you can fly with insides gripped by fury.

The window seat lady who had been in front of him in the check-in line tripped the alarm and was sent back through to remove her belt and large earrings. Her husband stood waiting, his hands on his hips, looking annoyed. Sam walked to his gate and sat down. He was still trembling. He closed his eyes and thought about Ellis: his face, voice, advice. Sam fingered the two gold bands on the chain that hung around his neck and replayed the things Ellis had uttered on the way to the airport.

"I've said it before, Son, but I want you to remember that you were chosen for this. I cannot go with you, but my spirit will be with you always." A long silence had ensued, and then Ellis added, "You're going to war."

When they had pulled up to the terminal, Ellis cupped Sam's face in his hands and said, "Don't worry, I'll be watching you."

JJ

JJ wished he could see her and attach a human face to the guilt he felt. Did he injure a tall girl? A short girl? A blond girl? A black girl? He knew that she was not in critical condition, but she was pretty battered nonetheless, with a fractured vertebrae and severe concussion. He just didn't know what she looked like.

And all he wanted to do was escape into sleep.

He had seen her car—it was a crushed mass of metal. The impact had crumpled the driver's side like paper and the emergency response team had difficulty getting her out. JJ had heard her weeping. A horrible, lonely sound. The police told him some of the other details. Bleeding from her nose and forehead. Deep gash from her shoulder to her elbow.

JJ woke up repeatedly from a nightmare in which a baby girl was trapped in a metal womb, scratching to get out.

He stared through his bedroom window at the park across the street. There were several small children, squealing and chasing one another around the slide, and three moms holding portable coffee thermoses and chatting nearby. He had occupied this room since he was a child. It had the same pink plush carpet that crept in under the door from the hallway—that he had hated, that he once tried to colour over with a blue marker and got caught by his older sister while finishing the first square foot. There were two large, discoloured Star Wars posters on the closet wall, sports medals and photographs pinned on a bulletin board next to his bed, shelves jammed full of old school binders and guitar music sheets, and a dilapidated beanbag chair in the corner by the closet. He had a framed photo of Andrea on his desk.

After two days spent in near darkness, his mom had insisted he open the blinds and the window.

"You're going to have to face the day at some point," she said, "and it reeks in here."

His broken arm and ribs were throbbing, but he refused to take the strong painkillers prescribed to him at the hospital. He avoided medication out of habit because of the constant threat of a random drug test. He imagined a doping control officer arriving at his door, with an empty cup and a threatening look, the moment the codeine went down his throat.

He wanted to suffer through this pain.

The pill container and a glass of water remained full on his nightstand. The clock read 10:46 a.m.

He had no idea if his teammates knew what had happened.

On the way back from the race simulation, the streets had been slick with rain. The route home from the rowing club was one he had driven a thousand times before. He knew the turns and the potholes. In the past he had safely made this journey with fatigue so intense he feared he might fall asleep

JJ

at the wheel. This time, his mind had been hyperalert, but it didn't matter. When he and the other driver hit a large puddle that had formed in the road, they both spun. He tried to steer, but the wheel was loose, tires completely off the pavement. The collision had happened midspin as their cars crossed over the yellow line. A horn blared. JJ's arm cracked against the steering wheel, and his body crashed hard against the tension of the locked seatbelt.

The doorbell rang downstairs. JJ knew that it was probably someone looking for him. He hadn't showed up for the morning row. He hadn't answered any calls. He had spent the morning curled up under his duvet wishing he could turn off his brain. He rewound his memory back to the moment he had climbed into his car. *What if I had avoided that section of road? What if I had slowed down sooner?* Sleep was the only way to stop his thoughts.

JJ listened to his mother's voice in the front hall.

"Glad you came," she said. "He doesn't know I phoned you."

"How's he doing?"

It was Pete's voice. His mother had been busy making calls, apparently.

"As I mentioned earlier, it's just his arm and ribs...and he's pretty bruised up. The doctor said he was lucky he's so physically fit—someone else might have ended up way worse off. Go on up and see him if you'd like. It will do him some good."

When Pete knocked on the bedroom door, JJ moved to the edge of the bed. *I need to get this over with, and then I can sleep.*

"Come in."

He wished he didn't have to have this conversation. He had no desire to think or talk about rehab or rowing, and Pete would surely bring up those subjects.

Pete opened the door slowly and moved quietly into the room. His body was huge and imposing, and he had a personality that matched. An American Olympic rowing champion from back in the sixties, he felt it was his duty to criticize the athletes for what he saw as a lack of mental toughness. "Your generation is a bunch of sissies," he had said more than once.

When the rowers were tired, Pete screamed at them to push through the fatigue. When they were injured, he pressured them to train through the pain; and when they expressed doubt about the program he had created for them, he told them that doubters always lose.

It had been less than two days since the accident, and JJ knew he wasn't ready to be told to suck it up and pull up his socks and get back on the horse and take the bull by the horns and get back into the ring. Or whatever. He needed to be allowed to sleep or agonize and run through every *what if* scenario until there was no more fatigue, agony, or *what if* scenarios left.

"Sorry I didn't call," said JJ, not feeling sorry at all.

"No problem. How are you?"

"Crappy, thanks."

"Oh." Pete collapsed his large body into the beanbag chair in the corner. The bag sighed and flattened, and Pete frowned—perhaps because of the chair, perhaps because JJ had admitted weakness. He straightened up as he began to speak in an all-business tone.

Here it comes. JJ studied a fleck of dried blood on his hand.

"Look, JJ. I know it's soon, and I know you're hurt, but I think we should go ahead and get a rehabilitation plan set up for you. There's no reason why you can't attend practices while you're injured. You can ride in the coach boat with me, instead of wallowing in self-pity here in this room."

JJ

Too much, too soon.

"I don't know." But he knew. He knew that his real injury was deeper than fractured bones. His drive was broken.

"Twenty-twelve is a year away...on the one hand that's a lot of time, but on the other hand, there's not a moment to spare. Your injuries are minor, and there're many rowers dying to grab that seat on the boat."

Pete had followed the expected script: starting in with a friendly message, then throwing doubt and fear into the mix. It usually worked, but not today. The idea of jumping up and focusing all his energy on getting back into a boat seemed ludicrous to JJ.

"What do you say? Should we get going on the rehab?"

JJ didn't want to respond. He wished he could pull the duvet back up over his head and say nothing. Even though they were not at the lake, Pete was his coach, and JJ knew he had to respond.

"Soon, Pete." He didn't mean it.

Pete smiled. "Great. I'll talk to a few people and set up a plan. We can get moving on it pronto." Pete wiggled himself out of the beanbag.

"Sure," said JJ. *Maybe never.*

After Pete left, JJ slept fitfully. The girl from the other car kept appearing in his dreams. First she came as a petite Asian and waved goodbye. Then she appeared as a pregnant blond in a wheelchair and she gave him the finger as he entered an elevator. Then he was standing outside of her crumpled car, peering in. Her face was obscured by blood, and she was screaming. He woke up drenched in sweat, panicked, heart racing. He sat up and began the relaxation breathing techniques the team psychologist had taught the rowers. *In the nose; out the mouth. Slowly, slowly.* Gradually his heart calmed, but sweat continued to bead on the back of his neck. He stood up and leaned his forehead against the cool windowpane. Rain began to fall. In the park, the mothers looked up at the sky and ran to grab their children by the wrists and collect stray buckets and shoes. Most of the children moved reluctantly, either not aware of the rain or just not caring that they would soon be soaked. One child wriggled out of her mother's grasp and ran to get a last turn on the slide. The rest were pulled away, kicking. Some screaming. They had no idea how silly they looked. It was a waste of energy to fight the inevitable.

JJ no longer sweated. He slept.

At 3:00 p.m. he woke to the sound of springs compressing as someone sat down on the edge of the bed.

"Please just let me sleep," he said without turning, assuming it was his mom.

A warm hand on his cheek. The delicacy of the touch surprised and irritated him. He pushed it away, hoping she would give up.

Then he felt a gentle kiss on his earlobe and Andrea's voice. "It's okay. It's me."

He turned carefully, wincing at the sharp pain in his ribs, and she was there, staring down at him, tears in her eyes. Her presence was at odds with this familiar childhood room. He affiliated her with the fast-paced world of elite competition, travel, late night phone calls, and kissing breathlessly alongside a highway. To have her here, next to the faded Star Wars posters, eyes soft with compassion, embarrassed him. He did not want her to see him this way, slow-moving and weak. She was not just a distant voice on the phone. He couldn't hang up.

She whispered to him, "Why didn't you call me? Your mom had to tell me on Facebook."

JJ

"You're friends with my mom?"

"Why didn't you call me?"

"Who else in my family are you connected with?"

She seemed to have missed or ignored the aggravation in his voice.

"It's so good to see you're okay. I flew here as soon as I could."

She touched his cheek again, and he wondered if she saw him as a pathetic broken man, mumbling silly things. She rose and paced slowly around his room, examining his trophies, giggling at the grade school headshots pinned on the bulletin board. He lay there, staring at her as she dragged her finger across his dusty dresser, her body alive with strength and confidence. After a while, he forgot his annoyance at the unexpected intrusion and told her about the day of the accident. The successful time trial and the slick roads afterwards. She moved back to her perch on the edge of his bed, listening carefully to his now calm, regular voice. But when he got to the part about the girl trapped in her car, Andrea's mouth opened sympathetically, and she reached for his hand. His voice cracked. He tried to hold back the tears, but they fell disobediently. He was not in control. He turned his head to hide his face and wipe his wet cheek on the pillow.

"It's good to cry," she said quietly, and his irritation resurfaced. He wanted to end the conversation and go back to sleep.

She sat there for a long time, diligently holding his hand. He knew she was waiting for him to continue his story. He would not. So, after several minutes, she began to speak, reciting the details of her decision to retire. She talked without pauses, like someone visiting the infirm and babbling to an unresponsive body. He imagined she felt it was her duty to entertain him like that—cheer him up, keep him company.

It was what Pete sometimes did with athletes who were cut from the crew. It was an attempt to distract the loser with an endless onslaught of words.

He needed her to stop. She described the difficulty of telling her coach about her decision to retire and the euphoria of seeing an unplanned life stretched out ahead of her. She explained her plans to move to New York for a while to focus on her photography.

When she finally took a breath, he knew he needed to punctuate the conversation. Then he could sleep.

He opened his mouth and simply let words fall out like a sigh, "I want to quit too." His unexpected statement floated in the ensuing silence.

It was true. Quitting appealed to him more than starting from zero at rehab, lifting five pound weights like an old man, and sitting on the dock or coach boat while the crew rowed.

Andrea responded predictably. "It's probably not the right time to make that decision. You should think it over."

Should. *Should* was the word his sport psychologist told him to avoid. He was trained to fight back and not give up, but the problem with pushing back was that sometimes the thing you're battling wins, and you lose. When it came to injuries, he knew so many athletes who had been hurt and worked hard at getting back into top shape, only to find they couldn't reach top shape anymore. And then they wouldn't make the team, or they'd make the team, perform poorly in competition, or get reinjured and be forced out.

One of JJ's former crewmates had once tried, against the advice of his doctors, to come back from a severe spine injury and make it to the World Championships. He ended up permanently damaging his back. For life. He was forced to retire midseason. JJ had heard that same athlete give a teary

JJ

motivational speech at a recent PacificSport event. "I had to try to get back into the boat. Otherwise, for the rest of my life, I would have wondered whether I could have made it. I chose to get up and start rowing again. I wouldn't let an injury tell me my dream was lost."

Some of the people in the audience had cried. The athlete had paused dramatically to let them bask in their goose bumps and tears, and then continued, assuming the earnest intonation of a typical motivational speaker. "So all of you, when you face challenges, get up and spit in the face of those challenges."

JJ had sat in the audience, holding back laughter. The truth was that his former crewmate's injury made the decision in the end. *It spat in your face, and you got dragged kicking and screaming away. Now you have to wear a back brace for the rest of your life as a reminder.*

Unlike that old teammate, JJ didn't want to put up a fight. He didn't want to get out of bed or even talk to his girlfriend.

Andrea tried to get him to say more. "JJ?"

The sadness was all around him, sucking energy out of his body. His eyes closed.

Her voice at a great distance: "We'll talk more about this later."

He responded from the fog of sleep. "Mm."

He woke up later to the sounds of Andrea and his mom chatting downstairs. Through the open door of his bedroom, he heard them discussing the things he avoided talking about with Andrea, like the seemingly innocuous questions she slipped into their late night phone conversations, which he ignored. He overheard his mother's delighted responses: that he adored spaghetti and meatballs with piles of shredded parmesan when he was a child; that he had lived in Burnaby with his father for the whole year of grade four. That was what they spoke about down in the kitchen, amid the clinking of cutlery on plates, and he could not stop them.

Nothing in his life seemed to be in the right place. It was all up in the air. His usual impulse to persevere had been replaced by a desire to escape. To avoid the path of resistance. To run away to somewhere new and hope that when the pieces of his life landed, they'd fall around him in a favourable way. He could not row, so he needed to leave this city. He'd head to Manhattan with Andrea. At least for a little while.

SAM

Despite the flight being an overnighter, Sam had not slept. He spent the first three hours rolling his rings between his fingers and vacillating between fear and excitement about the life that lay ahead. In the fourth hour of the flight, he drifted into a trancelike state. He imagined Ellis beside him, whispering about the war ahead—about how he might be tempted to doubt his mission but to keep faith.

The pilot's voice over the loudspeaker shook him fully awake. He smiled at the space where the imagined Ellis had been.

The screen on the seat back in front of Sam displayed a map of the Atlantic, with a dotted line marking the trajectory of the plane. They were soaring somewhere above Wales. In about forty minutes, he would land in the UK, the destination Ellis had chosen.

LEXI

Lexi Mason came home from a follow-up appointment with the surgeon. She had news to share, but it could wait. She was relieved that Brent was busy doing abs in the family room. She could have some quiet time. She hobbled as quickly as she could into their tiny kitchen, leaned her crutches against the kitchen table, hopped on one foot over to the sink to fill the kettle, and plugged it in. She turned around and leaned back to balance herself for a moment.

Some water had pooled along the edge of the counter and soaked through the back of her sweater, creating a dark line across her kidneys. She turned again to face the calendar on the kitchen wall.

"You been working out or something, Lex?" Brent asked, as he entered the room, grabbed an apple, and dropped down into a chair. His face was red and glistened with sweat.

"Huh?"

She didn't turn to look at him as she reached into the cupboard to grab a mug, a tea bag, and the sugar bowl.

"Your back is sweaty," he said.

"Oh. No, it just got wet," she said, flatly.

"Going back to the gym would do you some good, even if you just did upper body. Flies and bench and stuff, maybe some basic abs. Keep you looking good."

All of sudden she was conscious of her softening midsection. She wanted to cover up her butt and thighs, stop Brent from looking at them. She tugged at the edge of her sweater and put the sugar bowl, unused, back into the cupboard.

"How was practice this morning?" she asked.

His favourite subject: rowing.

"Pretty good, except JJ didn't show. I think Pete went by his house this afternoon to see what's up." He took a bite of his apple and talked through a full mouth. "My calves kill."

The water rumbled to a boil.

Brent swallowed and spoke again. "By the way, what did Dr Chen say? When can you get back in the boat?"

She stared at the calendar as she responded. "He said that my recovery from the second surgery is much better than expected. I can start training by the end of the month."

He jumped up. "That's awesome. London…here we come!"

He said the last part in a loud, deep voice, imitating a radio host, as he hugged her from behind. His lean muscular body wrapped around hers. He lingered. She wanted to pull away but didn't. He swayed slowly and her good leg started to tire. He pushed strands of her brown hair out of the way and kissed her neck. She focused on the calendar, covered with dark-inked notes about Brent's training and her doctor's appointments.

"Tea?" Lexi asked, peeling Brent's long arms from around her and reaching for the kettle. She hoped he'd decline, so she could sip away in peace.

"I've got water," he said, backing away slowly and sitting down at the table. His chair scraped against the linoleum floor.

She prepared her drink and turned back to Brent. She held out the mug in front of her to indicate that she needed him to take it for her to the table, so she could hop to her seat. He misinterpreted the gesture and raised his large stainless steel water bottle for a toast. "To London twenty-twelve!"

He closed his eyes and chugged, as Lexi stood there on her good leg, hot mug in hand, saying nothing. A moment later, he wiped his mouth with his sleeve.

"Just going to take a quick shower," he said. He placed his water bottle on the table next to his half-eaten apple and left.

Once he was safely gone, she returned to the cupboard to take out a few gingersnaps for dipping. She loved these small treats, even if Brent referred to them as *slippery slopes*. One time when he caught her sneaking an Arrowroot, he had said, "Those cookies are the difference between gold and fourth."

When she shot him a dirty look and made a show of cramming the full biscuit into her mouth, he added, "I bet Andrea never eats that crap."

The mention of Andrea had always made her feel uneasy. Though Lexi had never met her, Andrea had been heralded by Brent as some kind of infallible creature. A model athlete. She knew nothing turned him on more than that. She remembered exactly when Brent had first met Andrea.

It was at the regatta in Lucerne. Sixty-two days after Lexi's first surgery. Lexi was at home, getting stronger. She remembered the competition, because Brent had complained one night about the strong wind on the course. Apparently, a gust had blown the large white officials' tent into the water. Paper cups and napkins had flown around everywhere, and the races had been delayed. While they had been talking on the phone, Brent stopped the conversation to announce with great amusement that he had found a rogue serviette inside his backpack. She had pictured him discovering the napkin, most likely seated on a small European hotel bed, big black backpack in front of him. He would have extracted each item carefully, first his towel, then his extra training suit, then his lucky red sweater (the one she gave him during his first year on the national rowing team), complete with the wet napkin. She had imagined Brent pulling the wet napkin off the sweater carefully and meticulously, like the way he rigged his boat. And the way he removed the dressings on her leg after surgery: lifting a small corner of the clear hospital tape, stopping, looking up at her as she winced, and smiling. Then, he would repeat the action.

"Pain is just weakness leaving the body," he said each time. So he drew the torture out. *To exorcise me of my weakness.* There was nothing Brent hated more than a hint of weakness.

It was during a call on the last night of that same regatta that he had first mentioned Andrea. His words were slurred and cut by the crackling of the phone line. "Lex, (crackle) and (crackle crackle) Pickwick's, and I met a (crackle) kayaker named Andrea...Amazing pipes...(crackle, crackle) redhead. JJ thinks she's (crackle)...It's the middle of the night here and I'm (crackle) drunk. I'll call tomorrow."

She had not remembered Andrea from Beijing. After Brent's call she had pulled out her album from 2008 and flipped through all the photos. No redheads. She studied each picture, checking out the muscularity of her own arms, noticing people and details in the background that she had not noticed before. There was one shot of Brent and her hugging on the top of the medal podium, ten minutes after the medal ceremony, after all the medallists had cleared away to talk to the media and see their families. They did not have medals around their necks. Fifth and sixth. She was still in her red and white unisuit. A small, dark, lonely bird stood on the far-side of the bronze step. She had never noticed it before.

When Brent and Lexi had stepped off the podium to let other mourning athletes have their consolation photos taken, Brent had said, matter-of-factly, "We'll get another shot in four years."

This seemed to be a given for him. He was willing to continue training six hours a day and keep competing and travelling and hurting for four more years, so that he could stand on the podium in London with a gold medal around his neck. It wasn't a given for her. She was ready for an engagement ring, a three-tier white wedding cake, a real pay cheque, and a mortgage. She was eager for a garden with tulips and vegetables. For a life without the need for physiotherapy. For fewer airline points. But she never said any of this to Brent.

After their post-2008 Olympic break, when it was time to return to training, she chose to take the easy road, do what Brent did, and not change anything. She returned to the lake and allowed herself to fall into the hypnotic rhythm of life as a high-performance rower. The day-in, day-out exhaustion. The repetition.

Then a knee injury forced her out of training. And as easily as the hypnosis had come on, it fell away. She awoke again to all of the dreams and desires of a normal life. Visions of a golden wedding band loomed larger than the objective of a gold medal. She tried to ignore these thoughts. There was less than a year to go until London, and she knew that if she wanted to make the team and head to the Games with Brent, she would have to abandon fantasies of marriage and get serious about rehab. She would need to force herself to attend to all the little things, too: eat organic oatmeal instead of Corn Flakes, water and green tea instead of black tea with sugar, focus on her physio exercises instead of the Home and Garden channel shows, and maybe even get acupuncture (she hated needles). She wasn't sure if she was up for it. She wished they could just move on.

She dipped her cookie in the tea and listened to Brent sing "Eye of the Tiger" in the bedroom. She pictured him punching the air as he sang. She thought about what was ahead of her: the 4:00 a.m. wake up calls, the chill in the dawn air, the irritation of rigging the boat when all she wanted to do was row and get warm. But the thing she dreaded the most was getting pulled back into the numbing cycle of waking, eating, training, eating, napping, training, eating, sleeping.

The phone rang. Brent's song was cut off.
"Hello?" Brent said inside the bedroom.
Lexi strained to hear. She worried it was Andrea.
Pause.
"Hey, JJ. Where were you this morning? We called you...."
Pause.
She relaxed a little.
"What? Are you all right?"
Long pause. She wondered what was going on.
"Oh, man, that's rough. So, what's going to happen... when can you start training again?"
Very long pause. Lexi moved into the hallway so she could hear better.

LEXI

"What are you talking about? Don't be a loser. It's just a couple of broken bones...I've seen people come back stronger from worse injuries."

Short pause.

Brent's voice was getting louder, angrier. "You're acting crazy. This is idiotic. You'll change your mind, I know it. I know you. You're not a quitter...."

He was full-on shouting now. Fear rippled through Lexi. She had heard him speak like this before. "Is this about Andrea? That bitch...."

She was shocked to hear him refer to Andrea that way. Any envy she had felt before dissolved.

His voice turned to pleading again. A last ditch effort. "Come on, give it a week. Take some time off first...."

Brent swore. She heard the crash of the phone against the bedroom wall. She knew that it would be best to leave before he came out of the bedroom.

Sam

Sam walked up the ramp at Heathrow. Rows of people lined the walkway, waiting for their friends and relatives to arrive. A man ran to embrace a young girl. A couple engaged in a passionate kiss. People called out names and waved at each other. No one rushed to greet him. No Mom or Dad or Callie or Brent. He was anonymous and alone. He gripped his suitcase tightly in one hand. The weight of jet lag and the bag were the only things that anchored him to reality.

He searched the hordes of people for someone familiar, but they were all strangers. He imagined Ellis's face in the crowd, his eyes behind the security cameras that were everywhere. He moved with the people through hallways, down escalators, to the Underground. Ellis watching. Once on the Tube, speeding towards the city centre, he unfolded the white paper Ellis had given him a day earlier: *London Bridge Station, Pasty Shop, 9am.*

Sam hoped Ellis would be there, somehow, waiting at London Bridge. Standing in his dark suit against a wall. Perhaps coming to London was another test that Sam had to pass. Maybe Ellis was on the Tube right now, watching from behind a newspaper or through the window of the next car. Ellis would want him to be focused and serious, so Sam stared at the Tube map above the seats and planned his route.

At London Bridge, Sam disembarked and stalked the station, looking for something that might be a pasty place. What was a pasty place, anyway? He didn't want to ask anyone, so he circled the building, moving through crowds of late-rising commuters, and pictured Ellis lurking around the corner or hidden in a queue. Finally, he saw a stand with the word *pasty* on it and approached. He checked his watch and saw that it had stopped. He relied on the clock on the wall. It was nearing 9:00 a.m. No one was waiting for him. There was the familiar ache in his stomach. He had been too nervous to eat on the flight. He would not eat now, either. He ignored this need and leaned against the wall.

At 9:07 a.m., a man in a black suit entered the station and walked towards the stand. He was short, thin, bald, and probably close to fifty. *Not Ellis. Not even close.* Sam was disappointed. The man's lips were thin and his mouth downturned. He did not reach out his hand to shake Sam's.

"Hello. Welcome to London," he said, his *l*'s sounding like *w*'s. "I'm Paul, a friend of Ellis." He spoke in a monotone, and his eyes darted from side to side, checking to see if anyone was watching.

"Hi, Paul."

Sam wished it were Ellis. *Who is Paul? Paul doesn't want to be here. Neither do I.* He felt guilty for the thought. The man moved in fast, jerky motions as he pulled something out of his satchel. Sam felt a pang of jealousy. He wondered if Paul and Ellis spent time on the phone. If they exchanged emails. He wondered how well Paul knew Ellis, and if Ellis called him *Son*.

"I'm just here to give you this," said Paul, and passed over an envelope.

He snatched it from Paul's hand. A metallic jingle. *Another ring?* For a moment Sam was excited by the idea that there might be a note from Ellis inside—a message for Sam alone.

"It's just a key to flat number six. Building door code is three-three-two-two," said Paul.

Sam's excitement deflated. He had grown accustomed to the bigness of time spent with Ellis. He missed his moving speeches, his commanding presence, and his godlikeness.

He was already struggling with the mundanity of life away from Ellis.

"There's a cab outside waiting to take you there. Cabbie already knows where to go, and the fare is paid for. Stay in the flat and wait. We'll meet again soon."

Paul gestured towards the exit, walked further into the station, and joined the flow of commuters.

The cab sped along the busy streets of South London. Cabbie looked straight ahead, paid no attention to Sam.

Sam replayed Paul's words. "Stay in the flat and wait." *For how long? Will Ellis come to the flat? Will he call?* He needed to feel that Ellis would come for him. He pulled the key out of the envelope. No note. As more disappointment crept in, he reminded himself that Ellis had overseen this entire day. That Ellis was somewhere, somehow, observing and seeing everything. He had to have faith.

The cab slowed down outside a contemporary five-storey building.

"Here's your stop. That's your flat." The cabbie pointed at the building. "Good luck."

Sam stood on the sidewalk, his suitcase at his side, as the car sped away. His pulse raced. He felt disoriented and exhausted. These were the times when he would depend on the training exercises Ellis had him perform, like the Toronto rush-hour and food court observations. Ellis had advised him to use boredom, hunger, guilt, confusion, irritation, and any overwhelming emotions as fuel for their work.

"Breathe it in and convert it to anger. Let your fury burn big, bigger than anything you've ever felt, and then store it away to use for our cause," he had said.

Sam breathed in. Cars and trucks whizzed by a foot away from where he was standing. Exhaust fumes filled the air. A police siren sounded. The wind whipped his cheeks. Across the street a group of young black men talked animatedly in another language. Part of the road was blocked by construction barriers, and a couple of workers jack-hammered the pavement. He breathed in again and let his growing anxiety push against his ribcage from the inside out. He needed to preserve this tension; roll it into a tight little ball inside and keep it for when he'd really need it.

He approached the door of the building, pressed the code into the keypad, and entered the foyer. The floor was clean grey stone, and the walls were painted a flat white. The sounds of the street faded slightly once the door shut behind him. He moved through a doorway into the corridor. A camera followed his movements. At the end of the hall was number six. He unlocked his flat and entered.

There was an institutional sterility to the one-room flat. The white walls were unadorned with art, and the large white tiles on the floor were polished, shining, and not warmed by rugs. A small, round glass table and two chairs were placed just a few feet from the entrance next to a tiny kitchenette. In the middle of the room was a pale blue couch and low bleached-wood coffee table. At the far end of the long rectangular flat was a double bed wrapped tightly in a white comforter, two white side tables, and a door to a bathroom. On the wall to the right were two glass doors that opened up to a Juliet balcony, with the view of an old wall. Sam considered the fact he might be spending weeks staring out at that darkened brick. He did not know what Ellis had in mind for him, but he knew he had to trust that Ellis would tell him what to do. He put his suitcase down on the floor in the middle of the room and walked over to open the window. He sat down on the bed. On the pillow there was an envelope with his name on it. His heart jumped. A note from Ellis! He tore open the thick white paper and pulled out a folded letter, written in Ellis's careful hand.

My Sam,
Welcome to your London home. For now it is essential that you remain inside until someone comes to give you more instructions. I will send people to you, and everyone I send to you will only know their small piece of the puzzle. I can see the whole picture.
I am watching. Have faith. Be still.
Ellis

Ellis was looking out for him. A wave of calm settled on Sam. He lay down on the bed and held the letter up to his nose. He imagined that it smelled like Ellis. He envisioned his mentor leaning over the paper, and the soft swirl of his pen as he lingered over each word.
I just have to wait.

He fell asleep like that, with the letter open over his face.

When he woke up, it was dark in the flat. It took him several minutes to figure out where he was. He stood beside the bed, rubbed his eyes, and tried to gain some focus in the dark room. Then he remembered the letter. He threw himself onto his knees on the mattress and searched for the paper with wide violent sweeps of his hand across the bed. After five or six sweeps, he felt the sting of sheet burn on the back of his forearms and palms. His quick loud breaths filled his ears. Reaching too far on a sweep, he lost balance and fell to the floor. His arm crumpled beneath his weight. He stood and fumbled to find a light, a nagging pain in his wrist with each slap of his hand along the wall. He located a switch, and light flooded the room, stinging his eyes.

He squinted and returned to the bed, trying to spot the white paper. He ripped the covers off, pushed the mattress to the floor, and opened the drawers of the side tables. Nothing. Empty. He was frantic. Coming unglued. *What if I can't find it? I need it. I need it.* He tried to remember the exact words of Ellis's letter. Only a few came back, and he wasn't sure whether they were accurate: *Everyone I send…maybe…I will reveal to you…Wait?* The room was distorted and blurry. He knocked into the glass table. A chair crashed to the ground. Though he knew he was the one who had caused the loud sound, he scanned the dark room, imagining and hoping that the sound had in fact come from somewhere else, from someone else. From Ellis. Turning towards the window, he saw the ghostly billow of wind in the curtains. *He is watching. He's here!* Goose bumps blossomed on his body. He moved slowly towards the window. He stood and let the wind blow the sheer curtains against the front of his body, like a white veil.

He stayed still with his eyes closed as the veil was sucked away by the open window. When he opened his eyes, he noticed the letter pressed up against the wrought-iron swirls of the Juliet balcony railings. It was a euphoric revelation—a sign, a symbol, proof of Ellis's presence. He took the letter, read it until memorized, kissed it, refolded it, and placed it delicately in the impermeable plastic sack on the inside of his suitcase lid. He kept the lid propped open and moved through the flat to pick up his mess. At intervals, he looked back at the rectangular strip of paper and remembered Ellis's presence.

Jayna

Nate benched Jayna after she missed six rebounds in the preliminary round of a tournament in Quebec City. She was a player who usually out-rebounded her opponents, but not tonight.

"You're off your game," Nate said, before he smacked her on the butt and told her to take a seat. She could not look at him. Instead, she sat on the bench, pulled a sweaty towel over her head, and listened to the squeak of shoes on the court.

The night before, she had snuck out of the residence where the team was staying to hang out with Virginie, an old teammate who had moved to Quebec City to pursue a PhD. They met up at a bar where the grad students hung out during the school year. Virginie was a tall, gregarious, buxom blond. In conversation she was naturally flirtatious, giggling often and apt to place her fingertips gingerly on the leg or arm of her listener. She was already fairly drunk when Jayna arrived at the bar. Her arm was draped over the shoulder of a guy who was not disguising the fact he was staring down the front of her shirt. She stood up on the bench and shouted Jayna over, and the guy changed his focus to her thighs.

"Un pitchet de bière, s'il te plait," Virginie called out to the bartender.

Everyone in the bar looked. Virginie pushed away the guy she had been sitting with. He got up and returned to a table across the room.

"Hello, my love!" said Virginie as she gave Jayna a tight squeeze and peck on each cheek. The guys at the far table hooted.

A pitcher of beer and plastic cup was placed on the table.

"I got a head start on you, so you'd better drink up."

"Thanks," said Jayna as she poured herself a glass. "Who was the guy?"

"Don't know. Mathieu, Marc, Angelo? Who cares? They're all the same. I invited him over to sit with me, because it's sad to drink alone. Under some circumstances people don't mind being used. That guy was one hundred per cent okay with it." Virginie held up her beer cup. "Bottoms up!"

They chugged.

An hour later, after they had consumed a couple of pitchers and caught up on all the gossip about old teammates, Virginie had tried to describe her PhD research.

"We do a comprehensive assessment of mice, a series of injections and then analysis using imaging modalities. It's exactly what you would imagine we'd be doing in a lab."

Jayna slumped over the table, head rested on folded arms, eyes half shut, trying to follow. Virginie kept trying to explain.

"The whole experiment is like you on the court—the mouse is like you, and I'm like a coach, you know, like Nate, only better looking. I select the mouse based on a number of criteria, make it do all kinds of crazy activities over and over again, and watch what happens."

Jayna sat up straighter at the mention of Nate. Nerves fluttered. She remembered her tournament, where she was, and where she should be—in bed. She felt ill. Maybe it was the beer. Maybe the thought of mice. Maybe it was the image of Nate standing over her, injecting her with some kind of poison, and watching her panic, all the while taking notes on his clipboard. She knew she needed to get back to the residence.

Within minutes, she convinced Virginie that she had to go and stumbled out of the bar and into the back of a cab.

At the residence, she had removed her shoes outside the door and entered the dimly lit common area as quietly as she could. She fumbled in her purse for the keys to her room, which, thankfully, she did not have to share with anyone.

Even in her bleary-eyed state, she sensed that she was not alone in the room. There was someone in the shadows near the doorway. She stumbled to her left a little as she looked up and squinted to see who it was. But something in her just knew. She could tell from the fear that crept up her spine and balled up like a fist inside her throat. She could tell from the one bent leg, the sole of the foot against the wall.

"Do you know what time it is?" There was no condemnation in Nate's voice, just a hint of superiority. Just the knowledge that he had something against her. That she would owe him for his mercy.

"I just went out to visit a friend." She had tried to make her voice steady, but there was the telltale drunken slur and drawn-out words.

She couldn't prevent herself from tipping sideways and grabbing onto an old red couch for balance.

"Come here. Let me smell your breath."

He did not move from his spot in the shadows. She thought about running back out the door, chasing the cab that dropped her off, and begging the driver to take her away. With an infraction like this one, she could be sent home from the tournament. She might never be invited to the join the Olympic training camp. That would be the end of her Olympic dream.

"Come here, Bentley."

She had to do what he said. She walked slowly towards him, focusing on keeping a straight line. Her head was down, heart pounding. He leaned forward and sniffed loudly. "Your clothes reek like beer."

He grabbed her hair, placed it against his face, and let out a groan. She bit the inside of her lip to stop herself from saying anything. She was frightened and disgusted but stayed still.

"We should move out of this room, so you don't wake anyone up with your stumbling."

She fought the desire to spit at him.

But.

She wanted to hold on to her shot at the Olympics. And she was an adult. *I can handle this. If I pretend this is my choice, it will be easier.*

She let him to lead her by the arm to his room on the second floor, where no other rooms were occupied. He removed his hat. An identical pair of pants to the ones he was wearing was draped over the desk chair. She focused on the frayed navy hem. It was better than looking at him.

"Take off your clothes."

So she did, and he watched. *The mad scientist.* She did it quickly, though unsteadily.

"You're lucky that I believe in second chances." He stared at her, pale and naked, trembling in front of him.

She wanted to remind him that he was her coach. That he had his beautiful runner wife. That this was wrong. But she hadn't. Instead, she had crawled onto the bed, closed her eyes, and become the mouse.

On the courtside bench, Jayna kept the towel over her and studied her knobby knees. Previously, if she was off for a game, she would have been devastated. But somehow, today, she was just slightly disappointed. Under the shroud of the towel, she realized that what had happened with Nate was a kind of insurance for her. That now, more than ever, he couldn't afford the consequences of her not making it. He had already made the mistake of getting involved with his athlete; now she had a license to make mistakes as well. They needed each other in a perverse way. Perhaps Virginie was right: *Under some circumstances, people don't mind being used.*

She pulled the towel off and peered down the bench at her teammates, sweaty and screaming encouragement and directions to the players on court. Then she looked at Nate, who was waving his hands in the air, screaming something at the ref.

She swallowed and readied herself to speak to him in her sternest voice. "Put me back on."

He turned, and for a moment they did nothing but stare at one another. Her hands were shaking, but she held the gaze. She narrowed her eyes and waited for him to understand that he had no choice but to listen.

His brow furrowed. He spoke under his breath. "Next timeout, Bentley's back in."

It was a small exchange of power. A triumph for Jayna that ended abruptly when she turned to her teammates on the bench and saw their looks of confusion and anger. Many of them were to remain sidelined, while she was given another chance. She heard Jen say to no one in particular, "Coach's pet." Jayna's face burned with shame. What was even worse than screwing up or getting injured was the perceived favour of a coach.

Back on the court, she played a mediocre game, fuelling more whispers among her teammates. She knew they analysed and judged her every move, pass, and dribble, and she wondered what they were saying about her. She was unable to let go and let her instincts take over. Instead, she struggled against a hyperawareness: the man in the sixth row sipping a Coke, the seconds on the clock falling away, Nate moving a hand to his forehead, a teammate rolling her eyes.

She wished she could shut it all down and just play like she used to.

SAM

As the morning came, strips of weak light filtered through the window, and the flat began to warm up. Sam's wrist was swollen and painful to move, so he wrapped ice cubes from the freezer in a dishcloth and held it to the injury. Despite the discomfort, the memories of the night kept him dazed, happy, and desperate to see Ellis. All he had to do was wait. Ellis would send someone.

    He popped an ice cube into his dry mouth and sat down on the couch. He waited. Slept a little, sitting there, and then watched the room brighten. There was no clock in the flat, and, since his watch had stopped, he had no idea of the time. Hours and hours seemed to pass. Hungry, he got up and boiled some water and ate one of the two instant noodle packets in the cupboard. The only other food in the flat was a small jar of Nutella, almost empty. He dipped a spoon into the jar and sucked the sweet spread. He drank a large cup of water. His body ached for more food, but he wanted to make sure there was some left in case Ellis arrived. He went to the washroom, then over to the mattress and lay down. Sleep came, and when he woke up, it was dark again. The hunger pangs were strong again and his wrist sore. He drank another cup of water and pulled out Ellis's letter so he could touch it. It was alive to him now, imbued with the ability to speak, see, and hear.

Sam thought he should get some exercise to keep himself busy, so he switched on the light and began to walk a route around the table, to the bathroom door, across to the window, back around the table. He switched to a jog, stabilizing his injured wrist by pressing it tightly against his chest. He jogged 260 laps, switching directions at 130. His head spun.

The light in the room was changing. He drank another glass of water, snapped off a piece of hard noodle from the remaining packet, and sucked on it as he sat on the edge of the bathtub and ran the water for a bath. He savoured the saltiness of the noodles as the warm steam rose around him.

He had not taken a tub bath since he was a child. His memory wandered back to Brent, seated with him in their parents' little avocado-coloured tub. They had navigated bright toy boats through the soapy waters. It had fascinated Sam to tip the boats slightly and let them fill up. When he let go, some sank quickly below the bubbles, while others rebalanced and kept afloat. Often Brent grabbed the ones that remained at the surface and sped them around the volcano, which was his bent knee jutting out of the water, while Sam studied the slow descent of the shipwrecks.

When the tub was ready, he stepped in without testing the water. The water was too hot, stinging his right foot, and he swore aloud. The sound echoed against the bathroom white-tile walls—it was the first time Sam had spoken aloud since arriving at the flat, and his voice sounded strange, like it didn't come from him. He spoke again and listened carefully. "Hello?"

It seemed to be outside of his head, on its own, unrelated to him. It was a sad, hollow sound. When the water cooled a little, he sat down in the tub and listened to the drip-drip of the faucet. He felt the tug of loneliness, so he reminded himself that he had Ellis. He had their mission, too. It was something meaningful to pursue.

Pursuits without meaning are simply pastimes.

YASMINE

She couldn't pinpoint when she had stopped having dreams; she just realized over coffee one morning that it had been months since she recalled one. Immediately, she longed for the ethereal magic of dreaming—those extended blurry sequences when she could run through the air at amazing heights, free, weightless, and untouchable.

Nate stood near her in the kitchen, staring into the fridge for much too long. She sipped her drink and held her tongue. Silence was easier with him.

When he finally straightened up and closed the door, he raised a jug of orange juice in his hand. "This is almost empty." He opened the cap to verify the statement then shook his head in a gesture of disappointment. "You shouldn't drink so much juice. A glass of water and an orange would much better for you. I've told you this before."

He sucked down the remaining liquid, and with a dramatic lay-up, he tossed the empty container into the recycling bin against the wall.

She focused on the reassuring warmth of her coffee cup.

"Time to get you to the pool," he said, and made his way to the front door, which he unlocked and held open for her.

She rose slowly, testing her Achilles, grabbed her training bag off the stairs, and squeezed past Nate to exit.

Over the years Nate had become a compulsive clock-checker. He never went out without his watch, and he always seemed to be glancing up at the time on the wall or dashboard or reminding Yasmine of the passing minutes. She was already all too aware of the rapid movement of time: the approach of the Games, her ambitious goal of a sub-two-forty marathon time to qualify, and the quick passage of her prime years. Her sessions at the pool highlighted all of these things.

That morning, as she forced her limbs into an underwater stride, she watched the hand of the Speedo clock spin. Red on top, black on top. Around and around. Poolside, Vincent and Adam spun wet towels into whips and snapped them at each other, oblivious of their childishness. She watched the muscles of their long, narrow torsos tense and release as they lunged and recoiled. She envied their appetite for play and imagined that their sexual drives were equally insatiable. In her mind appeared a picture of Vincent, stretched out on a single bed in an almost bare room, with a woman; his large hands moving up and down, like swim sculls, the full length of her curved, lithe, young body. Yasmine pulled herself away from the image and tried to relax her tense muscles as she moved through the stride.

She thought of Nate. When he drove her this morning, he had placed his hand against her left thigh and massaged it roughly as they navigated the dark Montreal streets. He spoke of his team. There were the Olympic hopefuls and the ones labelled useless or hopeless. He was passionate about coaching. He saw it as his role to push individual athletes deep into discomfort; to show them how far they could go. It just bothered him that the coach eventually became invisible.

One night he had returned home from a tournament in Quebec City, fuming. Yasmine had been at the counter, carefully placing asparagus spears into the steamer, when Nate burst into the kitchen and threw his travel bag and baseball cap on the floor. As she turned to welcome him home, he began to shout, "I move my athletes beyond what they think they can achieve, and once they've gone there…into the far reaches of pain and success, they forget that they couldn't have done it alone. They give themselves the credit. They act like princesses. They make demands. Those selfish bitches." He had paced the room, breathing heavily, and Yasmine had turned back to her asparagus. It was best to remain part of the scenery and let him rant.

Adam and Vincent had put away their towel whips and were tugging tight bathing caps over their heads. She saw the way they watched each other as they used their fingers to force their hair up under the latex, goggles clenched between teeth. Vincent finished ahead of Adam and made his way towards the blocks. He did not appear to notice his teammate walking quickly to catch up, and turned only as Adam clasped both arms around him and pulled the both of them sideways into the pool. Yasmine had been alone in the lane, just metres away from where the two men fell in a tangled embrace, big feet flailing. Underwater, they separated themselves from one another and surfaced moments later in a different lane. Their coach, red-faced, strode down the deck and stopped to apologize to Yasmine. "Sorry about those two babies. I'll set them straight."

Later that day, while she waited for Nate to come pick her up, she saw Vincent on the street outside the pool. He stood ten feet away from a group of swimmers. He leaned back against the bus shelter and sulked. His posture bugged her. She didn't like the awkward forward-turned shoulders and convexity of his upper spine. She wanted to walk up to him and place her hand on his back to straighten him. She wanted to push him into the gaggle of teammates, but she was certain he would turn to her, like a teenager to a nagging mother, and glare. She felt too small. She wished she was in her tight running gear, racing by stealthily, but she still walked with a limp. She imagined that, like Vincent, she would never again join in comfortably with these twenty-somethings.

Nate's car pulled up in front of her, and the swimmers turned to watch her climb carefully in. It was in this moment that she wished her old friend Jeanette were with her, not Nate. They would head out for coffee, commiserate about their age, and laugh at the swimmers. But she had not spoken to Jeanette in three years. Not since Jeanette retired, got married, and gave birth to baby Jacob. Yasmine's world with Nate did not have enough room for friends anyway. Friends pointed out the way her energy dropped the moment she mentioned Nate. They asked her persistently why she did not accompany them to the cinema or bar. They suggested she visit her family in BC more often. They carefully avoided talking about Nate.

"Good practice?" Nate asked.

"Ok."

He placed his hand on her thigh as the car sped away from the pool and the swimmers.

SAM

It was impossible to tell the time of day. Sam leaned out the window and looked up at the strip of dark grey sky visible between the buildings. Cloudy morning or dusk? He had lost track of the days, and panic had set in. The need to see Ellis was physically intense. The suitcase was still open in the middle of the room, letter on display. Sam sat down against the balcony railing and whispered Ellis's name, over and over. It was the altar. He invoked Ellis. The hair stood up on his forearms, and the space in his chest tingled. *Ellis. Ellis. Ellis.* Two syllables, like a heartbeat.

Andrea

Andrea boarded her flight for New York City. She had a tiny Manhattan apartment lined up and plans to attend photography classes. She figured her savings from years of sponsorship earnings would carry her and JJ through for about ten months; then they'd have to find jobs or move. For the first time in years, she was travelling without checking in a kayak, paddle, and hefty training bag. After visiting JJ, she had returned to San Diego to plan for New York and put her kayaking gear in storage until she might need it again.

Andrea's mom had doubted the wisdom of retiring and moving East. "You're making a rash decision."

"I don't think so."

"You're sure?"

"Yes."

"This isn't about Danielle's death, is it? Maybe you should see a psychiatrist." This was the nature of these conversations with her mother. She seemed to think it her duty to say exactly what she was thinking, in case no one else spoke up.

Her mom left only a pause in the conversation before she added, "You need more time to think it over."

"Bye, Mom."

"Okay, we'll talk about this later then."

When the flight hit cruising altitude, Andrea pulled out her camera bag and began to clean each lens. She ran a cloth over the full frame fisheye, attached it, and then raised the camera above her head to take a test shot of the cabin. She looked at the photo on the screen: a widened, rounded view; passengers staring at the television screens in front of them, hemmed in softly by the blurred curve of the cabin walls. She wanted her life now to be like this—soft and fluid, almost undefined. She was eager to get beyond the constraints of a kayak, a narrow lane, and the strict boundaries of high-performance training.

At the airport, she collected her luggage and headed to a bench to wait for JJ. She propped up her feet on the baggage cart and watched passengers pass by. People of every shape and size, some smiling, some running, some holding hands. It occurred to her that she was now just like them. That before, she had felt she was somehow different. She had been focused, busy. *Better,* even. On the airport bench, without her USA tracksuit on, and without a training centre and coach to report to, she seemed ordinary. It felt good to not be trying to do anything extraordinary. She loved operating on a schedule determined by herself, not a coach or federation. It felt like the first real vacation of her adult life.

ANDREA

After three hours of waiting, bobbing between sleep and people watching, she made her way to the area where JJ would emerge. She was eager to capture the moment of his arrival and see the relief and joy on his face. They would not talk about sport. They would not compare workouts. She hoped his own accident had brought him the broadened perspective she had gained after Danielle's death. A sense that life was too short to spend focused on one activity.

She got out her camera and focused it on the door. After several minutes he came out, but all she saw was his downcast face, squinted eyes, and tense lips. She put down her camera and watched him. He focused on the floor in front of him, a large backpack on his back. Like a lost boy. Only when Andrea called out his name, from where she stood behind the temporary barrier, did he seem to wake up. A brief smile of relief formed on his face; he bent his arm and waved one of those small, single-stroke waves from the wrist to fingertips—an acknowledgement. She watched his head move in and out from behind strangers. The dark circles under his eyes and downturned mouth became more obvious as he approached. Eventually he was in front of her, forcing a smile. She stepped forward and wrapped her arms around him. They stood like that a long time, saying nothing. JJ's injured arm lay gently across her back. He sighed. Not a happy exhale, but one of exhaustion and sadness. It was the sound she had heard in the locker rooms at important competitions when athletes didn't qualify for the finals, when they realized they had failed, their race was over, and there was nothing that could be done about it. She had heard it coming from her own body after Danielle died.

It wasn't the reunion she had hoped for, but at least he was there.

"Welcome to New York," she said softly in his ear.

"Thanks." He spoke in the tone of a loser.

"Let's get out of here."

She took him by the hand and guided him out of the airport and into a taxi.

SAM

Sam figured it was the evening of the seventh day. He sat shirtless and still on the couch, rubbed the rings, and waited. His hunger had become manageable, but the thoughts of eating again were still very present. It was in the middle of one of these thoughts that Sam heard the door buzzer ring. The noise burst through the silence of the room, causing Sam's heart to beat quickly. *Ellis!* He leapt off the couch, immediately dizzy and stumbling. He steadied himself by placing a hand on the table, aggravating his still-sore wrist. He opened the door to the corridor. No one was there. He remembered: it was the buzzer from outside, not for the flat. He scrambled for the phone on the wall to let Ellis in.

"Come in," he shouted excitedly into the receiver.

His voice cracked from so little use. He pushed the button on the phone to unlock the door. There was a buzzing sound, a click, and a door opening in the distance. Sam dropped the receiver and looked out into the corridor. It was a woman walking towards him. *Not Ellis.* He had not even considered that it could be someone else. The woman was tall and big-boned, carrying plastic bags overflowing with food. *Not Ellis at all.* Disappointment filled him, then anxiety. He stepped halfway back into the flat, placing his hands over the rings on his chest.

"Sam?" the woman asked as she approached.

She had short hair dyed dark red and looked to be in her late forties.

What does this woman want? Was she sent by Ellis, or is she someone I should be wary of? Ellis told me I should be more careful.

"Pardon?" the woman said.

"I didn't say anything."

"You said something about being careful."

She stopped outside his door, put the grocery bags down on the ground, and extended her right hand. He held onto the doorframe and did not reach out to shake her hand.

She looked irritated. "I guess you're Sam? A friend of Ellis's?"

He nodded.

She stood a few feet back from the door. The bags were a barrier between them.

"I'm Susan...I just came to drop off some food for you. Ellis said that you're new to the city, and you might need some stuff for your flat."

"Yes," said Sam. "Who are *you?*"

"I just said I was Susan," she said and backed away, looking uncomfortable. "I better be off. Enjoy the food. Goodbye."

Susan walked quickly towards the foyer and was gone. Sam waited to be sure that the door clicked closed behind her before he moved from the threshold. His heart raced.

He grabbed the groceries and carried them inside, closed the door, locked it, and placed a chair in front of it. He tore open the bags and examined their contents: prawn cocktail crisps, Ribena, bananas, apples, a loaf of sliced bread, canned baked beans, and four small containers of yogurt. He laughed out loud, giddy to see so much food. He sat down on the couch to eat one of the slightly browned bananas. In spite of the hunger that had resurfaced, he only permitted himself a few bites of the banana. He focused on the slimy texture, savoured the perfect sweetness. He planned what he would eat later on, and the next day, and the next. But then a thought about Ellis surfaced, along with guilt. He saw how fickle his mind could be. Obsessing over food so completely. All he needed was to remember Ellis and think about grabbing the world's attention. He must remember why he was here.

He went to the suitcase to retrieve Ellis's letter, and he held it up to his face again. He willed himself to smell Ellis. To hear his voice through the paper. To Sam, it was proof of the plan Ellis had in mind. It was all he had to hold onto.

Over the ensuing week, Sam developed a pattern of sleeping, eating only a little, drinking water or Ribena, exercising, bathing, waiting, and talking to Ellis in his head. The food was almost gone again. The fear slithered back in.

It was night-time when Paul came. Sam didn't buzz him in right away. He waited with the receiver to his ear this time and listened. It was Paul's voice, all tinny and distant. "Hi, mate, can you let me in? It's Paul."

Sam found that he had forgotten how to respond. He stood there dumbly until Paul spoke again. "Sam?"

All he could think of to say was, "Yes," and then buzzed Paul in. The click of men's dress shoes echoed in the corridor.

Sam breathed in and out slowly, waited a few seconds, and opened the door. Paul stood there with a bag of food and a suit over his arm.

Sam managed a "Hi" and a nervous smile. He was eager to hear any bit of news from Ellis.

"Hello." Paul looked around. "Look, I can't stay. Here's some food. The basics...some bread, milk, butter, crisps, you know, and Ellis asked me to lend you a suit. I got one from one of my mates who's more your size." He handed the bag and suit to Sam. He then reached into his pocket a produced an envelope. "Here's some money to keep you going for a bit."

Sam took the envelope. "Come in, can you?" He realized how odd the question sounded after he said it—the words were somehow in the wrong order, awkward, like he had forgotten how to speak naturally. He felt anxious again.

"Can't tonight...have to get home, but, before I forget, Ellis found you some work—the suit's for your first meeting there. Go to Canary Wharf on September thirtieth. The exact address is in the envelope. It's a security guard position. Meet with Mohammed at half ten. Ask for him at reception. He'll set you up."

A series of questions layered one on top of the other in Sam's mind. What day was it today? What was the time? Where is Canary Wharf? Did he need a resume? He had so much to ask and Paul was already leaving—holding up his hand, stepping back, and turning away.

Sam forced himself to speak. "Am I allowed to leave? Here, I mean." He pointed at the door of the flat. "Would Ellis be okay with that?"

Paul looked desperate to depart but answered anyway. "Get some fresh air. See the city. And you should shave. I have to go. Take care."

SAM

He was down the corridor and through the door before Sam could muster a follow-up question.

When Paul was gone, Sam closed the flat door and stood still for a moment, smiling broadly. Ellis had not forgotten him, and he had his marching orders. Soon, he would find out what day it was and see the city, but most importantly, his mission would continue. He jumped, clapped his hands, and spun around the flat. And though it was clearly night outside, he grabbed the flat keys, put on his shoes, and raced out of the building into the streetlights.

He walked north to the Thames, where he stared at the twinkling lights of the city, and then turned south again. After days of near silence, the noise of the streets overwhelmed him, and he placed his hands over his ears in an effort to shut it out. He was resting beneath a streetlamp when he spotted two teenagers fighting on the steps of a church. They grabbed each other violently and struggled to remain standing. One of them pulled the other down onto the steps, where they continued to yank at each other's clothing. He realized that they were, in fact, making out. In their skinny jeans and oversized dark hooded sweaters, and with their dishevelled mid-length hair, it was impossible to tell whether one was a boy and one was a girl. He was disgusted and fascinated by these creatures, devouring one another in the darkness. One of the teenagers pulled back from the other and pointed at Sam.

When they turned to look at him, Sam still could not identify their genders. They had angular facial features and dark pencil around their eyes, which emphasized the angry looks they cast his way.

"Go away!" The young voice was shrill, crackling with fury. The teenager charged him. The other teen watched from the steps of the church.

Sam jumped up, turned, and ran.

The teenager pursued, shouting: "You pervert! Get the hell away from us, or I'll rip your head off!"

Sam raced across the street without looking; a cab driver honked. There were the heavy sounds of Sam's shoes hitting the pavement and fast steps and loud breathing coming up from behind. He picked up speed, turned into an alley. The breaths were close now. Then there were small bony hands on his back. Sam fell forward, his arms breaking his fall. Pain shot through his already injured wrist. A sharp knee pressed into his spine, and a voice said, "I could kill you, you freak."

Then there was the sound of retreating footsteps.

He sat up, holding his aching wrist close to his body. There was no one else with him in the darkness. He made his way through side streets and back to his flat. With each throb of his wrist, he cursed the teenagers. He despised their depravity, their self-absorption, and their evil devouring. They were this world he reviled. He was almost delirious with disgust. He understood why Ellis had not released him from his flat until now. *He was protecting me from the world. The world that hates me.*

Sam lay down on the couch and iced his wrist. He had a strong desire to express gratitude to Ellis. And that was when he learned to pray.

JJ

Andrea perched on the edge of the bed and ran her hands over JJ's back. He noticed her callouses had already softened. He lay facedown and couldn't make himself get up. His body was crushed by a heavy fatigue. It was the kind of exhaustion that went beyond his muscles into the marrow of his bones. It frustrated him that only a few weeks earlier, he had been able to drag his sore body out of bed in the middle of the night for rowing practices, but now, here in bustling New York with Andrea, he could not even respond to her touch.

"How are you doing today?" she asked.

He turned his head to the side to speak. He was ashamed of his inertia. He would continue to pretend he was ill. "Still sick."

Andrea pecked his cheek, which was covered with a few days of growth. "That's okay. Take another day to rest. We have all the time in the world."

He did not want to think about time stretched out endlessly in front of him. He resented her chipper voice and resilience.

She leaned away to tie her running shoes.

He needed a line of lane markers to guide him from this bed. He longed for a defined finish line. For a test he could win.

"I'm heading out. Just sleep. I'll bring you home some bagels," she said.

When she was gone, JJ closed his eyes and hoped sleep would come. It was his only defence against this strange feeling of defeat. When he landed on the decision to be with Andrea in New York, he had thought life would arrange itself nicely for him, but her happy voice and optimism made him more aware of his inadequacies and confusion. It had become a competition and she was five boat-lengths ahead. It was an agonizing, unbreachable gap.

When Andrea returned, he had not moved. She was red in the face and sweating. No bagels. Her voice was high-pitched with excitement: "I decided to turn my walk into a run. It was totally invigorating...I think I might want to train for the New York Marathon. Wouldn't that be awesome? I could even combine that with photography somehow...*photography on the run* or something."

JJ was silent. He could not relate to her ability to embrace new things with ease and enthusiasm. He wished he were able to imagine tomorrow, but all he could see were the twisted white bed sheets between his body and the edge of the bed, an uncrossable mountain range.

Andrea bounced away to the shower, rubbing it all in.

He felt he'd never be himself again. No one would ever again read his name in a newspaper article. He'd never again high-five his crew at the end of a tough race. His identity as an athlete was already lost. He'd be forgotten.

FALL 2011

Whether we fall by ambition, blood, or lust, like diamonds, we are cut with our own dust.
—*John Webster*

LEXI

Lexi pictured Andrea sitting in an artsy café somewhere in New York's East Side: flipping her red hair over her shoulder, playing with an empty raw sugar packet, tapping her fingers on her photo portfolio, and laughing at something an out-of-work-actor-slash-waitress just said to her. Truth was, she had never spoken with Andrea or even heard her voice. Everything she knew about her was what she heard through Brent or read on the Internet. It used to bug her when Brent talked about Andrea—but not since she retired the paddle, permanently or not, and moved to New York. Now he spoke about her with a brutal, acerbic tone to his words. When he said her name, his disgust was audible. Andrea had injured him, in a way. She had won JJ. And he had lost. He hated losing.

    Lexi had resumed rowing, under the supervision of Dr Chen and the team physio. She fell easily back into the repetitive pattern of training, and to her surprise, she was enjoying it. The day after weight training sessions, when her muscles were tight and sore, she stretched them whenever she could, just to feel the sweetness of the pain. She looked forward to the adrenaline surge that came in the middle of a fast run or row, or to the slap of a teammate's high five at the end of a tough workout. What she loved most was the definition coming back to her limbs, the power and confidence returning to her body.

When Brent walked in from his afternoon run, she was in the kitchen, finishing the preparations for dinner. So much of their lives as athletes was centred on food and eating. She pored over cookbooks to find recipes with the *right* amount of protein and ingredients that were low on the glycaemic index. She often found interesting dishes that Brent would subsequently veto, due to the inclusion of rich sauces or some other affront. He saw food as fuel only. She liked her meals to taste good, too. That afternoon, she arranged their dinners on two dishes and placed them in the oven to keep warm while Brent showered, then she carried the basket of clean laundry into the bedroom for folding. They were the same clothes every week: an assortment of Lycra training suits, white t-shirts, sweatshirts, shorts, and sport socks. They had the same set of national team garb, just in different sizes.

She had arranged the clothing in two neat piles on the bed by the time Brent walked out of the washroom, just a skimpy towel wrapped around his waist. He was in a playful mood, pretending he was on a fashion show catwalk. He paused at the end of the bed, legs wide, placed his hands on his hips and posed, made an exaggerated pout with his lips, then did a 360. She laughed. Recently, as a part of a game she played at a friend's bridal shower, she was asked to describe Brent. "He's athletic and fiercely competitive," she had said easily. Then, feeling guilty about her serious description, she added, "But he can be playful sometimes."

Sometimes. Here was the proof. And as though she was in an argument with herself, she thought, *I told you so.*

Brent sashayed over to where she stood and kissed her on the ear. A bolt of electricity shot through her body. He had not shown any sexual interest in her since the day of JJ's phone call about quitting. But now he was kissing her and moving his hands under her shirt and up her back. She leaned towards the bed with all her weight, trusting him to come along with her. They lay down amidst the athletic gear and scent of dryer sheets. They continued in a playful way: small bites, tickling, giggles, squeals. Now that she was back in training and feeling strong again, she enjoyed the sensation of pushing him or pulling him close with force.

When they were done, they lay tangled up with each other and the laundry. She was tempted to take advantage of the moment to mention Andrea and JJ; to tease him about his boyish crush on the redhead. She wanted to create lightness around these taboo subjects.

She turned to look at him. "I guess JJ loves Andrea more than he loved you." The spiteful, nasal tone of her delivery surprised her. It surged up from somewhere deep inside. She had not intended for the words to come out that way.

Brent sat up and looked down at her through squinted eyes. There was a sly half-smile on his face, and she thought he might be about to lean in and kiss her, but instead he placed one large hand on her throat and pressed, just a little. Enough to make her forget how powerful she had felt the moment before. Then he stood up without looking at her, dressed, and left the room.

Lexi stayed there for a long while, frightened, and studied the yellow-brown water stain on the ceiling. She held her hand to her throat. Lying still and silent, she knew there was a decision she had to make: get up and eat, or get up and leave. Or she could just sleep. Close her eyes and let the memories of the previous minutes get diluted by dreams. Her body felt suddenly exhausted, as though thinking about sleep made it impossible to consider any other option. She closed her eyes, pushed thoughts of Brent out of her mind, pulled a couple of the laundered sweatshirts over her body and fell asleep.

When she woke up, it was still light outside. She wasn't sure how long she had slept, but she knew she was hungry. It took her a few minutes to remember what had happened—and when she did, she forced back tears. She wished she hadn't mocked Brent. She wished she had said something else. Anything else, in any other tone of voice.

There was the sound of clanging dishes and humming from the kitchen. Brent's song was light-hearted and quick, which made her wonder if she was overreacting to what had happened. Perhaps it was a joke. Perhaps he was just being playful. Perhaps it wasn't a big deal.

Lexi dressed slowly, choosing her best pair of jeans and a shirt Brent had once told her was sexy. She hoped he would have forgotten about what happened by the time she made it to the table. She wanted him to see how good she looked and forget about what she had said.

In the washroom, she washed her face and fished out her makeup bag from deep in the cabinet. Hesitantly, she glanced at her throat. Brent hadn't left a visible mark, but she still sensed his hand hard against her windpipe.

She made her way to the kitchen, dragging her fingers along the papered wall as she walked, listening to the clink of

LEXI

Brent's cutlery against his plate. He hummed as he chewed. She entered the kitchen, saying nothing, and headed directly for the oven. He did not speak or look up. He continued humming, even as she took her plate and sat across from him at the table.

SAM

Since the day of Paul's visit, Sam had established a daily schedule of waking, nibbling on a bit of food, and leaving the flat to explore the city. He put himself through some of the same exercises Ellis had made him do back in Toronto. He wanted to feel the full measure of disgust for the ways of the modern world.

One morning he stood at the southeast entrance of Clapham Junction Station during rush hour. He checked his newly repaired watch. 8:15 a.m. Another mass of commuters approached. People ploughed into him; many knocked into his shoulders; one wave of people managed to sweep him backwards off his feet. The faces coming at him were sad, stern, serious, bothered. No one smiled. He saw mostly black suits. A tide of undertakers.

Twice he returned to the church on Bermondsey late in the evening to watch the teenagers on the steps. They were there each time, under the overhang, mouths locked together, pushing and pulling. He stayed away from the lamplight and peered at them from around the corner of a building.

On several evenings Sam visited the sidewalks of Piccadilly, stopping outside posh hotels to watch tourists in designer t-shirts, Louboutins, or shoes that looked like Hugh Hefner's slippers. The display of exorbitance piqued the fury in him. He stood in Piccadilly Circus and watched spitefully as tourists took pictures of the dark monument of Eros and his arrow, an angel losing balance and falling towards the traffic below. He scanned the blemished faces of the drunks and the eager faces of the men selling bus tours and show tickets to tourists. Flashes went off everywhere. These people manufactured their memories. They distilled their lives down to a few perfectly choreographed poses. It was all fake. He imagined what Ellis might say about the silly preoccupations of these people; about their self-centredness; about their pursuit of perfect memories. He felt Ellis's disgust.

One night Sam left the chaos of the streets to explore the relative quiet of St. James's Park. He walked alone down the wide, tree-lined paths. His hearing seemed sharper; behind his own breaths and the rumble of traffic around the park's borders, he heard the low whistling of the cool wind, the buzz of murmuring pedestrians, the rustle of crispy leaves. He had read somewhere that the park was once a swampy burial ground for lepers. He believed he could hear them all calling from beneath the layers of royal soil. He lay down and turned his ear to the wet, cold earth. He imagined that somewhere down there, deep down, the untouchables, the forgotten, the people without mouths to speak, reached up to him, begging him to remember them.

YASMINE

Yasmine's physiotherapist, Anthony, sat at the end of the treatment table and manipulated her foot and ankle as she lay silently, nervously clasping her hands over her chest. She feared that a particular angle or exercise might send pain rippling through her body, but that moment never came. The tightness in her Achilles had diminished over the past month, and the awkward limp was gone. She had begun a controlled training regimen that included walking, balance work, and other weight-bearing exercises, as well as her regular water-running sessions.

"Nice," Anthony said with a smile, and reached out to help Yasmine to a seated position. "Almost good as new. We need to get you fully checked out by your specialist, but I think you'll be back on the road and up to peak speed very soon."

She had not expected such a positive prognosis and let out a high-pitched squeal of delight. Her body was no longer her betrayer; it was back on her side. The athletes being treated around the room turned to look at her, some completely unenthused, others with expressions of undisguised envy. Yasmine ignored them and imagined being let loose on the streets, running Mount Royal, and feeling the pressure of her soles against the ground.

Anthony squeezed her hand. "I'll go pass on the excellent news to your coach." He walked towards the receptionist's desk, leaving Yasmine on the table to marvel at her healing body.

A female swimmer with patches and wires attached to each of her shoulders shouted from across the clinic. "What's the good news?"

Yasmine had seen this girl before, sitting on the blocks at the pool, perfunctorily icing her shoulders. She had stopped occasionally to peel away the sides of her Styrofoam cup and expose more ice.

"Just got two thumbs up from Anthony," Yasmine shouted back across the room.

"Sweet," the girl said half-heartedly and turned away, obviously unmoved by a virtual stranger's small victory, and more absorbed in her own deficiencies.

Two physios stopped manipulating their patients' injured body parts to applaud.

Anthony was back at her side. "Frederic is thrilled. We're going to set up all the appointments and testing. I want to come watch your stride in the water next week. Keep doing your daily exercises and lots of walking. I'll call Nate."

She barely heard the physio's last words as she dismounted, slipped on her shoes, and grabbed her coat. Eyes studied her as she walked between the two rows of treatment tables, whose athletic occupants were strapped to various machines or immobilized by the grip of sport therapists. She enjoyed the sound of the clinic door slamming shut behind her.

Out on the street, she considered calling Nate for a ride and even pulled out her cell, but she did not dial. She breathed in the autumn air, which was fresh and crisp, perfect for running. Today she would not run. Not yet. There was still more healing that needed to happen. She pushed the phone back into her jacket pocket, turned right onto the main road, and began the long walk.

SAM

You must be more careful from now on.

Sam shifted from foot to foot as he stood in the cold building lobby and waited for Mohammed to come down and meet him. A man behind a security reception desk had instructed him to sit in one of the chairs, but he was too nervous to stay still. The suit jacket Paul had dropped off was wide across the shoulders, and the pants sagged in the seat and were hemmed too short, exposing Sam's striped socks. He plucked constantly at his clothes and scanned the lobby for threatening people. He was too aware of the echo of dress shoes clicking across the white-tiled floor, the rasp of his own breath, and the distant hum of voices in conversation.

There was a man with a large black leather bag, not a suitcase or briefcase, a prop that might be used in a bank heist. Sam watched the man cross the lobby floor, drop the bag, and slump into one of the leather chairs. He was just metres away from where Sam stood. The man smiled at his iPhone. It seemed strange, so Sam moved across the lobby to watch from a distance. Close to the escalator a woman in a grey dress stood talking to a suit-clad security guard. She laughed loudly. He thought the interaction was unusual. The army of receptionists at the curved main desk chatted to one another, and one looked over. Sam turned away. A man seated in a chair nearby tapped away at a laptop. Sam wondered what he was writing. Reporting what he saw? He felt trapped in the midst of these suspicious individuals. He did his best to keep an eye on all of them by scanning left to right, much like he was watching a tennis match.

A tall black man in a navy jacket spoke to the guard behind the security desk. Eyes squinted, the guard looked in Sam's direction and pointed. Sam's hands shook. He reached up to touch the bump of rings inside his shirt—a reminder of Ellis and his mission. He had already come this far. He could do this.

The man approached, and Sam steeled himself against the nauseating swell of anxiety.

"Sam? I'm Mohammed. Call me Mo," the man said.

Sam nodded.

"I will explain how this will work once we are inside." Mo was already walking at a quick pace past the bank of elevators, expecting Sam to follow. He didn't know what Mo meant by *how this will work,* but he trusted that Ellis had already prepared the way. He believed Ellis was the mastermind behind a plan that was now slowly unfolding.

I can see the whole picture. I am watching. Have faith.

When they reached the first-floor security office, Mo led him into a windowless adjoining room and closed the door. He indicated for Sam to sit. There was no small talk. Mo moved quickly and quietly around the room, plucking a large brown envelope from the counter and pulling out a clip-on ID card, an SIA license, and some papers. He laid them on the table, one by one. The photo on all the documents was Sam's passport picture, obviously provided by Ellis. Sam was relieved that he could see Ellis's hand in what was happening. Daintily, Mo placed the brown envelope on top of the pile of papers, then slammed his huge fist down on top of it. Sam gasped and sat up straight. Mo leaned over him. He smelled of coffee.

"Look. Ellis talked me into this." Mo spoke in a hushed tone. "I'm doing this for Ellis, not you."

He dropped his volume even lower. "You have your pass now, and you'll start tomorrow night. The work schedule is in your papers here." Mo didn't leave space for questions. "Tell no one what I'm doing for you."

Mo paused for a moment and moved a heavy hand to Sam's shoulder. "I told the other guards that you're new here, that you have your SIA license, and that you trained in Canada. I said you're a quiet guy. Don't go making any friends here. Keep to yourself."

Sam glanced at the bulletin board next to the white door. There was a sign-up sheet for a local charity drive. Thirteen names were scrawled on it, one of which was scratched out. On the counter in the corner, next to the coffee machine, was a pyramid of mugs. Their curved white surfaces glimmered under the office lights. Obviously, people were supposed to take the cups from the top first, but he wondered what would happen if one of the mugs in the middle was removed, quickly, like a magician yanking a cloth from beneath a perfectly laid table setting.

His mind went back to when Brent convinced him to try that classic tablecloth trick, after their mom had set out the dishes for a dinner party. Sam had known it was a stupid idea, but Brent hopped from foot to foot beside him, prodding and insisting it would be "the coolest thing ever." Then came the part he later regretted: a split second in time when he did not make a choice to act so much as he suspended all thought and simply fell into action. He glanced at the eager young face of his brother, took the crisp edges of his mother's best white linen between his fingers, and tugged. It was precisely at that moment that his father entered the room and froze. Fortunately, the cloth barely moved. The unlit candelabra and empty wine glasses fell over and clanged against the china dishes. The plate closest to Sam teetered dangerously over the table's edge, but Brent grabbed it and held it safely against his chest. Their dad unfroze and strode quickly towards Sam, who already knew what was coming: the pinch of fingers around his ear; the angry huff of his father's breath; the violent slam of his bedroom door; and a long, hungry evening spent listening to adult laughter and the clink of cutlery against plates.

Mo grabbed Sam by the jaw and turned it upwards, so they were face-to-face, inches apart. "You gotta stop staring all around you, like a freak."

Sam had not realized he was looking around in a strange or noticeable way. He focused on Mo's intense dark eyes and the pressure on his jaw.

Finally, Mo released his face and stepped back. "You will always do what I tell you to. Right?" Rhetorical question.

There was no smile as Mo extended his hand, this time for a shake. He had the kind of crushing grip that ground Sam's finger bones together.

He felt he should say something, but he didn't know what was appropriate. Mo made a sweeping gesture towards the door with his right arm to indicate that Sam was free to go. He knew he had about five seconds before the door shut behind him and his chance to say anything would be gone.

"Thanks." It was all he could think of.

Without looking back, Sam left the office, brown envelope and papers in hand.

ANDREA

She crossed the avenue, peering into the cars lined up to her right. Rows of serious faces waited for the light to change. They had somewhere to go. She liked that. She caught a glimpse of her own shape in a windshield. Still strong and erect, emanating the confidence of an athlete. In that reflection, she also saw JJ, his slump-shouldered body peeking out from the far side of her. He had become impossible to talk to over the past weeks, flicking on the television the moment he woke up and raising the volume as soon as she spoke. He curved into their little couch, a bag of chips nestled between his lap and chest. It was the same concavity she saw when he stood that very morning, reluctantly, and agreed to walk with her to the park. He was a man hollowed out.

"Why are you standing like that?" she had asked, annoyed at the sight.

"It's my ribs. They hurt." These days he used anything as an excuse.

He refused to talk about rowing. For so long it had been their only subject of conversation, but now when she mentioned Brent or Pete or the Games, he went pale and sullen. When she introduced the topic of their future, her photography, or the logistics of a Canadian finding a job in New York, he turned up the TV.

They were on their way to Central Park to check out a performance artist who had been the buzz of the twitterverse lately. Andrea knew only that at 10:00 a.m., the artist would be somewhere near the boathouse, and likely easy to spot because of her gaggle of faithful followers. These impromptu outings were a perk of her new life. She no longer had a training calendar to tell her where she needed to be; she was carving out her own plan.

She moved quickly across the Central Park Loop, dodging runners and cyclists, and spotted a group of people gathered around a tree. From a distance, it appeared that a woman was crouched on one of the large branches. She surmised it was the notorious artist and stepped on to the grass, eager to join the group of spectators. When she reached out for JJ's hand to pull him along, he was not there. She spun around slowly and moved back towards the runners, thinking he might be roadside, watching the Manhattan masses perform their morning workout. Getting inspired, she hoped. But he wasn't there. She couldn't be sure when she'd lost him. The last image she had of him was of a curved shadow on a windshield.

As she walked along the edge of the Loop, she admired the heavy breaths of the athletes jogging by, but felt no urge to join in. And she realized that she did not want to find JJ. She did not want to be the one to resuscitate him from his current state. As easily as the thought slid into her head, there came the realization that this was the beginning of the end of their relationship. There was a tug of sadness, but she would not let herself give in to it, not just yet.

She turned back to make her way to the tree. That's when she spotted JJ, standing off near some bushes, staring through the fence at the lake. Dozens of tourist rowboats were lined up on the grass on the other side of the chain-link. She would not go over and join him. He had to mourn on his own.

These were the lingering effects of her life as an athlete—she could not be with someone in a constant state of losing.

SAM

The walk home from Canary Wharf after his interview took him close to two hours. He wandered in and out of some small roadside parks. He berated himself for not being able to say more to Mo. For not sitting straighter. For not looking Mo directly in the face as he spoke. For not being more like Ellis. The critic inside his head became loud and shrill as he continued the walk. It rose above the din of Tower Bridge, drowning out the banging and drills of roadside construction crews.

Once inside the apartment building, the silence of the foyer greeted him, and the critic in his head departed. Sam leaned against the cool white wall and sighed. The activity of the morning had exhausted him. He dragged his feet down the hallway and had to use his remaining energy to push open the door of his flat and step inside. Out of the corner of his eye, he noticed the movement of the white bed sheets. He walked closer and saw that there on the bed was Ellis, sleeping. A divine vision.

Sam froze, shins pressed against the foot of the bed, and clasped his hand over his mouth. He fell to his knees. Ellis's body, still clothed in a dress shirt and black dress pants, lay prostrate on the bed. He snored. Sam imagined that in each of Ellis's noisy exhales, he heard the breathy murmurings of a prophet, so he listened intently and even dared once or twice to reach out and touch his foot. It was an hour before Ellis began to show signs of waking.

When Ellis finally sat up and rubbed the sleep out of his eyes, Sam struggled to stand, his legs numb from kneeling for so long. He was mesmerized by the vision of Ellis in his bed.

"It's wonderful to see you," said Ellis with a voice deepened by sleep. Ellis did not appear at all surprised to see him there, at his feet. He took his time to get up, then walked to the end of the bed and pulled Sam into a tight hug.

Stunned and delighted, Sam leaned into Ellis's body. After a moment, Ellis released him.

"Don't look so terrified. I'm here now. That should be enough," said Ellis.

He forced himself to speak. He was frustrated for not knowing how to act naturally. "Yes. Welcome." *I should offer him something.* "Would you like water?"

"Not now." Ellis moved casually around the room, running a hand along the furniture.

Sam followed him with his gaze. He imagined that Ellis's fingertips left glowing traces on the table, chair, and counter.

"I hope you're enjoying the space I provided for you," Ellis said, stopping to peek inside the refrigerator.

"Yes. Thank you." Sam reminded himself to show more gratitude and added, "You have been good to me."

He hated how his words came out so tight and formal. He was worried that Ellis would be turned off by his awkwardness. Ellis had continued pacing and was now in front of the open window, leaning forward against the railing and straining to see what was out in the space between the buildings. Then he turned and spoke.

"Susan called me," he said. "She said you behaved strangely and frightened her when she stopped by with the food."

Sam's stomach dropped.

"You mustn't invite any suspicion. I sent you here because I thought you could handle the pressure of this calling." Ellis paused and looked out the window again, the gauzy fabric of the curtains pinched between his fingers. "Can you?"

This time Sam did not hesitate. He was desperate to reassure Ellis that he could manage being in London. That he could make Ellis proud.

He made certain his voice sounded strong and eager. "Yes, I know I can do it."

"Good. Now I'm ready for some water."

They sat at the small table. Sam recounted the story of his meeting with Mo. Ellis spoke for a long while about the blessed life of simplicity and the horrors of the Western world. Sam was reminded of his days with Ellis back in Toronto. There was the familiar chill up the spine, the prickle of goose bumps, the desire to hear more.

When the teaching session came to a close, Ellis took something out of his pocket and extended his arm so that his fist was resting on the table. Slowly, he unfurled his fingers. There was the clink of metal hitting the surface of the table, but it was still covered by his hand. Immediately, Sam knew what it was and smiled easily. Ellis pulled back his hand slowly, revealing the third gold ring.

"This is the ring of solitude. Any man who wants to achieve something great first has to learn how to be alone."

Sam picked up the ring. It was smooth and perfect in his hand. He held it tightly, creating the deep red imprint of a circle in his palm. This time gratitude came naturally: "Thank you, Ellis. I owe you everything."

VINCENT

Vincent zipped up his track jacket, looked at himself in the mirror, and grinned. He had been asked to wear his National Team gear to a sponsor's black tie gala. He was a grown man in a red and white tracksuit amid a crowd of martini-sipping millionaires in sequins and tuxes. Instead of feeling pride, he was embarrassed. He would rather be in a pool.

Every swimmer anticipated the glorious moment when he or she received their first team parka and kit; and he had been no different, excitedly sorting through his pile of new Speedos, maple-leafed socks, and red flip-flops. But the moment he donned his Canadian team uniform, years ago, the job of being an athlete had transformed into an entirely new role, with a wide range of responsibilities. Like a superhero pulling on a leotard. It changed things. He could deal with the fast swimming part, but the national representative, role model, public speaker, and political figure aspect of the career? Those were responsibilities he hadn't signed up for.

Tonight was another one of those out-of-pool extras. In their cloud of chlorine cologne, he and Adam joined some current and former swimmers at a fancy Montreal hotel for the gala, where they were each expected to entertain a table of business people. The athletes gathered in the lobby, waiting for the emcee to announce their entrance. Vincent peeked at himself in one of the mirrors on the wall, and ran his finger over the red goggle indents below his eyes and across the bridge of his nose. The chemical scent and raccoon marks were the parts of the uniform he could not easily remove. The emcee's voice boomed over the loudspeaker inside the ballroom, stirring up the diners' excitement as the door burst open and the swimmers filed in. The guests welcomed them with a standing ovation. Vincent cracked his knuckles, took a deep breath, and entered the glittering room of tables.

He walked to the front with the others and waved as his name was announced: "Vincent Beaulieu, Twenty-twelve Olympic hopeful."

He blushed and tried to ignore the nervousness stirring in his belly. He was not yet an Olympian, and now everyone at the gala was aware of his goal to make it to the Games. It was just more unwanted pressure from a group of strangers.

At his assigned table, he endured the slap of his fellow diners' hands on his back before taking his seat between a middle-aged woman draped in pearls and a bald man in a shiny tux. The conversation focused on Vincent, who did what he could to respond with humour and confidence. When the keynote speaker stood behind the podium, the deluge of questions ended, and Vincent relaxed into his chair. Starving, he shovelled some potatoes and steak into his mouth while he could. As he chewed, the man to his left whispered something about his twelve-year-old son being a talented hockey player. Vincent nodded and grabbed a second bread roll from the basket.

The speaker wrapped up his presentation with a video montage of the 2008 Olympic Games. The lights dimmed as the highlights played. The woman to Vincent's right pressed her nose against his neck and inhaled.

"I love the smell of chlorine," she purred into his ear.

He felt a shiver of excitement, followed by revulsion. Rather than respond, he took a sip of water and turned to the bald man, who wanted to talk more about his hockey-playing son.

"I want him to focus more at practice. I think it's all the video games he plays. They reduce his attention span. What do you think I should do?" the man said.

This was an all-too-familiar scenario. These were the other roles he was sometimes expected to play: boy toy and parenting expert.

When the lights went back on, Vincent scanned the room. Two tables over, Adam laughed and clinked glasses with his fellow diners. Quickly, Vincent turned back to his group, lifted his water goblet and proposed a toast: "To winning."

The businessmen and women around him raised their wine glasses and echoed, "To winning."

When there was a break in the evening's program, Vincent sneaked away to the lobby and joined a group of swimmers and guests who were crowded around Michael Pointer, a former Canadian Olympic Swim Team member. He was in the midst of a story of how he had underprepared for his 200m freestyle event at the 1988 Games and had never earned the Olympic gold he was slated to win.

"The gun went off, and I flew off the block, and it was magic," he was saying. "I was surging through the water, perfect streamline, already ahead of the American to my left and the Russian to my right. I had a great feel for the water that day. Everything was going well, and then my body just died. BAM! I was totally fried, suddenly, less than one hundred metres into the race."

Pointer dropped his voice and the group leaned in closer. "I struggled to finish. My legs were lead. My coach was pissed, and my girlfriend was getting ready to break up with me. That was in front of twenty thousand spectators, and a huge TV audience watching." He paused dramatically. "Then in the media corral after the race, some reporter asked me, *What the hell happened to you?* Just like that too, *What the hell happened to you?*"

Pointer was clearly intoxicated, leaning much too close to one of the young female backstrokers on his right. Drops of sweat appeared on his balding head and upper lip. His shirt was unbuttoned too far, and a curled grey chest hair poked through a buttonhole. The deep V of his shirt opening pointed down, like an arrow, towards the deflated sag of his belly.

The whole scene disgusted Vincent. As a child, he had had a poster of Pointer in his prime (Speedo-clad, pecs and six-pack abs well-oiled) taped to the back of his bedroom door. It bothered him to see his former hero aged and buffoonish. As Vincent backed away from the group, Adam appeared at his side and spoke under his breath, "That guy's a walking cautionary tale."

It was true: Vincent worked harder at practice because of guys like Pointer. He never wanted to become one of those *has-been* athletes—the kind who showed up to gala events years after their retirement from sport because they hadn't found the same level of success in any other area of life and needed to be reminded that they once did something well. He didn't want to be known for anything other than having swum fast and won. Vincent believed that if he was good enough in the water, he wouldn't have to play any of these other roles at all.

"Let's go back inside and charm the sponsors," said Adam, nudging Vincent roughly with his shoulder.

Vincent grunted, pushed Adam back, and returned to the ballroom.

SAM

Still giddy from a day spent with Ellis, Sam sat alone in a subway car filled with cleaning staff and security guards on their way to the various office buildings of Canary Wharf. A group of men huddled around the open window at the end of the car and chatted quietly in another language. Everyone else sat silent. Sam kept a hand flat against his chest over the place where the three gold rings hung. He had asked Ellis if he could wear one of the rings on his hand, but Ellis insisted that they should be hidden from public view. "They're our secret," he had said.

The tube door opened, and the passengers spilled out into the busy station. There were long queues of commuters anxious to travel home. Sam scanned their faces; dead-tired clones. They appeared to be too exhausted to notice him—or anything, besides the approach of their train. They had no energy left at the end of their busy days to consider the impoverished.

Ellis was right about these people; they were asleep in their self-centred way of life. They were money-driven zombies, and they needed a wake-up call.

He pushed his way through the lines of travellers, knocking over a couple of briefcases and one portable coffee cup, and entered the serpentine shop tunnels that would lead him to his new place of work, the bank building where he had met with Mo a day earlier. When he arrived, an older man in a navy suit and blue tie welcomed him at the door in a loud, cheerful voice that shook Sam out of his angry thoughts. "Hello, sir. Can I help you with something?"

Sam was discomfited by the unexpected warmth. "I'm the new guy."

"Ah, yes. Mo said you'd be coming. He's not here. Go to the security office, and Marcus will show you around." The man nodded and turned back to the door as Sam rushed off, eager to distance himself from the suspicious wide smile. He hurried past the elevators. When he pushed open the security office door, a blond man in a navy uniform looked up from the table where he was reading the paper and rolled his eyes.

"You're early. I'm Marcus...and I'm not cutting my break short for you."

The abrupt delivery came as relief to Sam. This man was just like all the others.

"Your uniform is in the other room. Back of the door. Put it on," Marcus said and returned his focus to the news.

Sam entered the room where he had met with Mo a day earlier. The pyramid of clean white mugs was significantly depleted. The sink was stacked full of coffee- and tea-stained cups. His father used to pour himself a large, steaming coffee each morning, sip some of it while scanning the sports pages, then dump the rest down the drain and leave his dirty mug on the counter. Sam grinned and imagined what Ellis would say about these scenes: *Filthy pigs. Too busy and important to clean up after themselves.*

Sam tore open the clear bag that covered his crisp navy jacket and dressed for his new job. He affixed his new ID tag to the lapel, stood tall, and wished Ellis could see him now. With the full garb on, he'd be able to blend in and slide around unnoticed, able to do whatever Ellis asked him to. There was a loud knock on the door.

"Done in there? Let's go."

Marcus was already pacing the hallway when Sam emerged from the office.

"Let's get this show on the road, Princess," Marcus mumbled, then slapped the elevator button.

They travelled towards the thirtieth floor in silence. Marcus studied the TV newsfeed to the left of the door. Sam glanced at it briefly: sovereign-debt crisis, Syrian unrest, the latest on Will and Kate. He used to devour those kinds of news clips. Now he saw them as distractions. There were millions of people starving around the world whose stories were untold. Ellis's voice sounded in his head: *Mourn for those who cannot speak for themselves.*

He turned away and focused on his unpolished shoes.

"Are you getting off?" Marcus stood outside the elevator with one hand on his hip, the other holding the door open.

Sam looked up, shocked that they had already arrived and irritated by Marcus's loud sighs. The old rage stirred in his belly. He reminded himself to remain calm and neutral. He fell into step with Marcus.

They toured the floor, beginning with the kitchenette, moving past the expansive glass-walled meeting rooms. Everything glittered. Flashes of corporate money in every polished surface. Three men in black designer suits sat, huddled and plotting, around one of the board tables inside their see-through box.

"Some of these guys regularly work sixteen-hour days. That's how they pay for their Paul Smith pinstripes," Marcus said, deadpan.

They moved to an open area where Marcus pointed out some expensive artwork and the locations of the security cameras. Then they turned to look out the floor-to-ceiling window. The lights of the newly built Olympic site sparkled in the distance.

"Behold London's white elephant!" said Marcus.

"Wow," said Sam, as he admired the shining, orblike main stadium. He pressed his hand against the window.

"Don't smudge the bloody glass," Marcus said sharply, and walked on.

Sam pulled his hand away, leaving his mark over the distant Olympic site.

JAYNA

Jayna raised her arms, a beer in each hand, as she navigated through the throng of dancers. She extended her neck to scan the crowd but could not spot Will or any of her teammates among the Friday night revellers. Will was likely near the back of the club at his table, enjoying bottle service. She continued to push forward, and a good-looking Indian man wrapped his arms firmly around her waist. She tried to wiggle loose, careful not to spill the beer held high above her head, but the man simply emulated her moves like they were engaged in a strange dance. He pressed his body hard against hers, his forehead at her eye level. She was certain she could smell Nate's musk in that moment, and a shot of fear passed through her. A woman crashed into her back, and Jayna stumbled—a splash of lager landed in the man's dark hair. He squeezed tighter to balance her and glanced up. Her arms ached.

"You're tall," he called over the pounding techno.

"Let go of me!" The beginnings of panic in her throat. Like Nate was there.

"What?" he shouted.

She jammed her black heel sharply into the top of his foot. He released her and fell, wincing, into the couple grinding behind him. They shoved him back while Jayna rushed past, desperate to get out of the pulsing crowd.

Safe against the wall on the periphery of the dance floor, she realized she had been crying. The beer bottles shaking in her grip, she used the back of her right hand to wipe away a stream of hot tears. She lifted one brew to her lips and chugged it down. The panic was still there. She took the second bottle and drank it too, hoping the claw in her throat would loosen its grip but aware that she'd have to down a few more drinks first.

As expected, she found Will lounging in the back of the club, an ice bucket and open bottle of premium vodka on the table. A long-legged blond in a short white skirt was propped up on the bench, her bare limbs stretched out across Will's lap. The woman's red-soled shoes claimed the only remaining spot. She recognized the blond: a contestant on one of Quebec's popular reality shows. One of the programs where the stars pretended to be friends, then went off and bad-mouthed each other in a sound-proof booth for the viewing audience's enjoyment. Already Jayna did not like her.

Will glanced up and offered a quick smile. "Wondered where you'd gone."

"For a beer."

"Oh. Sit." He gestured to the place occupied by the woman's expensive shoes. Jayna placed the heels on the table, sat, and poured herself a tumbler of vodka and ice. She had to get the stunning starlet to leave, so she could grab Will's full attention. The desperation was overwhelming; the shakes from

JAYNA

moments before returned to her hands. It wasn't Will in particular that she wanted, but his complete attraction to her.

She decided suddenly that she'd be funny tonight. Charming. Ironic. She would never win the beauty battle.

"Don't I know you from somewhere?" Jayna said in an overdone sultry voice, across Will's lap to the woman. The ice in her tumbler rattled. She put down the drink and hid her trembling hands.

"Sorry," said Will. "My bad. Tori, this is Jayna. Jayna, Tori."

"Nice to meet you," Tori said. She was unbelievably perfect. Skin smooth and unblemished. A bottom lip so plump, it had that lovely seam vertically down the centre. Her voice was deep and sensual. For a full minute, the three of them sat without speaking, just sipping. Jayna decided she would entertain them with a story. She would own their attention. She sat up straight and spoke. "Have you ever had a mouse in your house?"

Will tilted his head to see her better. A curious smirk on his face. "Not that I remember, why?"

"Last summer I had a fat little rodent visitor," said Jayna.

"Totally icky," said Tori.

"It was after the big fireworks at the Old Port. It was like one a.m., and I was still pretty loaded when I got back to my building, but I knew I had to be completely quiet, or Mrs Gendron, my grumpy eighty-year-old neighbour, would get all mad and lodge a complaint. I was already on the landlord's blacklist, so I had to be super careful....Anyway, I take off my shoes and tiptoe down the hall. You've never seen a girl my size move with such grace, worthy of the Bolshoi. Then I pull out my keys with the silent precision of a surgeon." Jayna stood and made a huge show of reaching into an imaginary purse with her fingers in a pincer grip. Her face contorted in concentration.

Then she dropped her voice and continued the tale. "I make sure the keys don't rattle as I turn them slowly in the lock. I push open the door ever so slowly, expertly avoiding its signature squeak, and finally I'm in. I breathe a sigh of relief that the old lady hasn't caught me this time. And then I flick on the light, and he's there." She pauses for a moment as she sits back down, and her listeners lean in.

Her voice turned animated, frantic. "There's this little furry monster, incredibly fat and cheeky, taking off in all directions. Over my rug, up the leg of the coffee table, down the other side. I'm still standing there, stunned, when it scurries under the couch. I wait, but it doesn't come out. I wait a little longer, but still nothing. I realize that I won't be able to sleep until I get this nasty intruder out of my apartment, so I make a huge, flying leap from the welcome mat to the sofa. I need something to poke and prod under the couch, and all I have is the TV remote."

Will's eyes widened and narrowed in synch with the telling of her tale. Tori moved her lips perceptibly to Jayna's account.

Jayna wondered why she started telling it in the first place. Part of it was true, but she wasn't sure where the truth stopped. The problem was that there was no real end to the story that she could think of. She would have to improvise.

"I creep onto the floor and reach my arm and the remote under the couch, and as soon as I do, the disgusting creature bursts out and makes a dash for the baseboard heater. I'm totally determined to get him, so I try to yank my arm out, but the sleeve of my jean jacket is caught on a spring. I pull and pull, but it doesn't come loose, and I'm getting seriously furious. I look over towards the wall, and there's the stupid rodent, paused near the heater, watching me. Wiggling its tiny pink nose at me in mockery. So I crawl towards the wall, dragging the sofa noisily along with me, the weight of it ripping my jacket. And I'm screaming, *I'll get you, you little bastard*!"

Tori choked with laughter and snorted as she took a sip of her vodka. Will looked approvingly at Jayna, placed his hand on her knee.

She foresaw what the rest of the night would look like. A typical Friday, she guessed. She would drink more vodka, clink glasses with the reality star, maybe even French kiss her on a dare. Then, in a fog of drink, she would return to her apartment with Will and do whatever he wanted. She would bend and toss her hair and wait for things to go numb. Maybe he wouldn't notice that she didn't have baseboard heaters.

SAM

On his last day in London, Ellis took Sam to the centre of Tower Bridge, where they looked out over the Thames and watched boats move slowly below. Sam already felt the loss of Ellis's imminent departure. Anticipating the separation, he tried to open himself up to Ellis's every thought and move: what he felt as he shielded his eyes from the sting of the cold wind and the thoughts in his mind as he cleared his throat to speak.

"Mo says you're off to a good start," Ellis said suddenly, keeping his eye on a rusty barge creeping out from beneath the bridge. Sam couldn't help smiling at the unexpected praise. His body ached with the desire to make Ellis proud.

"Continue to lay low at work. There's been a change in plans. I'm setting things up for your next move. You won't be there long."

Sam was comforted to know that Ellis was the mastermind of the mission. He had faith. He grasped onto the bridge railing and squinted at the towers of Canary Wharf in the distance. Ellis reached over to grab his hand. Electricity shot through Sam's body.

Ellis spoke as quietly as he could above the traffic noises. "I've taught you the importance of being called, the value of sacrifice and solitude, and soon you'll prove to me that you are a man of action." He squeezed Sam's hand then let it go. "Without action we will accomplish nothing. It's that simple. A man can plan and train, but if he doesn't enter the race, he loses."

For a long while they stood without speaking.

A couple stopped near them and affixed a gold lock to the white chain-link fence in front of the railing. They took the key from the tiny device and tossed it into the Thames. They embraced, faces crashing together amid the yammer of passing vehicles. Sam watched the woman pull back, mouth something tender, and nestle into the man's chest. Callie flashed through his mind, an unwelcome spectre from the past. He tried to shield himself from her image—from the thought that they could have been here, scarring a lock with their initials, her wide grin shot directly at his face, her soft fingertips mocking his cheek. How carelessly she would have launched the tiny key into the depths of the river.

Sam knew Ellis's commitment to their cause was deeper and more selfless than these silly tourist superstitions. Every shake of his fist and sound from his lips carried with it purpose and importance. He was the voice of the voiceless. The hand of the helpless.

After the couple sauntered away, Ellis spoke directly into Sam's ear, words choked. "It will be necessary for you to cause pain. Be prepared." Then Ellis stepped back and held his hand delicately over his mouth. He trembled, face contorted.

Tears pricked Sam's eyes, not because of the content of the statement, but because Ellis suffered intensely. Sam's body ached to cling to this shaking god, reassure him of his own eternal devotion. But Ellis was unreachable, immersed in some otherworldly agony.

"I'll do whatever it takes."

Ellis did not respond, eyes transfixed on something painful and frightening Sam could not see in the grey sky.

Sam tried again, louder. Desperate. "I will do anything for you."

Ellis dropped his gaze, then raised it to Sam's face. Slowly. "Son, I have never been so proud."

A tide of exhilaration flooded Sam's chest. Heat shot through his body. The quickening of pulse and breath. A raging need to collapse and be covered, crushed, consumed by his master. He held tight to the side of the bridge, fingers turning white, and closed his eyes. In the rush of yearning, he had learned to move to the side and wait for a hand to be extended: the invite to intimacy. This was a show of ultimate self-discipline.

The invitation arrived. Ellis slithered one long arm across Sam's shoulder and back and wound him inwards. Strangling with pleasure, Sam absorbed the pressure and heat and harboured it deep in his mind.

They walked down the bridge towards Potters Fields Park. Sam glowed with satisfaction as Ellis maintained a protective grip on his shoulder. A line of vehicles passed to their right. One black Mini slowed, opening the gap between itself and the car in front. The passenger side window opened and a man leaned out. His eyes were ablaze and his mouth cavernous as he hurled words their way. "Poofs!" was all Sam could make out.

The car sped on as the window wound up. It was a blow to the stomach, stirring up fury. He slid sideways towards the barrier between the road and walkway, and Ellis dug his fingers into Sam's arm to steady him. Clearly, the man in the car had not recognized the purity and perfection of the moment.

Ellis said nothing as he ushered Sam towards the park and home.

Vincent

He dropped onto his bed and held his breath until the tension in his back subsided. The pain was not a fluke thing or injury, it was routine. The residue of a long training day. The further along he got in swimming, the more he realized that he could never escape his athletic vocation. It was not the kind of job he could leave at the proverbial office each day. Success in sport depended on the strength of his mind and body. After he left the pool, every step he took or morsel of food he ingested had a particular impact on his body and, therefore, on his swimming. He had to be wary of his thoughts and dreams, because they had the power to drain him of a steadfast belief in his gold medal potential.

He stared at the poster pinned to the ceiling above his bed. It was the London 2012 Aquatics Centre. There was the crisp blue rectangle of water, split into ten lanes; the 17,500 seats that would be filled with rowdy spectators; the curved lines of the ceiling that would guide him to the finish. He envisioned gliding into the wall and slinging an elbow over the lane rope to get a glimpse of the scoreboard through black-lensed goggles.

This was the image he studied each night before bed, mentally moving himself through the motions of race day. He felt the thick air of the ready-room crammed full of his rivals. He engaged in the fog-preventing ritual of spitting into his goggles and rubbing them with his fingers before placing them firmly on his head. He studied the view from behind the blocks—the ultimate test laid out before him in a slice of pool water. He visualized bending over the side of the pool, scooping up a handful of cool water and splashing it on his body. He saw himself swinging his arms in fast windmills and shaking out his hands. He heard the sound of water running in the drains.

He populated the stands with people from the various parts of his life. The first section was the most crowded, filled with the red-cheeked ball-hockey-playing boys from the wintery streets of his St. Leonard childhood. The second section, bustling with his relatives—Uncle Gilbert's whiskered mug in the centre of the group, half-hidden behind a book. The third and last section held the characters from his life over the past few years. It was sparsely occupied. A wasteland. Besides Adam, he did not really have any friends. It was easier that way—fewer relationships to manage while he focused on his Olympic dream.

Tonight as he sank into sleep, he added Yasmine to the mix, a lonely head bobbing above the bleacher railing. She smiled at him. He saw that she knew his secret: isolation begot success. Yasmine understood that he raced alone.

He slept dreamlessly.

VINCENT

At 5:00 a.m., the alarm stabbed through his thick slumber. He slid long and slow out of bed, rubbed his eyes with warm water, and crept down through the dark house to his parents' kitchen to breakfast from the store of food in their pantry. They often boasted to friends and family about his magnificent consumption of food, claiming he'd cost them millions in groceries since he began swimming as a child. But he never ate with them. He was long gone by the time they rose for work, and they had already dined when he returned from training at night. They did not see him when he slunk into the house at midday for a large lunch and nap.

The early morning was the most frightening time of day for Vincent. He did not always know what Robert, his coach, had in store for him at the pool. It could be a low-key, technique focused, stroke-drill day, or—if he was really lucky—starts and turns. But it could also be the dreaded 50 x 100 set. Or a set involving lots of butterfly. Either might kill him. Whatever the content of the workout, Vincent would hammer through it. That was what he was known for.

A recent article in the *Gazette* described him as relentless. "This is a young man who will do anything. He'll leave no stone unturned in his courageous pursuit of Olympic glory," it had said.

He never told anyone that fear was what truly motivated him. If he didn't push and pull and sweat and bleed and vomit, failure loomed.

Yasmine was already at the pool when he arrived. She stood in her black bathing suit, stretching. Her perfectly sculpted leg was up on a starting block. It was her loneliness, he imagined, that made her so beautiful and successful. A woman turned inward. He couldn't help but peer into her bubble and wonder if she saw him standing there. She leaned over her extended limb and picked at the nail polish on her toes.

"Vince." Adam appeared beside him, talking through a wide yawn. "Stop staring, you ass."

Irritated by the interruption, Vincent pretended not to hear his friend and busied himself with his backpack. He pulled his goggles out of the side pocket and clamped them between his teeth, placed a towel around his waist and removed his shoes and pants. He pulled up two baggy Speedos, formerly black, but now chlorine-faded to brown.

When he glanced back at Yasmine, she was seated on the block with three men around her. One of them squatted at her feet and clamped her ankle between his hands. A very tall, man wearing a baseball cap was behind her, his oversized paws gripping her delicate shoulders. The third smiled and clapped at something the crouching man had said. Yasmine's facial expression remained stony as the entourage manipulated and discussed her body. He heard her answer their questions flatly: *Yes. No. Yes. Yes. No.*

Robert's shrill cab-whistle, an essential skill for every swim coach, beckoned the swimmers to the white board behind the blocks. Vincent, Adam, and the rest of the high-performance group dragged their large feet to where their coach waited. They had to pass behind Yasmine. Vincent's heart rate picked up as he approached, but it was Adam who spoke to her. "How's the Achilles?"

"I'm cleared to run," she said. "You'll get your lane back sooner than we thought." Then she smiled. For Adam.

The tall man moved closer and hovered over her petite form.

Vincent's hope slumped; it was a feeling like dropping a body-length behind, mid-race. Yasmine was returning to the road. He had never even spoken to her, and that was it. Back to his water world. Back to her solid ground.

The swimmers gathered around the white board, memorizing the set, and Adam whispered, "The tall guy's her husband."

Vincent pushed the surge of jealousy down. He suppressed the desire to turn and imagine her delicious lonely bubble pressed up against his own.

He faced the pool, his slice of the world; moved to the right of the lane-four block; and watched the Omega clock tick towards red on top.

Sam

In Trafalgar Square a clock counted down the minutes to the Opening Ceremonies of the Olympic Games. When Sam had read about it, he thought it seemed an ominous reminder of the rapid passing of time, a monument stabbed into the ground amid the crowds, like a ticking bomb. He went to see it on a Saturday, when the tourists were in full flock. Hordes of people milled about the square. They stopped to snap pictures of the clock. Quickly bored, they turned to admire the fountain or aging edifices.

Sam stood transfixed by the jagged structure, watching the minutes fall away. It reminded him that time never moved forward but rather counted down. There was always some final event hovering in the distance. Sam didn't know exactly what it would be for him, but he knew it was coming. He knew he had to be prepared.

LEXI

Lexi and her teammate Joanne lay down on the filthy floor of the boathouse without bothering to spread out a towel. Lexi's body vibrated with exhaustion. Her limbs shook and contracted on their own. Practice was over for the day, and she could not move. She could only sip from her water bottle and wait it out.

This was the way it had been since the bedroom incident. She threw herself into training until the muscle ache helped her ignore every other pain. Formerly, the draw of home would have been enough to force her body out into the cool air to drive, autopilot, all the way back to her house. Not anymore.

"I should go now," said Joanne.

Lexi grunted a response. "I hear you. I'm not sure I'll ever be able to get up."

The two of them stayed there, off to the side of the room, bathed in the musty scent of old wood. Other teammates walked by, laughed at them, and continued out the door to the parking lot.

"These are the moments we'll remember," said Joanne. Lexi could tell from the breathy sentimentality of the phrase that Joanne was getting ready to move on. To groan to a stand and find her car.

"I should go home," said Lexi, without moving.

"Me too," said Joanne. With considerable effort, she got up and reached out her hand to Lexi.

"I'm not ready yet."

Joanne shrugged, waved goodbye weakly, and dragged her shoes along the boathouse floorboards as she left.

Brent was probably at home, packing for his training camp. Later tonight he'd be on a flight. Gone for more than a month. She hoped the time apart would eliminate the habit she'd developed of inching backwards when he spoke, or of wincing, just a little, when he reached for his fork and knife.

Yesterday evening they had argued about Andrea. Again. They never spoke about JJ. In Brent's mind, Andrea was the guilty one. The Delilah.

"I respect that she stepped away from her career when she did. Obviously she had other priorities," Lexi had offered, trying to be the voice of reason in the midst of a ridiculous argument.

"You do not respect her. You just don't. She's an idiot. End of story."

Lexi ignored him. She imagined JJ and Andrea lingering at a restaurant, sipping lattes and whispering about marriage and rings and life. Brent was adamant that he and Lexi not consume anything with caffeine. They avoided cafes. They never ate out either. There was no time—or money, in their tight budget—for weekend meals at local restaurants. They never even spoke to each other over breakfast.

LEXI

They rarely held hands.

One time, two years earlier, when they had gone for a walk in downtown Victoria, Brent surprised her by grabbing her hand. She was too aware of their calloused palms rubbing together when they leaned forward to admire an overpriced, white knit sweater in a shop window. Lexi saw their breath form and recede on the glass-pane.

For half an hour they had moved around the town and talked about stuff that had nothing to do with boats or nutrition or team selection issues. While they walked back to the car, Lexi had closed her eyes for a second, to try to memorize the sensation of the clutch. She stumbled slightly sideways into Brent, who bumped back, playfully, thinking she had nudged him on purpose. The romance departed. Brent's competitive nature was piqued.

"Last one to the car is a dirty rotten egg," Brent had said, as he began to sprint towards their little grey Honda.

With Lexi following in a half-hearted jog, Brent ran until he slapped his large hand against the side of the car and shouted, "I won!"

The boathouse was deserted. *I should really go.* Lexi rolled slowly to her side, pulled in her legs, and finally dragged her body to standing. Reluctantly, she made her way home.

When she entered the house, she kept her running shoes on and went straight to the kitchen to grab something to eat. On the counter was a tower of small food containers, filled with vitamins, soy nuts, and quinoa.

"Don't touch my food," Brent shouted from the bedroom.

Lexi rolled her eyes and sighed.

"Where are my weight gloves, Lex?"

She wanted to call back that weight gloves were for sissies. Real men go barehanded. But she restrained herself. Those were someone else's words, anyway. She had recently overheard a man in the weight-room mutter them. He had been resting after a set of chin-ups, puffing out his chest under his black muscle shirt and talking to a teenage boy who was waiting to use the bar.

Irritated by his tone, Lexi had walked up to him in her light blue gloves and spoken in a silly falsetto voice: "Oh, sorry to interrupt boys, but could I jump in and do a quick little set?" He stepped out of the way, and she did a set of twenty-six chin-ups, counting aloud. Seven more reps than the muscle-shirted man.

"Hall closet, top shelf," she called to Brent, then leaned against the counter and sipped her glass of milk.

She heard him rummaging around in the hallway. A few minutes later, he strode into the kitchen, opened one of the clear boxes, and popped a handful of soy nuts into his mouth. She listened, disgusted, as he crunched and breathed through his nose. He fiddled with the container lid. She wanted to tell him that soy contained oestrogen, something that could cause the feminizing of his body—some pseudo-science she had gleaned from one of his men's health magazines. She watched his jaw work violently as he studied the cover, pressing it down in the corners, and grunting when it popped back up.

"You do it," he said, and thrust the container at Lexi's chest.

Several nuts tipped out and plinked against the floor. He squinted at her, as though she was to blame for the finicky cover and the spill.

She gripped the box, a funnel cloud of frustration gathering force inside her belly. A swirl of retorts flew through her mind. All the things she could say to stump him. Humble him. Make him sorry.

She stood and fumbled with the container. He lingered in the kitchen doorway, watching. The box closed.

"That was easy," she said, pertly. Petulant. Defiant. She lifted her chin and caught a glimpse of Brent's pursed lips. She was flirting with danger.

"It's hard to be a big girl, isn't it?" he said.

A man jabbing in his knife. He smirked and left the room.

A strange film of calm fell once he was gone. Lexi moved slowly to the sink. She looked around the kitchen, wide-eyed, noticing the hum of the fridge, the rust on the oven knob, the linoleum bulge near the doorway. Every detail observed in photographic contrast. There was no sudden blast of thunder or snap. In the minute that followed, she moved with deliberation. She squatted slowly, legs still shaky from her workout. She reached into the cupboard to collect the old round glass casserole that once belonged to Brent's mom, who had died several years earlier. She noticed the dark burn marks on its bottom, the beginnings of a crack on one of its sides. She placed its matching lid carefully on the countertop. She took a long, measured breath and raised the heavy dish high above her head. A child on the soccer field sideline, positioning a perfect throw-in.

Lexi admired the curved trajectory of the vessel as it moved from her hands towards the blue and green striped wallpaper. On impact, it burst into three large pieces, and a hundred splinters of glimmering glass shot across the floor. There was a pleasant granular crunch as Lexi stepped sideways to pick up the glass top.

She had the lid lifted high when Brent raced back in.

"What the hell?" His voice was strangely high-pitched.

She launched the cover, full force, at Brent in the doorway. He jumped aside and it smashed against the wall behind him. For five seconds they stared at one another, their relationship glittering at their feet. Lexi was amused by the way his mouth opened and closed but no words came out. She stepped forward, unsure of what she should say or do next, and he shuffled backward. There was nowhere to go from here.

He broke the gaze first, looked to the floor, nudged some of the shards with his slippered foot, and mumbled something indecipherable. He retreated to the bedroom. He would be gone in an hour, and she would wait until then to tidy the mess. She would sit down to finish her milk. She would not speak to him. Not wish him the best at his training camp. She would hold on to her small win.

It would amaze people to know that this was part of her life. That things could move so smoothly on the water and be so messed up at home.

SAM

It was another day spent alone, staring at the wall outside his window. He knew he should get off the couch and eat or bathe or walk the city streets, but he was transfixed by the dark brick and exhausted, unable to move. These were the days he dreaded most. No work shift. Nowhere to be. The mortar lines blended together and blurred more the longer he looked. He was embarrassed by the thought that Ellis might be watching him now, but still, he could not stand. He begged for forgiveness and, after a very long while, lay down on the couch and slept.

Yasmine

In the middle of Jeanette's miniature apartment living room, Yasmine stood staring at the chubby eleven-month-old sleeping in the battery-powered baby swing.

"I wondered when you'd come to see him," said Jeanette, slouched on her couch, chewing on her thumbnail.

Yasmine leaned her oversized blue gift bag against the wall and bent to take a closer look at the tiny human. He was a miniature version of Jeanette, all scrawny limbs and long fingers and toes.

One night, during the last month of university in Oregon, when it had been too hot to study, the roommates had stripped down to their underwear, propped their feet up on the window sill, and painted their toenails. Yasmine had dreamed aloud about her life in Montreal, and Jeanette reminisced about the college nights of beer drinking and silly pranks they'd leave behind.

"Nice rainbow underwear," Jeanette had joked.
"Nice prehensile toes."
They had leaned into one another and laughed.

Now they were strangers.

There was a lump in Yasmine's throat. She would not let herself cry. She was here to pretend it hadn't been three years since they'd last seen one another; to see the child; to ignore that she had missed the baby shower; to not mention her marital problems; to act normal.

She refocused her attention on Jeanette. "You look good." The words came out with a tone of incredulity. "I mean it."

"Sure."

Yasmine cleared her throat and fidgeted with the swing settings. A tinny version of "She'll be comin' round the mountain" began to play, and the baby twitched in his sleep. Frantically, she pressed buttons to make it stop. The volume went up.

"No, no, turn it off!" said Jeanette as she leapt off the sofa, swatted Yasmine's hand away, and deftly flicked the right switch. Their bodies were touching in that small space next to the baby's swing. They separated quickly, accentuating the awkwardness of the moment.

Yasmine, desperate for some of the tension to dissipate, reached for the gift.

"I got this for Jacob." She shoved the bag into Jeanette's hand.

Her friend flopped down on the couch and extracted two white onesies and pair of baby running shoes.

"Thank you. They're adorable," Jeanette said, unenthused. She placed them next to her, and Yasmine watched as she slowly, meticulously, folded the soft yellow tissue paper.

YASMINE

Jeanette looked up, finally. Her eyebrows were raised as she gathered in air. Yasmine recognized the expression as the prelude to a parting statement. An *it was good of you to come* or *great to see you* utterance that killed any hope of further conversation.

"Thanks for stopping by," Jeanette said. Then she sighed.

Yasmine could not get herself to interrupt her movement towards the door. It was not Jeanette nudging her, either. She collected her own coat from the floor, slipped on her boots, and muttered something made up, about not wanting to disturb the baby's routine. She ignored the intimate memories hanging in the air. Jeanette seemed to go along with the charade of being strangers—not mentioning the past or their long commute from the West Coast. Yasmine turned at the door to say a final goodbye and good luck, and she thought back to that day, years ago, when they had arrived in Montreal, and she stood terrified in Nate's hard, lifeless front yard. When Nate had appeared, Jeanette had shouted "Bye" out the car window and drove away. That was the real beginning of this painful distance. She could see it now in Jeanette's bowed head and impatient wave: guilt. And she was well aware that people hate the things that remind them of their guilt.

She should go.

Through her tears on the long walk back to her house, Yasmine studied the barren trees and listened to the violent crack of ice beneath her boots. There was clear finality to each step. She crushed the past underfoot.

When Yasmine failed to make it to the 2004 and 2008 Olympic Games, then got injured, her family, coach, and Nate had mourned for her. *Olympic dreams are born early and die hard.* She was now resurrected and ready to tear off her grave clothes.

She would let nothing tie her to this place anymore. Her injury had healed, the Olympics were in sight again, and her body ached for home. Her recent return to Mount Royal paths, as well as the indoor tracks and streets of the city, had renewed her strength. *Crunch of gravel; crack of ice; thumping pulse; and long, long exhale…crunch of gravel; crack of ice; thumping pulse; long, long exhale.* Running was beautiful music to Yasmine. A favourite song played only for her. It propelled her forward, and now it moved her away from here.

SAM

When the elevator door opened, Sam walked slowly into the hallway. It was 10:00 p.m. on the second-to-last workday before the long Christmas weekend. This floor of the building was fully lit, and a couple of heads were visible above the low cubicle walls.

Sam made sure no one was watching before he walked around the corner to the employee kitchen. He stood and stared at the espresso machine—the water canister was open. Ellis's words pushed their way into his mind: *It will be necessary for you to cause pain. Be prepared.*

Sam imagined placing a dishwasher detergent tablet in the open slot and filling it with water. He wondered what would happen: the next day, several employees would greedily consume soapy espressos. He pictured them spitting at their desks and grasping their throats.

He shook away the idea, left the kitchen, and executed a standard slow round of the floor. The employees working late did not even lift their heads to acknowledge his presence. When he finished the round, he returned to the elevator and descended.

In the past weeks, he had thought of a thousand different ways to cause pain. To move the fury inside, outside.

But he waited for Ellis's call.

VINCENT

Yasmine had stopped coming. As Vincent moved along the pool surface during practice, he no longer saw her lean, vertical body inch forward in a neighbouring lane, feet slicing through the water. Her spot had been reclaimed by a line of fellow swimmers, gliding horizontally through tiny bubbles.

Without her, the pool was once again a place for the aquatic-only crowd: the roar of fifty swimmers doing laps; the synchro music on replay, metallic taps in the background; the rumble of the diving boards; the shouts of the water polo players. He turned his focus to the tiles on the bottom and the rhythmic nature of his sport. He counted his strokes and breaths: *One, two, three, four, breathe; one, two, three, four, breathe.* Every reach, pull, and glide moved him closer to the Olympic Games.

He had never spoken to Yasmine, but already he missed her painted toenails and rigid body. Her frowning face above the wash of water. Her fierce, lonely determination that surpassed his own. He wanted to be harder, like her.

After practice, he stood under the burning stream of water, head hung forward. Three teammates walked through the shower area, laughing about something that had happened at a party two nights earlier.

Vincent had not attended. Long ago, he had stopped communicating with the other swimmers, besides his exchanges with Adam, and they had stopped inviting him to social events. Most mornings he dropped his swim bag far from the rest, shadowed his face with his hoodie, and sat in silence.

Twenty-eleven was winding up. Each day he moved closer in time to the year of *his* Games. A sense of urgency consumed him. He had to focus on what mattered. He would no longer waste energy on activities that did not contribute to an Olympic berth and medal performance. He figured that people forgave top athletes for the way they cut themselves off from the world when they were deep in training. Especially if, after all the isolation, they won.

SAM

At 11:30 p.m. on New Year's Eve, Sam ventured out for a walk. He was just minutes away from his flat when the sky opened up and freezing rain slapped his face, soaking through his clothes. To escape the downpour, he pressed into a huddle of bodies on the sheltered threshold of a pub.

Shouts from inside: "Ten, nine, eight, seven, six…"

The people around him joined in: "Five, four, three, two, one…Happy New Year!"

Sam peeked into the dingy bar. Drinks were raised in the air. Couples kissed.

The bouncer in the doorway extended his hand to Sam. "HNY, mate," he said.

Sam shook the man's hand and nodded.

"Go on in," the bouncer said.

Chilled by the wet clothes that clung to his skinny frame, Sam could not resist the offer to move into the warmth. He wedged through a pack of young women just inside the door. Their curves and bumps were visible through tightly fitted dresses. Their sweet perfumes mingled with the pub scents of beer and damp. His body responded to the press of their arms against his back. His pulse quickened, and his skin warmed. Ellis had warned him about the fickleness of the flesh.

He would remain in control.

He ignored the painful yearning and moved further into the dark room. He narrowed his focus on the large, pink mouth of a man, opening and closing in animated conversation. The teeth inside were yellowed and crooked. The nose above, too big, too red. The chin below, sagging. Within a few seconds, Sam was pinned between a dancing couple and the cocktail table where the fellow stood talking to three other men. Sam was close enough to see the fingerprints on his beer glass, the hair in his ears, the sunspots on his cheeks.

Sam wondered if he could clench his fist and pound the man right in his big mouth. Although he was able to imagine causing pain, he wasn't sure if he was truly able to do it. He had never punched anyone in his life.

Brent had been the fighter. As children they had wrestled in the piles of autumn leaves on the front lawn. Once, Sam had manoeuvred Brent in what he thought was an impenetrable half-nelson, but Brent wriggled free and snuck in two violent jabs to the gut that left Sam doubled over in agony. Their mother had watched them from the kitchen window, wagging her finger. Elbows flapping, Brent circled his crumpled body and shouted, "Chicken! *Bawk, bawk!*" Sam did not have the nerve to hit back.

"Can I get you a drink?" the man said to Sam, as his three companions stared. "You look like you need one."

SAM

This display of generosity from the man he had contemplated hitting a minute earlier inspired deep embarrassment and guilt. He looked away, turned, and pushed back through the crowd of revellers. He broke out alone into the night, his body heavy and useless. The rain had let up, and people stumbled along the puddled streets in pairs.

Sam fixed his eyes on the wet pavement and rushed away from that place. The unshakeable faith he had felt that day with Ellis on Tower Bridge had already melted away. He was disgusted with himself because of it. If Ellis were here, Sam would not be able to look him in the face.

Ellis had been clear: the mission would require him to cause pain, and Sam wasn't certain he had the strength for it. He stopped walking and pressed his forehead against the glass front of a darkened shop. A sliver of cold shot through to his brain. His reflection was obscured by the condensation and water droplets. He hated this inescapable fog of inadequacy. He breathed heavily and looked past his mirror image to the merchandise inside. It was cheap, gaudy costume jewellery. The pink and green baubles and yellow-brown beads of the vain world. He loathed the sight of them—already tarnished, pointless. *Corpse dressings.* They lacked the purposeful beauty of the rings Ellis had given him. Sam pressed his hand against the chest of his jacket to feel the necklace and three rings beneath. His reminder.

He stared into the eyes of his reflection, bottomless black circles. He had seen Brent do the same in the locker-room mirror years ago, to pump himself up prior to a regatta. Brent had whispered, "I'm all in." He had been ready to compete. Ready to conquer.

Sam glared into the glass. *I'm all in. I'm all in. I'm all in.* It was the build-up to a crescendo. He let out the roar of a weightlifter and tore himself away from the shop. He sprinted towards Bermondsey, ears filled with the pounding of his heart, hands clenched in tight fists. His body pulsed with electric fury as he turned the corner and neared the church.

He stopped there, near growling, at the foot of the stairs. Up against the door were the twin-like lovers. They clutched a large grey blanket around them and rubbed noses and kissed. Sam stomped one foot on the ground to get their attention. They dislodged from one another and looked his way sharply, like birds disturbed in their nest. One of them stood quickly, the cover dropped and pooled around his feet.

"Go away!" he shouted. The voice was shrill.

Sam stood his ground. This time he would not run. Even as the hooded teenager leapt down the steps towards him, he widened his stance and tightened his fists. *I'm all in.*

The teen struck first. It was a violent shove. Sam absorbed it and readied himself to thrust back. Both of his palms slammed into bony collarbones and knocked the teenager off-balance and back onto the steps. Sam's body reverberated with the seductive power of that moment. He was suddenly on top of the teenager, hitting hairless cheeks with bare knuckles. Over and over. Blood was smeared on his hand. A girl's high-pitched scream came from the perch at the top of the steps, the bell to end the round. Sam did not look up to acknowledge his victory. He simply stepped back from the whimpering child, whose face was now painted warrior red.

The game was over now, test completed, adrenaline retreating. He would not let himself feel remorse. No shame. No regret. He jammed his wet hands into his pockets and rushed home.

YASMINE

Yasmine smiled as the plane emerged from within the thick cloud cover and land became visible below. The mountains slept in the foggy distance; the towers of the city stood in welcome; the busy arteries snaked over the rivers and still-green trees. In the months to come she would take to these roadways each day; tie up her laces and hit the wet B.C. pavement. She could almost smell the scent of the pines. She was home again.

    She had found it surprisingly easy to unwind her life in Montreal. She began by announcing her decision to leave to her coach, then her physio, then her agent (who launched into frantic preparations for her new training life in Vancouver). They barely flinched at her request to not tell Nate about her decision. Perhaps they had sensed the inevitability of the moment. Perhaps she was the only one who had not predicted the end of this chapter. She had not realized that her shackles could be so easily shed.

Even her mother, thousands of miles away, responded with such calm to the news that Yasmine was leaving Montreal. It was as though her mom knew all along that this was an eventuality.

"I'm coming home," Yasmine had whispered to her over the phone.

"Is everything all right?"

"I'm just coming home to train. My flight's on New Year's Day."

"Is Nate coming with you?" Her mother had asked this perfunctorily, without a tone of true curiosity.

"I haven't told him yet." This, no doubt, confirmed everything her mother suspected.

"Let me know your arrival time, and I'll be there to pick you up."

Yasmine had waited until the last possible moment to tell Nate. Already, she had become a master at avoiding him: going to bed before he returned home on the nights he coached; eating dinner on a tray in front of the television when he was around; staring at the screen when he spoke. He hadn't seemed to notice her complete withdrawal from married life.

On New Year's Eve, he had gone out with some old high school buddies, and she stayed home. It took her less than an hour to pack most of her things into two large suitcases. Then she had stalked slowly through the rooms of the house, noticing for the first time how little of her there was in the place. The posters on the walls were his. The worn furniture had been there since before she moved in. The only real evidence of her residency was the bookcase in the hallway, loaded with tarnished trophies, plaques, and medals with ribbons of every colour. All these she would easily leave behind. They meant more to Nate than to her, anyway. The top shelf sagged under the weight of the hardware. She stood, tearless, before this shrine to her athletic prowess, slipped off her wedding band, and dropped it into the gold bowl of one of the trophies. *Plink.*

She had moved her cases to the front door and sat on the stairs, heart pounding in her ears, wondering if she should just go. Maybe it was best to depart before he staggered in after the bars closed. But that had seemed like leaving the race with the end in sight. This was a finish line she had to cross. A frightening thought had passed through her mind as she waited in the unlit hallway: *If worse comes to worst, I can outrun him.*

Sneakers on, suitcases at her feet, Yasmine sat in the darkness and listened to the clock tick in the next room. She checked her watch: 3:22 a.m. She stared at her naked fingers. Finally, on the other side of the door, the rattle of Nate's key chain. It piqued her nerves. She stood up on the first step. And then he was there, turning his back to her as he entered, two arm lengths away. He eased the door closed with a gentleness he rarely displayed. She smelled the sweat on his body, heard his heavy breathing.

"Nate," she said sharply, ripping him out of his sleepy skulk.

He sucked in breath. "You scared me."

Panic filled her throat. She had not planned what to say.

In that short gap of silence, he stepped towards her and bumped into the suitcases. They crashed to the floor.

He spoke. "What are these for?"

She had to tell him quickly. She would make the first move before he took control. "I'm going home."

He just stood there. A dark silhouette, looming between Yasmine and the door.

She had not trained for this. She had not rehearsed the lines or planned the actions. The words came out rugged and unpolished: "I want a divorce."

"What?"

She did not answer or repeat the line. She needed to get out now. She would walk to the corner of the main street, where she would find a taxi, head to the airport, and wait for her flight. She would leave and not turn back.

"You have to stay."

He edged the fallen suitcases out of the way and was face-to-face with her. Beer on his breath. She did not want to say anything else.

He placed his hands on her arms and whispered, "What about the Olympics?"

She did not want to tell him that she would still train. She would still try to qualify, without him. That would be too much for him to handle.

"You're just tired," he spoke softly into the grey air. "It's been a tough year, but we're so close now." He ran his hands up her arms, to her neck. She remained stiff and cold. She would not let him claim her.

"No," she said, and slid out of his grasp. She stepped around him and opened the door. The streetlamp lit up the hallway. She reached for the upset cases and dragged them out onto the threshold. Nate watched in silence, arms limp at his sides, his mouth a black hole.

There was one dangerous moment when she had turned back and said "Goodbye," and noticed the sad stoop of his shoulders, all the confidence and charm drained from him, and felt a pang of pity. She could not submit to those emotions. She would not.

"Stay," he said.

"Goodbye," she said again. She wheeled her bags down the step and onto the sidewalk, leaving him standing in the open doorway, staring out at his barren yard.

There was the jarring pull of brakes beneath the plane. The passengers applauded. Yasmine joined in, grinning widely, as the aircraft taxied to the gate.

"Welcome to Vancouver," said the voice over the intercom. "Happy New Year, and thank you for flying with us."

She was home.

WINTER 2012

God made everything out of nothing, but the nothingness shows through.
— *Paul Valery*

SAM

Sam dragged himself out of bed. Dried blood from his hand dotted the white sheets; his aching knuckles reminded him of the night before. He pulled his fist up to his face and stared at the raw skin and open cuts, amazed and frightened that he had been able to lash out with such force and then walk away. But not without incurring damage himself. He sat on the edge of the bath and ran cold water over the bad hand, watching the red-tinged water swirl down the drain.

He returned to the main room and closed the bathroom door behind him. A white slip of paper was on the floor near the door. A rush of hope—perhaps it was a message from Ellis. He ran over, picked it up, and read: *Centre of the Millennium Bridge. Noon.*

He opened the door to the hallway and peered out. There was no sign of Ellis or anyone else. His pulse quickened. He wondered whether he'd see Ellis or learn about his mission today.

Within minutes Sam was dressed and bursting out of his flat. He leaned into the frigid wind and strode towards the Thames, the note clutched in his left hand. He scanned the faces of people walking by. One man looked away from Sam's glare. Another clutched the collar of his coat and tugged it up to protect wind-stung cheeks.

Sam arrived midbridge several minutes early and turned in a slow 360. No one lingered on the bridge. People simply rushed over, passing by, shielding their faces from the wind and trying not to slip. He waited, shivering with cold and excitement, and focused on the London skyline. Greed was visible in every aspect of its elaborate design. He looked at the almost complete Shard, its jagged, violent edges menacing and hovering above the neighbourhood.

An adolescent girl in a multicoloured knit hat tapped him on the arm. "Excuse me," she said. "A man asked me to pass this on to you."

She pressed a puffy white envelope into his hand and proceeded to walk away.

"Wait!" Sam called out.

She turned to him.

"Who gave this to you?"

"An old man with a cane over there," the girl pointed to the north side of the bridge. "I was just passing by...he said he had to get this package to you but finds it difficult to walk on the bridge's deck. Too slippery or something."

"What did he look like?"

She shrugged and frowned. "I have somewhere to go. Go see for yourself, he's probably still there." She continued walking.

Sam tucked the package under his arm and ran towards the northern bank, slipping a little on the deck. There were no old men with canes in sight. He raced down the steps and scanned the street frantically. There was no one who fit the girl's description. He sat down on the cold steps and caught his breath. He wondered why the package could not have been delivered directly to his flat like the note. Was Ellis watching this? Maybe this was what Ellis had wanted. These layers of mystery. These tests of faith and obedience. Anonymous soldiers following disjointed orders? Perhaps this was the safest way to operate. *I have to trust.*

He turned the package in both hands for a minute. With security cameras everywhere, he knew he needed to keep moving. He made his way home.

When Sam entered his flat, he perched on the couch and tore open the envelope, desperate for it to be something from Ellis. Some sign of encouragement. Anything. Inside there was a thin white mobile and a smaller envelope full of SIM cards. No note. He swallowed hard and turned on the phone.

A message popped up on the screen: *Contact me.* It was from an area code he did not recognize. Immediately, he called the number. His heart thudded in his ears.

A woman's raspy voice on the line: "Hello?"

Sam wasn't certain what he should say. He did not respond right away, so the woman said again, "Hello?"

"Hi," he said. Then hesitated again before adding, "You texted me."

"Who are you?"

"Sam."

There was a moment of silence; then the voice said, "Ellis has a message for you." At the mention of the name, Sam's body flushed with heat.

"Next Tuesday at three p.m., your time, Ellis will call you. After that conversation, change your SIM card. And watch your back." Then she hung up.

Sam held the mobile in his shaking hand for a few seconds before placing it on the couch at his side. In his head he replayed the woman's words. Ellis was going to call on Tuesday. That was wonderful relief.

And watch your back.

He instinctively looked around the room. It was only then that he noticed the bathroom door was partly open. He remembered shutting it. He always kept it closed. The hair on his arm stood up and his pulse raced. Rising slowly, he crept closer to the washroom, ears alert to every sound now. His short, quick breaths. The rubber squish of his soles against the floor. The noise of trucks outside.

He nudged the bathroom door open and peered in. The dark, windowless room was empty. He exhaled and backed out.

His eyes darted around the main room, noticing details, like the way his black pants hung limply over the corner of the bed and how the curtains were open a crack. He could not be sure whether he had left these things in their current positions. Every object appeared to radiate with the touch of an intruder. He was sure someone had been in his flat, looking at his things.

He hoped it was Ellis.

Sam placed his hand on his chest where the rings were. He reminded himself that Ellis would look out for him. No matter what, Ellis would be there.

JAYNA

She closed her phone and crumpled to the apartment floor. The conversation had not been one she'd expected. The head coach of the Canadian Women's Basketball had called to offer her a spot at the upcoming training camp and national team trials. Nate, who was the assistant coach, must have done something to make this happen. Pulled strings. This moment should have been infused with the satisfaction of fulfilling a dream. She should have felt euphoria. Instead, she was huddled on the cold linoleum, clinging to her cell and shaking uncontrollably.

She tried to focus on the distant barking of a dog from somewhere outside and the water running in pipes behind the apartment walls. She looked at the microwave clock, flashing twelve o'clock. It was at times like these that she wished she had a roommate. Then she would have to pick herself up and pretend she was okay. Alone, she'd wait it out.

When she felt calm enough to stand, she moved to the fridge, pulled out two beers, and opened them both. She sat on her tattered couch and drank. The liquid was cool relief to her tightened throat. She stared at her headless reflection on the blank television screen: body slumped forward, a bottle clutched in each large hand. If someone saw her right now, they wouldn't believe she had just been invited to join the national team and was possibly heading to the Olympic Games. She swallowed the rest of the beer and wiped her eyes and lips with her sleeve.

She would have to celebrate; she would have to dance and carouse until the occasion lived up to her expectations. She put away her empties and picked up her phone. Twitter: *Hey party people! I got invited to try out for the Olympic Team. Come celebrate with me at Will's club at 10.*

She put down the phone and grabbed another beer.

Jayna entered the club just after 10:00 p.m. She joined her teammates Helen and Vee in the centre of the dance floor. Arms flung above her head, she closed her eyes and spun and bounced with the crowd. People fed her cocktails, which she consumed skilfully without interrupting her groove.

"Congrats," yelled Helen over the pounding bass.

With each drink, Jayna felt the disappearance of anxiety and the slow entry of something like courage. Her hair had come loose from its ponytail, and strands stuck to the sweat on her face. She removed her heels and placed them on the edge of the floor before joining a group of dancing strangers. Her teammates had been absorbed by the pulsing crowd.

After a while, the lights, people, and music in the room began to feel distant, and she found herself wandering to the back of the club, where she thought she might find Will. Where she might be able to pull him close and feel less alone.

He was there, hedged into his usual booth by a fat man she did not recognize and the gorgeous reality star, Tori. They were engaged in subdued conversation: subtle hand gestures and delicate sips of their drinks. Tori giggled softly about something. It all seemed very adult to Jayna, who now teetered before them, barefoot, dishevelled and sticky with perspiration. They looked up, amused. She was beyond controlling herself. She couldn't be sure how long she had been standing there in front of them. Time was sliding around.

"Can your bimbo make space for me?" She heard the slur of her own words. She felt the sideways sway of the room.

Tori frowned. There were no wrinkles when she frowned.

The fat man said something to Tori, which Jayna could not hear. Then Tori laughed.

"What did you say?" She said to the man. He recoiled. She was too loud.

"Don't embarrass yourself, Jayna," said Will, coolly.

A sense of desperation crept up in her. She had to get a space there at the table next to Will. She needed him.

"I'm trying out for the Olympic Team." It was all she could come up with to say. She spat the words. She wanted them to respect her for a moment. She hoped they would make space and let her sit down. The room was spinning. Faces were watching.

"Good for you," said the starlet flatly.

"I'm practically an Olympian. I'm better than you." This was not what she had wanted to say, but the angry words flowed, and people glared. She stumbled and grabbed onto the table's edge for balance. In the next booth there was a man who looked like Nate. Dark hair, chiselled jaw. He was laughing. She hated him sitting there, making fun of her.

"Shut up. Shut up!" she screamed at him.

"You're drunk and acting obnoxious," said Will. He was next to her now, holding her arm firmly. Steering her through the lines of faces. She leaned into him as they walked out onto the sidewalk. The pavement was slippery under her bare soles. He pushed her into a taxi, and she tried to turn, to hold onto him, to kiss him. He extricated himself from her grip.

"Go home and get some sleep," he said, from what seemed like an incredible distance, before the cab door slammed shut.

There was no place for her here.

SAM

Ellis's phone call came at the appointed time. Sam was sitting at his table, anticipating the ring.

He picked up immediately. "Hello?"

"You've shown great obedience," Ellis said. "I've seen that your life has remained Spartan. I like that. It's time for your next assignment."

Maybe it was Ellis who had been in his flat? He smiled at the thought and stayed quiet, awaiting his instructions.

"I've found a new job for you with London Twenty-twelve security. You will attend a meeting at the Olympic site on the first Friday in February. Eleven o'clock a.m. Arrive early to pick up your ID at the security screening area."

The instructions sparked Sam's nerves. "What else do I need to know?"

"That I need you working inside the Olympic site, and that I'm looking out for you."

"Should I talk to Mo?"

"His role is now complete. He does not need to know anything. Sometimes we have to adjust our plans and leave people behind for the sake of our mission. I still need you, but not him. We're moving on."

Sam wondered what that meant. Did Ellis's network of soldiers have limited roles? *Will my role end suddenly too, without warning or explanation?*

He knew he should trust Ellis and let go of his insecurity, but the question just slipped out: "What else do I have to do?"

Ellis's voice was tinged with impatience. "You need to remind yourself who we're doing this for. The voiceless. The poor. I'm depending on you. You're my key player."

"Yes. Sorry," Sam said quickly, hoping Ellis would accept his apology.

"Call me once every two weeks on a Monday."

Sam wrote down Ellis's number, switched SIM cards, and placed the phone in his pocket.

On the Friday morning of the meeting, Sam followed a group of uniformed men out of Pudding Mill Lane station towards the security screening area. They moved into single file as they approached the gate. Two frowning guards stopped them, one by one, pointed scan guns at their ID badges, and ushered them through. There were three security cameras visible from where Sam stood, one aimed in his direction. Waiting there at the back of the line, he endured the press of anxiety in his bladder. A patch of sweat spread under the arms of his shirt. He was thankful for his dark coat.

He wished Ellis could be there guide him through each step. He was now at the front.

"Where's your security badge?" asked the guard.

SAM

Sam's body filled with heat. *I have to look calm.* "I'm here to collect it." There was a slight shake in his voice.

"Can I see some photo ID, please?" Both security personnel were eyeing him. Surely, he looked suspicious.

He was desperate to quiet his trembling hand. Slowly, he reached into his pocket and pulled out his passport. The guard closest to him snatched it up and looked closely at the name and photo, then at Sam's face. He moved away, unlocked a large metal cabinet, and pulled out a mesh bag.

"Here's your kit and badge," the guard said gruffly, when he returned to where Sam stood. "Sign here." He held out a clipboard with a paper.

Sam signed, surprised that the process was so absurdly simple. Had Ellis really orchestrated all this?

"You're on the main stadium ground team. Follow those guys ahead. There's a meeting at eleven," said the other man. "There's a loo in the building, where you can get changed."

Sam walked swiftly to catch up to the mob of security personnel, careful not to look too relieved or too rushed.

Inside the building, which still reeked of paint and new vinyl, Sam followed the men to the door of a large meeting room. It had concrete floors lined with chairs. There were about one hundred people in the room, all wearing the same dark uniform, some holding fluorescent yellow or orange coats over their arms. Sam found a nearby washroom and changed. He tucked his clothes into the mesh bag, clipped on his ID, and moved into the meeting area, where a tall woman dressed in civvies had already begun her address to the group.

"I worked security during the Winter Games in Vancouver," she said. "It feels like working at Disneyland at times. You have a serious job to do, but you need to do it with a smile... you want the public to feel like they're in a happy, safe place.

You'll meet all types: the stupid anarchists who will throw rubbish at you and the people who want you to smile for their photo. Leave the frowns to the military."

The room laughed.

Once she sat down, a stern man in a suit took over the podium. After clarifying to the group that they were in fact instructed to take their role seriously and discourage photograph-taking on the Olympic site, he led the group through a PowerPoint presentation on the different types of Olympic accreditation and security scanners. Sam had a flashback to a U of T lecture hall, sitting staring idly at the backs of people's heads and at his professor's slides. That seemed like a lifetime ago. He had been a different person, someone he had come to hate.

"Before I let you go," the man said, "I just want to remind you who you are not. You are *not* police officers. If you see a potential menace within the Olympic grounds you should not investigate it, you just tell me. You are *not* media stars. You will *not* advertise any threats or talk to the press and throw the world into a panic. You will tell me, and I will deal with it, quietly. That's it, that's all. If I hear that any one of you is trying to be a hero, I will have you released from your duties. Clear?" Heads nodded. And with that, he closed the binder on the podium and adjourned the meeting.

The room emptied quickly. Outside the door there was a table with large flasks of coffee, and a crowd gathered around it. Sam hovered on the periphery of the group, not certain where to go next. As he stood there, his anxiety returned. He scanned the area, counting four security cameras. He looked away from them and stared blankly into a huddle of coffee drinkers. Each face was a suspicious one. Each hand raising a vessel of steaming liquid, threatening. Each scrape of a shoe, startling. He needed Ellis more than ever.

SAM

A tall, grey-haired guard approached. Sam's heart shuddered, but he did not move. The man stopped in front of Sam and held out his hand. Sam wiped his palm on his pant leg and accepted the shake.

"I'm Alan. I know who you are," said the man.

Sam felt the flutter of nerves. *How does he know me? What does he know?*

"I've been inside the venue for a month already. We're already active."

"Nice to meet you," was all Sam could think of to say. He wanted to know who *we* were, and if he was included.

Alan moved to Sam's side. They stood shoulder to shoulder for a few seconds, watching people.

Alan spoke again. "Ellis says hello." And he walked away.

Andrea

After JJ left, the apartment had seemed much cleaner and brighter. No more dimmed lights and closed curtains for midafternoon television marathons. No more empty chip bags left on the ground next to an overflowing garbage can. All that was left of him was an imagined dent in the sofa and the weight of his departure—not the most recent departure, but the one that took place after his car accident. When he left everything he used to be behind.

Andrea wondered if she could have done something to help him, instead of leaving it too long, saying nothing, and then giving up. But she would not dwell on those sad thoughts anymore. She had survived Danielle's death. She would manage this, too.

Eventually, she would let go of the image of his blank face, turning away from her as he climbed into a cab and sped off to LaGuardia. The back of his head. The beautiful waves of sandy hair that revealed nothing of who he had become.

She deleted the photo of him from her cell phone.

He was much like a lost race to her. Something she had analysed through tears and now needed to leave behind.

She closed the door of her light-filled apartment and descended the staircase to the lobby. She was on her way to the NBC studios to begin preparations for her role as a canoe/kayak colour commentator for the Games. She would be the clarifying, critical, or congratulatory voice behind the athletes. When the offer was made for her to take on the role, she had jumped at it. It was her chance to let the world know what really happened inside the boat. She would enlighten the audience on the real pain of competition: the burning agony of lactic acid, the years of hard journeying that led to the finish line. She planned to remind viewers that the competitors were actual people, not just athletic winners and losers with a duty to the nation.

She walked out onto the cracked city sidewalk outside her building and scanned the street for a yellow cab. She never knew what a day might bring. The driver might turn around mid-ride and say, *I've seen you on TV. You are the rower whose teammate died.* She would not correct him to explain the difference between rowing and kayaking. She might run into one of the producers at the television studios who would encourage her to *hang in there* and *get back in the boat for 2016*. She would not explain that she was happier now. That she might eventually return to kayak, but that she also might not. That now she understood she was much more than just a paddle-wielding athlete.

Somehow, in the middle of the big city on a cold Friday morning, her friend dead, her boyfriend gone, her body just beginning to soften along its sharpest edges, she was still winning.

Sam

He stood, staring upward, mesmerized by the shoots of white metal that curved up the sides of the main stadium. He felt the same sensation of smallness he had experienced as a child one of the first times he went to see the Blue Jays play.

After one memorable game, he had gazed up in awe of the Toronto Skydome and squeezed his hotdog so hard that the ketchup oozed out. His father had reached over with a fistful of napkins to wipe the red sauce dripping down Sam's shin and onto his white tube socks. Brent must have been there, too, somewhere in the background, but he had no primary role in the memory. It was Sam who had played the starring role.

In the third inning, he had heard the sharp crack of a bat and stood to watch a fly ball rip through the air towards his section. He even climbed onto his seat and reached out his gloved hand in hope. The man sitting behind him had tapped his back and urged him to sit down, but Sam held out his tattered Rawlings with the laces ragged and loose, and the ball fell towards him, backlit by the stadium lights. It felt like minutes passed as it descended and he waited, noticing how the CN Tower peeked into the open roof of the dome. Eventually the ball landed, *plop*, in the soft leather of his palm. He had caught it sweetly, easily. He had gasped, and the spectators around him burst into surprised applause. His dad had jumped up and hugged him, in that spontaneous and genuine way that only happens when something unexpected and joyous occurs. They collapsed into their seats, and the game resumed, but the two of them alternated turning the ball in their hands and laughing at nothing, except for, perhaps, the absurdity of hope.

Sam looked away from the stadium, not certain how long he had been poised with his head back at an awkward angle.

In a few months, Brent would be here with his teammates, bursting into the Opening Ceremonies wearing his Team Canada garb, probably taking photos of himself or tweeting on his mobile.

Sam imagined his dad on the couch in front of the TV at home in Elora, watching the Games, Bex at his side. He would probably scan the mob of parading athletes in the search for his youngest son, The Athlete. Sam pictured the smile spreading on his dad's face as he located Brent in that thick crowd. He guessed that his dad would experience a rush of pride that sprouted from somewhere even deeper inside than what he had felt back at the Skydome with Sam. In this moment of joy, he wouldn't wonder where his eldest son Sam was.

Sam's chest tightened. He shook away the image of his dad. He focused on the grumbling of trucks in the distance.

Then he noticed Alan, standing about fifty metres away. At his side was another security guard. A tall brunette. From this distance, he could not see the details of her face, but he was sure she was watching him. Quickly, he turned his back to them and began to walk as casually as he could towards the basketball stadium.

He had seen Alan earlier that day. They had passed through the security checkpoint at the same time to start their shift. They had not spoken to one another or acknowledged each other's presence. They had played the part of two security guards on their way to work. Alan had been busy, carrying a large, open box that appeared to be filled with fluorescent coats. The man on duty appeared to notice Alan struggling with the load, so he dutifully scanned his badge, then held open the gate. Alan passed through easily. A wave of guilt had washed through Sam as he watched Alan turn towards the stadium. Then the guard faced Sam and pointed the scanner.

SPRING-SUMMER 2012

VINCENT

It was the Olympic trials. The prerace rituals for the finals of the two-hundred-metre backstroke were in full swing inside the crowded, damp-smelling ready-room. A Vancouver-based swimmer named Gallagher was in the corner of the room, hopping from one foot to the other, smacking his palms against his shaved pecs and grunting. A guy named Patton from Toronto mumbled to himself, "I'm ready. I'm ready. I'm ready. I'm ready." Next to Vincent, Adam had pulled his hoodie over his head and had his iPod buds crammed into his ears, techno music thumping and audible to all.

Vincent put his goggles strap in his mouth and chewed. He just needed to block out the noise and movement in the room. He had to stop noticing the stain on the floor and the buzz of the lights. He had to narrow his own focus and make the moment all about him. There were too many people near him. He was too aware that only two of the eight swimmers in the room could earn an Olympic Games berth in this event, *if* they finished within 1:58.48 minutes.

The door to the ready-room opened, and an official in white entered. "Gentlemen, line up in order from lane eight to one. Quickly," said the man.

Vincent moved to his place. He was lane 3. He hated lane 3.

His heart picked up pace. He wanted to slow things down: his pulse, the movement of time, the bobbing people. He tried a drawn-out exhale. He attempted to talk himself down: *I've done this a million times.* Someone's hand was on his shoulder, the team psychologist. Vincent shrugged it off and launched into his prerace ritual. He licked the insides of his goggles and put them on. With shaking hands, he pulled his bathing cap over the top of his head and jammed any protruding strands of hair up under the latex. He heard the swell of cheering in the stands. Someone else's race had ended. Someone had won. Someone had lost. It was his turn now. He let out a long, jittery exhale.

When the ready-room door opened, Vincent gasped at the true volume of the audience. Horns blared, clappers clacked. He stepped out into the bright lights of the pool deck. He had the urge to pee, but it was too late now. The line of swimmers moved towards the blocks. Vincent ducked to avoid the moving camera boom.

He slumped into the white plastic chair behind his lane and pressed his hands against his ears as the announcer called each competitor's name. He closed his eyes behind his goggles and waited. A sensation like the heaviness of sleep was coming. This was not what he was supposed to feel. He had to snap out of it. *Get up. Get up!*

Vincent dragged himself to standing. He stripped off his track top and tear-away pants and dropped them into the bin next to his chair. *Wake up. Wake up.* He slapped his legs and chest and arms and stared straight ahead at his lane. The water was too blue.

Someone in the audience yelled, "We love you, Gallagher!" No one shouted Vincent's name.

He approached the block and knelt down to splash the pool water on his face and limbs.

Vincent stood again and looked up at the stands. This was always part of his race routine, a blind glance at the colourful crowd. But today he noticed details in the noisy group of spectators. A little girl with a large yellow sign caught his eye. "Go Adam!" it read in shimmering pink letters. A couple climbed the stairs. A Canadian flag upside down. The whistle blew to indicate that the swimmers could get in the water. He jumped in. There was the sharp shock of cold liquid around him. He tried not to think about the fact that this was his only shot at making the Olympic Team. He pushed off the slippery bottom, popped up into the loud air, turned, and swam back to the wall for the start. Adam was already in front of his block, ready. Vincent pushed his goggles lenses with his palms, to make sure they were well suctioned, and reached up to wrap his hands around the block start handle. He had never noticed the way his thumb curled over his other fingers. He wasn't sure his grip was right. It was something he just used to *do* and not think about. His heart pounded hard, and the race had not yet begun.

The audience went silent, and a voice said, "Take your mark...." He curled himself up and inwards, towards the top of the block. He was more aware than ever of being coiled tightly. Beep. The spectators burst into cheers as Vincent exploded backwards into an arch, arms arcing over top, and he was back underwater. Sound muted. Bubbles around him.

His right hand on top of the left, elbows extended and upper arms squeezed against the sides of his head. Ten fly kicks. He emerged, switched to flutter, pulled with his left arm and began his stroke.

A camera moved along a rail on the ceiling. Maybe Yasmine was watching from somewhere? He imagined her alone up in the crowd. Frowning at him.

He had to regain his focus. The clock would not wait. To his left, Adam's strokes mirrored his own. He had to speed up, because Adam was stronger on the second hundred. He turned, pulled, flip-turned, kicked, and emerged again. Adam moved slightly ahead. Vincent fluttered harder in an attempt to get back up in line. Adam remained slightly out of reach. Vincent saw nothing but a small splash from the lane on the other side. He flipped over for the second turn. Acid burned his throat. One hundred metres to go. Adam was at least a half-body length ahead. Vincent thought about the pressure of water against his hands. It was not enough. His kick lost some of its force. He was falling behind. His breaths shortened. He turned again, pulled, flipped and began the final length. Arms were getting harder to bend on the pulls. Legs heavy. He wanted to die. The crowd's voice burst and faded and swelled and faded again. His last strokes. Two, one. He reached towards the wall. The spring of the timing board against his fingertips. It was finished. He lifted his head quickly to see the scoreboard, before the nausea of exhaustion hit.

Fourth.

In the next lane, Adam pressed himself high onto the rope, pointed his index finger into the air and let out an exuberant primal roar.

Vincent did not want to see or hear anything else. He dropped down to the pool bottom and screamed into the bubbles.

VINCENT

It was over. In just under two minutes.

Sick heat flowed through his bone marrows and veins. The double death of a body and a dream.

Weaving under and over the ropes, he slowly dragged himself to the side and climbed out with the other losers. On the jumbotron appeared the image of Adam and Gallagher, still in their lanes, waving and celebrating their Olympic berths. Vincent looked away.

He walked to the locker room. He focused on his toes and avoided the sympathetic faces of the swimmers and coaches who were lined up along the pool deck. At the doorway, he looked back. No one was watching him any longer. Their attention had turned to Adam. Triumphant. Beaming. Someone slapped Adam on the butt. Adam's girlfriend Callie appeared from behind the swimmers and fiercely embraced her man.

Vincent entered the changing room and found an empty bench. He wished he had a hoodie and towel he could bury himself in. Instead he sat, exposed, in his race suit. Water puddling below him, head in hands. He pictured his parents up in the stands, huddled together. A million dollars of groceries wasted. His mother wiping away tears. Their disappointment his fault.

"Vince." It was his coach Robert's voice. Solemn.

Vincent could not look up. Said nothing.

"You put up a good fight."

But Vincent knew he hadn't. He had let his mind wander.

"This just wasn't your time. You're young. You'll have another shot at the Games in 2016."

Just six thousand more hours of training before I get another chance.

The announcer was already calling out the names of the athletes in the next event. Everyone else was moving on.

SAM

Time moved quickly. Sam sat up in his white bed, tired from another restless night, rubbed his eyes, and wondered what might be asked of him. *Is today the day?* It had been over two months since Ellis had given him any significant instructions. Their biweekly calls now were like the perfunctory repetitive exchanges of most long-distance relationships.

"How are you?" Ellis would ask.

"Fine."

"Be patient."

The phone calls left Sam wishing he had said more. He often regretted that he had not proclaimed his love for Ellis or his dedication to their mission. Instead, he spent the calls listening carefully to every inflection in Ellis's deep voice, worrying that he was falling short of expectations, worrying that Ellis was losing interest in him. For days after these conversations, Sam would dwell anxiously on particular words

Ellis had used. He dissected these words. Searched for special meaning. He bit his nails roughly and ached for his mentor.

Sam got up and went to the fridge. There was sour milk, a quarter of a baguette, and a block of mouldy cheese inside. He pulled out the bread and nibbled on it as he paced the apartment. Stale. He chewed slowly. He had lost his interest in food lately. His body had narrowed and collapsed inward under his clothes.

He finished the heel of the loaf and fingered his mobile. Nine o'clock in the morning. Three hours to wait before he was scheduled to call Ellis.

In the washroom, he splashed water over his face. His eyes appeared sunken and dark. His facial hair growth had slowed. He pictured Ellis appearing behind him, strong hand on his shoulder, mouthing the word, "Son." He held on to this image.

When he was dressed, belt pulled to its tightest notch, he retrieved Ellis's note from his suitcase, sat on the couch, and stared out the window at the brick wall. He looked at the letter, soft from being opened, read, and refolded repeatedly. He read the last line: *I am watching. Have faith. Be still.* He sighed.

Finally, the appointed time arrived. He dialled and waited. Hope and nerves welled up.

"Hello?"

"Ellis, it's Sam."

"I don't have much time, but I have something to ask of you."

Sam felt the joy of the fly ball landing in his Rawlings. "Yes."

"Tomorrow at noon, go meet with a woman named Francine in Peckham." He gave the specific address. "She has instructions for you."

SAM

Like a shot of adrenaline, a sense of purpose came rushing back to him.

"Thank you, Ellis." He could not disguise the excitement in his voice. He was already imagining some future moment where Ellis would thank him for his good work. He envisioned Ellis greeting him with open arms and a broad smile.

After the phone call ended, Sam switched SIM cards and lay down on the bed, happy.

LEXI

Sweat flowed from Lexi's skin, ran in streams down her face and arms, joined and separated into more rivers, then dripped on to the floor beneath her stationary bike. She glanced at her teammates. They grunted and winced along with her. One of them shouted out, "Thirty seconds! Drive to the finish!" and the buzz of increased rpms filled the exercise studio. Lexi stood on her pedals and pushed, letting out an animalistic shout as the instructor counted down from ten.

"Awesome workout," Joanne said to Lexi between heavy breaths as they cooled down. They high-fived across the space between their bikes.

Lexi loved the intimacy of the team during these workouts. She forgot about Brent and the silence of their home. In the embrace of this physical pain, she forgot about the cold cushions of the couch that she stretched out on each night as Brent snored under the duvet on their bed. There were no more dreams of marriage and gardens.

She counted down to the Games. Each evening she fell asleep reviewing her focuses and goals for the next day of training. She knew now that one can only serve one master at a time.

SAM

Sam descended the steps of the train station and wove his way down a busy street, past shops selling electronics, hair weaves, exotic fruit. With each step his nervousness grew. On a leafy side street he found the cafe. It was run down and almost deserted. At a worn table along the wall of the room, a middle-aged woman with wiry black hair sat sipping tea. He knew from the way her gaze was positioned on the entrance that it was Francine. She fidgeted nervously with the delicate cup.

There was something familiar about her.

Tentatively, Sam approached and spoke softly. "Francine?"

Her voice cracked as she spoke. "You're Sam."

He sat down slowly in the rickety chair across the table from her.

"I've been waiting for this moment," she said. She had a French Canadian accent. She seemed jumpy. "Why don't we get you something to eat? Are you hungry? Some tea? There's a chill in the air."

"No thanks." He would not be distracted. "You have something for me?"

Francine pushed her dark bangs to the side. Her eyes were wild and dark. She spoke as though she had not heard Sam's question.

"I'm happy to finally meet you. Ellis spoke about you with real pride."

Sam was pleased to hear this, but the woman's jerky speech bothered him. He looked towards the counter from where a man in a yellow apron watched them.

"He said you understand your place," she continued. She spoke in the too-loud voice of the unstable.

"Quiet down," he said, then glanced over at the man in the apron, who was now busy stacking cups.

Francine bowed her head for a long while, Sam thought perhaps in embarrassment, but when she looked up, he saw tears on her cheeks.

"I've been looking forward to my part in all this," she said in a hoarse whisper. "I've been here in London, waiting for my turn to play a part in this mission, just waiting and waiting...." She wiped her nose with her sleeve. "And here it is... my big moment."

She reached her hand across the table, palm up. An invitation Sam ignored. He worried that the man at the counter might suspect something. He peered through the window of the cafe at the houses across the street. Perhaps there were people spying on them behind those dirty panes.

Words from the past came to mind: *You must be careful.*

He faced Francine and repeated flatly, "You have something for me."

She slumped a little and curled her fingers inward. It took her too long to reach into her purse. Finally, she placed a small scrap of paper on the table and kept her hand in a tight fist next to it.

"This is it," she said.

There was a phone number on it, written in blue scrawl.

He was impatient now, desperate to get what he needed and leave. "What do I do with it?"

Francine breathed in before reciting the following instructions: "Memorize it and throw it away. Listen carefully...." She dropped her volume. "During the Opening Ceremonies, listen for the announcement of the team from Great Britain, the last of two hundred and four countries to enter the stadium for the Parade of Nations. Wait sixty seconds, then dial. Your call will initiate the IED firing circuit." She stopped abruptly.

Sam's hands fell limp against the table, causing the spoon to clatter in Francine's saucer. Even though he knew he'd be asked to do harm, to do something significant, he hadn't quite expected a mission like this. He wasn't sure he would be able to go through with it. His head hurt. He thought of the clock in Trafalgar Square, rapidly counting down.

"If it's just a phone call, why do I need to be there in person?" He wanted to pick holes in this plan.

"Television coverage can sometimes be delayed, so you have to be onsite. Everything will be set up and ready. All you have to do is dial."

Sam glared at her twitching mouth. He was about to challenge her again, but she spoke first.

"Stay focused and remember our cause. We're fighting for the poor. We're battling greed. That's it. That's the message from Ellis."

The invocation of Ellis's name stopped Sam's mouth. Shivers shot up his spine. This was not about Francine. It was Ellis's plan, his words. A holy calling. The baton had been passed on to him, and he was desperate to leave Francine as quickly as he could. He tucked the slip of paper into his pocket. "I have to go," he said.

She grabbed his wrist as he stood up. "Wait, there's one other thing…I have something else." She unfurled her other fist to unveil a ring. His heart raced. He sat down.

"This is from Ellis…because of your obedience."

He carefully plucked the beautiful shining band from her shaking palm. He ignored her lonely, wet eyes. This was the fourth ring. One to go. *Thank you, Ellis.*

"Please stay and eat with me," she whispered, desperately.

"Thanks, but I have to go."

Sam stood again and stuck out his hand, and she pumped it weakly. He thought of her then as one of the team members who would be cut off and left behind.

Once outside the cafe, he glanced through the glass at Francine's profile. She was hunched over the table, fingers tented. It hit him suddenly. He had seen her before. At the red-doored church in Toronto, kneeling in the aisle in desperate prayer. Quickly, he faced the wind and walked on, trying not to wonder why Ellis had sent her. Not willing to think about the strange network of people involved in this mission. Not letting a single doubt enter his mind. He would focus on Ellis's goodness and wisdom instead, and on the people they were destined to help: the impoverished, the abandoned, the forgotten. Apart from his rings, that was all he had to hold onto.

JAYNA

This was not her usual gym. The court floor was worn, but the nets were new. She was thousands of kilometres away from Montreal on the fifth day of the selection camp. The women passing the ball to her were not her usual teammates. They were aggressive, frighteningly talented women who were only there to win a spot on the Olympic team. With every pass, throw, and step, the players tried to show off their individual strength and dominance on the court, while at the same time trying to demonstrate that they were team players. After Jayna managed to drain several three-pointers during a shooting drill, a skinny blond from Nova Scotia slapped her on the butt and said, "You go, girl!" in a voice loud enough for the coaches to hear. An hour later, when they were in the midst of another drill, the same woman slammed her shoulder into Jayna's back, knocking Jayna's lanky frame to the floor. Another player had helped her up. Observing courtside, Nate and the other two coaches scribbled in their notebooks. Jayna tried not to notice the furious movement of their pencils.

Lunch break came about thirty minutes too late. Jayna's left ankle was sore. She was unaccustomed to the long runs the athletes had been forced to do each morning of the camp, but she had pushed herself through them and made sure she kept up with the pack in front. She ignored her body's protests. She could not wince or limp or show any sign of weakness.

Now she chewed on her protein bar and watched the clock on the wall. Thirty-eight minutes until another scrimmage. The last of the camp. Later today the coaches would announce who made the team. Until then, she would ignore every ache.

"This camp is way tougher than the last one, isn't it?" asked Marianne, a ten-year veteran of the team.

Jayna was surprised to hear Marianne address her. Up to this point, they had never spoken; they'd simply jostled one another on the court.

"Oh," Jayna said in response.

"Sorry, I forgot that you had never been invited to one of these camps before." There was no condescension in Marianne's voice, but the comment made Jayna even more aware that she was the underdog. Something else she would have to ignore.

The buzzer went off to signal the end of their lunch break.

It was Nate who assigned the teams for the scrimmage. He read their last names from his paper. Jayna studied her shoelaces.

"Bentley," he said. *Bentley. Bentley.* She suppressed the swell of panic in her chest.

She exhaled slowly and moved towards her scrimmage team. Marianne was already there. Going through the motions of being a teammate, Jayna high-fived her.

JAYNA

The women huddled and strategized. Jayna breathed in and out slowly. She scanned everyone's faces, brows furrowed in concentration. She wondered if any of them was as nervous as she was. Within five minutes she was positioned on the court. Her heart pounded. She wiggled her fingers and focused on the ball in the head coach's hands. Up it went into the air, followed by a burst of action and the sound of squeaking court shoes. Her team won the ball. Jayna moved up the court, received a pass from Marianne, dodged a defender, turned, and sharply passed to another player. She found an open slot and waited. She would not notice Nate on the sideline. She would not watch the clock.

Someone shouted her name, and she poised her hands to catch. It came, arcing through the air, landing in her grasp. She would not overthink this. She would not let herself miss. Her body took over, leaping just a little as she pushed the ball above the waving hands and jumping bodies. Swish. First blood.

The game continued. Jayna pulled herself constantly back inside her own body. She ignored Nate on the side. She missed only a few opportunities. She tried not to let the knife in her ankle distract her. Sweat soaked through her tank.

The scrimmage clock was about to go off. Her team was winning 34–29. She widened her stance, boxing out an opposing player, and kept her eye on Marianne, whose feet had just left the ground and whose long arm stretched up to intercept the ball. Bodies shifted balance, turning to tear back down the court. Jayna moved with the flow. Her heart raced with the effort. The choreography of the moment was magical: Marianne's long strides, Jayna breaking away from her man, lead hand out as she cut to the basket. The ball was airborne and heading towards her as the buzzer sounded. Game over! She let the ball hit the floor and bounce away. A strange shot of joy filled her chest. Jayna let out a primal cry of exultation. "*Wooooooo!*"

The women on her team threw themselves into a messy group embrace. If Jayna could stay in this moment, everything would be okay. But the players separated and turned to file off the court, once again competitors vying for a few precious spots on the team.

Nate stood next to the head coach, mumbling. Jayna's sweat was still warm, but a wrinkle of cold fear formed in her mind. The power over Nate that she had felt courtside months earlier had dissipated. What if Nate decided she wasn't good enough? Would she ever have the guts to tell people what he had done to her? Would anyone ever believe her?

She wasn't sure she would ever be strong enough for this. She sat against the cool wall, grabbed her hand towel from her bag, and draped it over her head. The elation of the scrimmage win was replaced by silent tears.

The women were dismissed. They were free to roam the campus for a few hours while the coaches developed their final team roster. Jayna located the campus pub and cloistered herself in a dark corner.

"A pint of whatever's on tap," she said to the waiter. Her body reverberated with panic and pain. She was sure she'd be sent home. Her dream officially crushed. She would choose never to play basketball again.

Two other players entered the pub and waved warmly at Jayna but sat near the door and ordered ice water. Jayna picked at an old burn mark on the tabletop. It had obviously been glazed over, and she was determined to scratch away at the clear coat until she exposed the blackened wood beneath. She dug her nail in and worked at it, but couldn't reach the damaged surface. She drained her beer, and a second one.

JAYNA

"You coming, Bentley?" one of the players called to her as she made her way out the door.

"Be there in a minute."

Jayna picked up her bag and walked to the washroom. She sighed at her reflection: hollow eyes, green pallor, messy hair. She brushed her teeth, applied some mascara, and tidied her ponytail.

She was the last to enter the room where the announcement was to be made. Chairs lined the walls, and the women sat biting their nails or chattering nervously. Jayna found a spot near the door. If her name was not on the list, she would disappear.

The coaches stood up. The head coach cleared her throat. "I'm proud of you, ladies," she said to kick off her speech. Nate held a stack of papers in his hand. The list of names.

Jayna stared at the untied shoelace of the player to her right. She could not listen to this feel-good preamble to bad news. She wished she had consumed another pint.

Finally, the speaking ended. Nate circled the room and handed each player a paper, face down. Jayna cringed as he laid the sheet in her lap. Her throat tightened.

"Okay, the list of team-members is arranged in alphabetical order by last name. You can turn your paper over now," he said when the last handout was given.

She flipped it slowly and placed her finger next to the first name: *Appleton, P.* Down to the next: *Barrette, K.* Still down: *Bentley, J.* She stopped. Placed her hand on her mouth. Shook her head and started from the top again. Was she reading it wrong? *Appleton. Barrette. Bentley.* She did not continue further down the list. She made it? She looked up, pulse throbbing in her veins. A few of the players sobbed. Looking dazed, one woman stood to leave. Cut. The women whose names were on the list remained still and quiet. From his chair across the room, Nate stared at her, a pleased grin on his face.

Her face flushed with embarrassment. She wondered if anyone noticed.

After several minutes the head coach spoke again, "You are welcome to stay if you need to, but you're free to go. Those who were selected to the team must report to practice in the gym tomorrow morning at seven."

Jayna struggled to stand. A couple of people patted her on the back and whispered words of congratulations as she passed through the door to the hallway. She trembled. She stood against the wall, eyes wide, and hoped that a glimmer of joy would shine through the confusion.

"Don't worry, it will sink in eventually," said Marianne, as she passed by and gave Jayna a congratulatory punch in the arm.

She rubbed her hand on the spot Marianne had hit. She knew that hovering under her skin was a layer of thick, dark shame.

SAM

After several hours spent outside in freezing cold rain, Sam was chilled to the core. Though he usually avoided the security lounge, he couldn't resist today; he quickly ducked inside. Even in the warmth of the room, his teeth chattered. He kept his heavy guard coat on and rushed towards the coffee machine. He passed a table where four men in security garb played cards. They did not look up from their hands.

He hovered in the corner, clutching his mug, waiting for the shivering to stop. One of the card-players glanced over and smiled. Sam turned away. He studied the bulletin board. There were business cards of various service providers tacked on haphazardly and some out-of-date notices. In the centre of the board was a large poster that reviewed the emergency drill protocol for the Opening and Closing Ceremonies. He felt queasy in his stomach—the sickening sensation of nerves, like he used to feel as a child prior to hockey games.

He distracted himself by carefully reading the document. He knew it all. He had already taken part in dozens of emergency drills: terrorist threats, bombings, environmental disasters. During each rehearsal, he followed instructions and did his best to ignore the rush of guilt and excitement. He blended in with the other guards.

Below the poster someone had jokingly plastered a "Keep Calm and Carry On" sticker. Sam was surprised that no one had removed it. But he was glad it was there. It reminded him that no matter what happened, he had to remain collected and confident. He was supporting a good cause. He needed to remember that it was all worth it.

Now warmed up and somewhat calmed down, Sam turned to leave the lounge. Rushing towards the exit just ahead of him was the familiar tall brunette he had seen standing with Alan near the main stadium a few weeks earlier. He pursued closely and followed her out the door. They stood side by side under the overhang. He caught a glimpse of her profile as she glanced to each side and then out at the pounding rain. That's when Sam fully remembered her. The lady from the church with the red door. The woman with the shoes that clicked. Another one of Ellis's soldiers.

Sam stepped towards her and she looked his way. Her eyes grew wide with recognition and she placed a hand on her chest. Sam simply stared, not sure what to say.

She broke the silence, her voice apologetic. "I'm sorry. It's just the way these things turn out sometimes."

Sam did not understand what she was talking about. Perhaps she was being sent back to Canada. Perhaps she was off the team.

If there were things Sam needed to know, Ellis would tell him. He was sure of that.

SAM

"Goodbye and good luck," said the brunette. She snapped open her black umbrella.

Sam stood there, incredulous, and watched her slim silhouette disappear into the downpour.

YASMINE

She entered the final two hundred metres of the marathon. The crowd behind the course barriers was layered fifteen people deep. The volume of the last stretch took her by surprise every time—after many kilometres of relative quiet, the deep, hoarse cries of fans, shrieks of children, and the booming voice of the race announcer. Her legs throbbed. Her lungs burned. She pushed away the rising nausea to absorb the swelling sound. A competitor from Kenya crossed the finish ahead, her name shouted through speakers. Yasmine imagined the ribbon falling to the ground. In moments she would trample it underfoot. She rounded the corner and saw the finish. The clock bright and counting upwards: 2:35.39.

She was ahead of pace. This was it. Her last chance at an Olympic berth. Her body wanted to shut down, but she would not let it. She had to sprint. This was a choice. A horrible, painful choice. She would rise. She would push.

Yasmine summoned every ounce of energy left in her exhausted body, literally grunting, "Come on, body," and bearing down. She entered fully inside herself now, the cacophony around her dimming to a constant flat note, the colours and camera flashes melting to a stream of grey.

She soared, legs extending forward, her breath strong in her ears, a distinct throb in her heart. It was a strange euphoria, this intersection of human drive and otherworldly pain. She dug into it as she moved closer still. Every nerve and muscle roared as she surged towards that finish.

In the days to follow, she would study the photos taken of her at the exact moment she crossed over the finish line. Her face was contorted and ugly, but her body was graceful, in a wide stride, fully off the ground. She was floating. She would reflect on the worthwhile torture of those mornings suspended in the pool, of the horror of learning to fly.

A large entourage greeted her on the other side of the finish line. Her parents, brother, physio, coach, and representatives from Athletics Canada, jumping and hugging. Her time was 2:36.23.

"You did it," said her mother, firmly, proudly, into her ear.

Yasmine sank to the ground then. Sitting on the cold pavement, her father's hand on her head, she began to laugh. A rippling joy from deep in her core. A refrain of relief.

SAM

Sam awoke, breathless, from a dream about his mother. He had been standing behind her in the dim hallway of the Elora bungalow, begging her not to leave. He pleaded to the back of her head. She had not responded to his words; instead, she babbled on about the terrible change in weather and the unfortunate demise of left-wing politics.

"Stay," he said, and it had been his young boy's voice. The sound of Sammy, although he felt like Sam.

"Who's going to push back against capitalism?" she asked.

"Please," he had said.

"It's raining now."

He wiped the sleep out of his eyes and walked to the shower, feeling guilty about where his subconscious had taken him. Back in Toronto, Ellis had asked him to wipe the slate clean, but Sam could not control this invasion of the past. All of his dreams were set in the house of his childhood. It was a place and time engraved in his brain.

He sat on the edge of the tub and let the water run, testing its temperature with his fingers, and pushing away the thoughts of his mother. As irrational as he knew it was, he imagined Ellis was aware of his guilt and weakness. Ellis hovered somewhere deep inside his heart and read his every thought. The tap still running, he stood and stared at his emaciated body in the mirror. Behind his own eyes were Ellis's eyes, judging.

He was a bad soldier. "Forgive me," he whispered into the thickening humidity.

Steam had filled the room and fogged up his reflection. The jagged lines of his body retreated into the cloud. He fixed his eyes on the blurred image, sure that the silhouette was no longer his. It was Ellis. He squinted to see better. The arms were raised to ninety degrees on each side in a gesture of acceptance. Forgiveness. Sam wept.

Before stepping into the shower, Sam leaned forward and used his index finger to trace something into the condensation: *18 days.*

JAYNA

As the London-bound flight reached cruising altitude, the captain's voice came over the speakers: "We are proud to welcome to this flight members of the Canadian Olympic basketball Team. We know you've all worked hard to get to the Games, and we're proud of you."

Jayna tuned out the French translation of the announcement and the applause of the passengers. Certainly, she wasn't filled with pride, and she was sure no one else would be if they knew how she had gotten here. She wondered if her guilt was obvious to others—she imagined it radiated from her as she fidgeted in her seat. The fact that her parents could not afford to fly to London for the Games was a source of relief; they would not be close enough to observe her shifting eyes and fingernails bitten to the quick. If they saw her now, they would inevitably ask her what was wrong and inspire the release of the tears she was working so hard to suppress. If she could just make it through to the end of the Games without letting these emotions rise to the surface, she might be okay. She would retire and move on. She might be able to forget.

Jayna plugged earphones into the armrest and clicked through the stations: pop, classical, children's music. She stopped on a channel that played a form of new age jazz—saxophones, breezes, and birds twirping in the background. She hoped the sounds of nature would ease the swell of anxiety. As she settled back into her chair, she heard, over the melody, the familiar rattling of ice being dropped into a plastic cup. She twisted in her seat to watch the flight attendant wheel the drink cart down the aisle. She ran her thumb along her lower lip.

She wished she could have a glass of wine. Prior to boarding, Nate had reminded the players that it would not be appropriate to consume any alcoholic beverage on the flight. They were wearing Canadian team outfitting, after all. The women had agreed. It seemed logical at the time, but Jayna had not expected this desperate need to hit her so soon.

She looked at the teammates along her row; they were sleeping or scribbling in journals. They weren't like her university teammates. These girls were professional players or NCAA champs. Every day of the pre-Olympic training camp, someone had reminded the team that they wore Canada on their backs. These were intense, competitive women. They didn't joke about Nate behind his back, and they didn't add vodka to their water bottles for a little extra fun at training. They talked about being responsible ambassadors for Canada. They spoke about how it was the first time in twelve years that the Canadian women's team had earned a spot at the Olympic Games. They warned each other about not letting the country down.

Jayna knew she didn't fit in. She was not as good as them. In so many ways.

JAYNA

She decided she would not order wine. She would get water. It was a display of discipline no one noticed. As she sipped it, unsatisfied, she glanced up the aisle. Four rows ahead, Nate was asleep, head at an impossible angle. His long arm was draped over the armrest. He snored in his Canadian team gear. She loathed him deeply.

She wondered if he thought she was up to the team's standard. She hated that she still cared what he thought. She squeezed her empty plastic cup until it cracked.

The teammate in the seat ahead of her peeked over, eyes sleepy. "Stop bumping the back of my chair," she said, annoyed, then plunked back down.

Jayna heard other accusations in her voice—like *You don't deserve to be here*—hidden behind the words. She saw the same messages in her teammates' glances and felt it in the rough way they chest-passed her the ball at practice. She felt helpless.

In a few hours, they would land in London, collect their belongings, line up for their accreditation, and settle into their rooms at the Athletes' Village. This was supposed to be the pinnacle of an athlete's career. Olympic-bound competitors were meant to feel happy and prepared. They should be confident that they'd left no stone unturned. Jayna had many stones that she was afraid to turn over.

SAM

The Olympic site had opened, and the athletes and officials had begun to fill in the empty spaces. It was today that Sam experienced his first significant bubble of doubt. It snuck up silently from within, as he stood in his security uniform outside the main stadium, watching a team of synchronized swimmers rehearse their routine on land. The eight athletes moved in perfect synchrony, goose-stepping from one pattern to the next, arms rising and falling, bodies turning, fingers snapping, with militaristic precision. It was a performance punctuated periodically by the loud, sharp, synchronized clap of sixteen hands.

A coach stood close by, shouting corrections and nodding with satisfaction. It bothered Sam that these women seemed to know exactly where to go and exactly what to do, without being told or prodded. They all moved together, never leaving a teammate behind. Their faces were fierce and focused, nothing like the beaming, clownlike synchro parodies he had seen on late night television. Their unison was strangely beautiful, which saddened him. He felt isolated and awkward standing there, holding his walkie-talkie, studying them. He could not say where Alan was. He had not seen him in over a month. He had simply disappeared. Perhaps he had switched shifts. Perhaps Ellis had cut him out of the mission. He could not say where Francine or Paul were. He simply did not know. Perhaps he was the anchor for the team now. Or, perhaps plans had changed, and his team had moved on without him, without warning.

Two days earlier Sam had called Ellis at their regular appointed time. A woman had answered. She had a lovely, deep, soft voice. Sam had asked for Ellis, and the lady had responded that he was out. That Sam should try later. He had hung up, confused. Where was Ellis? Who was the woman? His confusion led to worry. When he had called back an hour later, he was greeted by Ellis's voicemail, which said only, "Please leave a message." Sam had not.

He had hung up the phone, changed the SIM card, and leaned against the wall of the flat. He waited for the nausea of disappointment to pass. He told himself that Ellis would find a way to communicate. Somehow.

Now he wondered if that was true.

Quickly, he turned away from the synchro swimmers and looked towards where he had seen Alan and the brunette standing three months earlier. There was another male guard in their place, monitoring the open area. Sam knew that the man's name was Ravi, but he was sure that Ravi did not know his name. Athletes and coaches walked by, many deep in conversation, proudly sporting clothing with their country's colours or flag or name. Sam wasn't entirely sure what nation or team he belonged to anymore. He felt completely anonymous. Invisible.

YASMINE

She pulled on her new running top, red with a maple leaf printed boldly in white on the chest. It was smooth and dry against her skin. A perfect fit. She collected her training flats and walked out the front steps of the London house she was sharing with some of the Canadian track and field athletes.

There was no scent of pines here, no lush green forests, just concrete and grey all around. It was 6:00 a.m. and she was about to head out to perform mile repeats. She was still jet-lagged. But none of this bothered her. She sat down on the steps, breathed slowly, and waited for her coach to come out and join her. She had no desire to be anywhere else.

A week from now, her parents and brother would arrive in London for the Opening Ceremonies (they had managed to wrangle three tickets). Then they'd travel to South Wales, where they planned to visit with relatives and wait out the week until Yasmine's race day. Her parents had had to dip into their retirement savings to pay for the flight, but they did so ungrudgingly. "It's worth it, Yazzie," her dad had said, and she believed him.

She suspected Nate would be somewhere along the marathon route on race day. She pictured his tall, muscular body peeking out above the cheering crowd as she raced by. She knew she wouldn't be able to avoid him until then, either. He'd likely be at the Canadian Team welcome party a few days from now, and at the Opening. He was hard to miss. She, on the other hand, could glide her small, slight frame quickly through any crowd and hide herself within the noise and protection of others.

She stretched out her legs and flexed her feet. There was not so much as an ache or pull from her Achilles. She beamed. Recently, a fellow athlete had insisted that properly rehabilitated ligaments were stronger than they had been prior to being torn. Yasmine doubted the science behind the theory, but in a strange way it felt right. She ran with a lightness that wasn't there before her injury. Being healed made her feel free and untethered. Her times had improved, and she had made it here, to the Olympics, after all.

SAM

He entered the coffee shop where he had met with Francine months ago. The table where they had sat was now occupied by two men, deep in conversation. Sam had hoped Francine would be here. He wanted to pretend that the months had not passed by. Like she had been sitting here each day, faithfully waiting for him to return. Like he had never left her crying, by herself. He had been in such a hurry to leave that day. She had been a virtual stranger to him. Tonight he needed her. If she had been here, he would have begged her forgiveness. He would have run his hands through her untamed black hair. They would have been okay. But she was long gone, and he returned to his flat, alone.

Tomorrow was the Opening Ceremonies. All he had to do, at the right moment, was press the right key. Maybe then Ellis would come for him. He touched the four rings on his necklace. This was his last test.

They were doing this for a reason, after all. They were going to awaken people to the needs of the impoverished. Sam would play his part in getting the world's attention, and Ellis would find some way to deliver the message. Ellis always found a way.

He must have faith in Ellis, as Ellis had faith in him. He had to repress every doubt.

Sam stood in the middle of his flat and wondered what he should do next. It was nearing dawn now. He could not sleep. An ambulance screamed by on the street outside his flat. His hands shook, and his heart pounded. He walked to the kitchen sink and turned on the faucet. It ran cold and loud. He cupped his palms and placed them below the stream of water, closed his eyes, and thought of Ellis until his hands went numb.

A weak light filtered through the window. There was a knot in the pit of his stomach. He wasn't hungry, but he knew he should eat to sustain his energy for this day.

With shaking hands, he replaced his SIM card and programmed into the phone the number Francine had made him memorize months earlier. Everything was ready.

He checked his watch: 6:20 a.m. He needed to be onsite by 4:00 p.m. for his shift. This might be the longest day of his life.

Lexi

Upon her return from the Eton rowing venue after training, Lexi dropped her bag on her bed. She loved this sparsely decorated Olympic Village room she shared with her teammate Joanne. White walls, light wood flooring, small beds. No broken glass. No Brent. He was in another Village room with one of his crew. Being apart felt so natural, so right, that it made her wonder why they had ever tried to be together. They had been working against nature.

As soon as she had stepped into the Village a week earlier, she had the distinct feeling that it was much better to be an Olympic veteran than a first-timer. Because she had experienced the Village before, she was mentally prepared to fight the draw of free fast food in the dining hall; ignore the distraction of impossibly fit young bodies; push aside the frustration of team-issued clothing that didn't fit her large frame; decline the tickets to other sporting events; and sleep through the celebrations that grew in volume and chaos as the Games wore on.

In 2008 she had fallen victim to new distractions. She had thought that a couple of late nights in the athlete lounge would be no big deal. She had figured spending the afternoon before her finals at the swimming venue wouldn't affect her. But she had been wrong. The free attractions had never been part of her finely tuned performance plan, and she had paid the price in the form of exhaustion crippling her body too early in her race. This time around she remembered.

She was here to row well and win a medal. She recalled what it felt like to miss the podium four years earlier; the burning disappointment and regret followed her throughout the day. It was a dream remembered and dying over and over again, every time she woke up. She did not want that this time around.

"I'm going to grab a snack at the dining hall. Want to come?" said Joanne.

Lexi had eaten her bagged lunch on the way back from the venue. She was planning on a long nap. "No thanks. I'm good."

Joanne headed out the door, and Lexi moved to the balcony, from where she scanned the open space below. People dressed in their team gear moved back and forth. A couple of muscular athletes had rolled up their sleeves and pant legs and were sunning themselves on a patch of green grass. Some young girls, probably gymnasts, sat on a bench, writing postcards.

As she stood overlooking this scene, she was filled with warmth. For a few seconds, she wondered if it was happiness. Or perhaps a sense of security and control. But then it became clear, suddenly, mysteriously, that she was going to be successful. It was like she had already won. It was a knowledge and satisfaction that poured through her that she could not explain. An experience so exhilarating and irrational, she would never be able to share it. She tucked the feeling away. It would be her secret confidence.

OPENING CEREMONIES: PART TWO

YASMINE

Waiting in line for the Parade of Nations was much like the starting corral at a running race. People crammed together and edged forward, and there was a palpable current of nervous energy and excitement in the air. Yasmine imagined that for many of the athletes around her, the moment of entry into the main stadium was what they had worked for. It signalled their arrival. For her, it was one of those moments she had dreamed about since the first time she failed to qualify for the Olympics, but there was no finality to it. It was just another important milestone in a long journey that started long ago and stretched out into the future well beyond these Games.

Ahead of her, the main stadium audience roared with cheers as the team from the British Virgin Islands was announced. There were close to two hundred nations left to enter before the host country made its appearance, but the crowd sounded riled up by the mere mention of the word "British."

"The announcer could yell fish n' chips, and the audience would go mad," said a tall, blond pole-vaulter to Yasmine. They were all a bit silly with excitement.

"Or bangers and mash," suggested a bulky shot-putter in a mock English accent.

Yasmine was laughing along with them, when she felt a weight on her shoulder. Still giggling, she turned.

There was Nate, his large frame a dark wall. He looked down at her with the expression of a disappointed parent, lips pursed and brows furrowed. Her laughter dissipated, and the frustration of the past eight years returned suddenly. She would not let this happen. Since she left Montreal, she had refused to talk to him on the phone or over email. She had masterfully avoided him, so she could focus on her training. And even now, she thought about turning and forcing her way through the queue or ducking off to the side and creeping into the Ceremonies, hidden in the shadow of another athlete.

"Hi," said Nate.

Nervously, Yasmine glanced back towards the pole-vaulter and shot-putter, who were already conversing with someone new.

"Don't worry, I won't bite. I just wanted to see you. How are you?" he said. His words were harmless, but his hand was heavy on her shoulder.

She had no one to turn to and nowhere to escape. She thought about her family out in the packed stadium, excitedly awaiting her entry. This was supposed to be a joyful occasion for all of them. She would not let this man steal her lightness and ground her with his heavy hand. Nor would she run this time. He was the one who needed to go.

She brushed his hand away roughly and spoke forcefully. "I'm doing very well."

The disappointed look returned to his face. Now he lifted his hand to touch her hair. She recoiled and steeled herself against his advances. She would no longer let him take anything from her.

"Oh," he said. "I knew you'd think you didn't need me, but...."

"I don't," she said, truncating his statement, remaining in control. She ignored the fact that he was technically still her husband. That they had shared a home for more than eight years. He would not wrench this happiness from her. They would talk one day, but not now.

He opened his mouth. "Okay...I...."

She did not let him finish. She turned back towards the pole-vaulter as she mumbled to Nate, "Good luck to your team."

As Yasmine reintegrated herself into the conversation with the athletes around her, she sensed Nate hovering. Then the crowd shuffled forward, and he was gone.

The volume of the audience swelled as she approached the entrance. The stadium lights shone through the opening to the field and down the dark hallway, over the heads of the waiting athletes. It was like an incredible sunrise. She smiled and kept her eyes looking forward.

JAYNA

In the hallway on the way into the Opening Ceremonies, one of the male rowers led the Canadian athletes in cheering. His cheeks were red from the effort of screaming "CA-NA-DA... CA-NA-DA." The swimmers were the most enthusiastic in joining in. A few of them had their long arms draped over one another, and the force of their voices was mesmerizing. Jayna watched all of this unfold around her. She looked at their faces, fierce and focused as they chanted.

The group budged forward a little, and she turned around to move. Up ahead she spotted Nate. He was speaking with someone. Through the gaps in the crowd, she saw that it was his runner-wife. Rumour was that she'd left him, though Nate had not said a thing about it. A moment later Nate was headed back through the packed crowd of athletes towards the basketball team. His face was pale, and his mouth drooped. This look of deep injury and helplessness was not what she had expected. A brief surge of pity surprised her. She thought no emotion would ever be strong enough to overwhelm the hate that consumed her.

Her tears were much too close to surfacing. She looked away from Nate and surveyed the athletes around her. They grinned and laughed. The Games were about to begin, and everyone gathered in that hallway had hopes of success or glory. She was desperate for a happy ending as well but was too aware that the story never unfolds as one hopes it will. For most of these competitors, there would be no shining gold or podium to climb. Many would leave London crushed by defeat, perhaps even limping and sidelined by a fall.

She had been falling for a long time.

Jayna's teammates had joined in the raucous cheering. She leaned into their huddle and let it all out. The syllables were angry and loud. Her voice crumbled beneath the pressure. Everything inside her was released recklessly into the air and echoed off the walls.

Two minutes later, an official came and asked the athletes to quiet down and straighten out their formation. They would be entering the stadium shortly. They unlocked their embrace and spread into tidy lines of ten. Jayna felt good to be thrown back into order. It was what she needed—someone to shove her into place and send her in the right direction.

They inched forward and finally entered. Jayna looked up. With thousands of camera flashes all around, it was like walking into a lightning storm—the crowd, a distant thunder.

SAM

From his position outside the stadium, Sam listened carefully to the announcer belt out the nations of the world in alphabetical order. As the list neared its end, Sam's stomach tightened, and his body temperature rose sharply. His jaw ached from clenching his teeth each time the crowd noise grew and receded. He distracted himself by picking out the countries formerly known by other names. Some had been conquered or divided and forced to make the switch. Some had wanted to announce reclamation of power and independence. Some were still being silenced and oppressed. Some would go on to change names again. Naming was a human instinct and weapon.

Focusing on this did nothing to reduce his dull chest ache and heart palpitations.

There was a great swell of cheering for the host nation, the last to enter, and what sounded like the booming voice of God: "Great Britain...."

Sam checked his watch. As he counted down, he touched the rings hanging from his neck and wrapped a sweaty hand around his mobile. He could not find his focus. He ached for Ellis's help.

Sam looked at the dark grey sky and turned away from the closest security camera. He could not stop a rush of memories like a movie reel: A swimming pool. Brent's little voice from the water below. His knees buckled under the pressure. There was the tenuous security of his mother, watching from somewhere off-screen.

The time arrived. Sam swallowed and his finger found the right key on the dial pad. His breathing was too fast, and his heart squeezed into a tight ball. He pressed and held the button as splinters of pain shot through his body. *The sensation of falling through air.*

He crashed to the ground, and the sky turned to ashes.

Behind closed eyes he saw the beaming people who had filed by him earlier in the evening to enter the stadium. They clasped their tickets in anticipation. Then they surrounded him. They touched his face and arm. Someone sat on his chest. There was the distant wail of an ambulance. He turned to see Brent, bloodied and pulled out on a stretcher; his mother, running alongside.

Sam's body convulsed with pain.

"What's your name?" asked a man, staring down from a halo of light. His voice was soft and comforting.

"My name?"

The man asked again, "Do you know your name, sir?"

He could not remember.

"You collapsed, but you're going to be okay," said the man. "I'm a paramedic, and I'm going to escort you to a hospital."

He let out a groan as they rolled him away, and he felt the world burning behind him.

SAM

When he woke up in the hospital, his entire body was locked in the agony of a cramp. He was hooked up to a drip. A nurse sat on a chair in the corner of the room, staring at a television set on the wall.

Through blurred vision he saw that it was coverage of the Opening Ceremonies. The scene panned out to show thousands of Olympians, coaches, and officials gathered closely midfield, admiring the lit Olympic cauldron. Confused, Sam attempted to prop himself up on the bed, but the tightness in his chest tied him down. He breathed heavily, lay still, and cocked his head to see the screen. The camera view sped along the periphery of the cheering mob, scanning athlete profiles. There was a sudden blur of red and white outfitting. Sam could not make out the details, but he was sure he saw Brent's face: the high-bridged nose, tight jaw, and pink cheeks. He gasped with sudden relief. And then Brent was gone. Sam lifted his hand towards the screen, but the IV tape and tube tugged back, and his arm collapsed against his belly. He strained to hear the broadcaster's baritone: "It's been a perfect night here at the Olympic stadium in London...."

Sam had not detonated anything. The world had not burned. A tide of joy flowed in and out, followed by horror. He could still sense the impression of the dial pad key on his fingertip. He had been capable of killing. Of erasing the small face that had peered down from the top bunk. Of tearing apart families and terrorizing a generation. A single tear slipped down his cheek, and he did not move to wipe it away.

He noticed his mobile in a small wire basket on a table to the right of his bed. He struggled through shots of pain to reach for it, then held it delicately in his hand like a bloodied knife. He needed to call Ellis. He prayed he would have the right words. He hoped Ellis could explain what had happened or failed to happen. Maybe he could make it better.

The nurse was still there, with her back to him, engrossed in a replay of the cauldron lighting with musical accompaniment. Sam didn't care. Alone on his hard bed, he dialled Ellis's number. It did not ring. A recorded voice said, "The number you have reached is not in service."

Sam would not believe it. In a flush of panic, he redialled. It was the same polite, automated female voice. He clung to the mobile, to the dead air. Even his desperate listening could not invoke Ellis. His god had abandoned him.

Suddenly he remembered the words of the brunette on that rainy day outside the security lounge. "I'm sorry. It's just the way these things turn out sometimes," she had said.

He dropped the phone on the bed, grasped the four rings on his necklace—heavy and incomplete—and pulled with all of the energy left in him. The chain snapped, and the bands clattered to the floor and rolled in circles.

The nurse rushed to his side. "Are you all right, Mr Gottschalk?" she asked.

In his shame, he wanted to wave her away, send her back to her chair to watch coverage of the athletes filing out of the stadium at the end of the ceremonies, but he did not. Her eyes were wide and kind. He let her take his hand and hold it softly as she whispered, "Everything is going to be okay. The doctor will be here soon. You'll be fine."

She remained close to him as they waited, his cramped body slowly loosening its grip. Eventually, they returned their attention to the screen. To the voice of the television anchor, rambling on and filling time as the athletes departed. "Athletes sacrifice everything to get here, and only a chosen few make it in the end. And here they are tonight, ladies and gentlemen. Let the Games begin."

Made in the USA
San Bernardino, CA
12 November 2012